THE VIENNA GAME

MICHAEL GLENN

PAGETURNERBOOKS LLC

PageTurnerBooks, LLC

Pageturnerbooks.llc@gmail.com

Interior Book Design by Vellum

Cover by Wayne Joyner

The Vienna Game

ISBN: 979-8-9893595-6-1 (paperback)

979-8-9893595-7-8 (e-book)

❀ Formatted with Vellum

CONTENTS

A Note to the Reader — v

1. Planting Seeds — 1
2. Settling In — 11
3. "Nothing Lasts Forever" — 21
4. Reality — 29
5. Portents — 35
6. Anschluss! — 41
7. Desperation — 49
8. Closing Jaws — 59
9. "Whatever It Takes!" — 67
10. Storm Clouds — 75
11. No Smiles — 83
12. "Im heil'gen Land Tirol" — 89
13. "I will, with God's help!" — 103
14. Powder Keg — 111
15. The Belly of the Beast — 119
16. Tempus fugit — 127
17. Sudetenland — 135
18. Thunderbolt Out of the Blue — 145
19. Roller Coaster! — 153
20. Broken Glass — 167
21. A Piece of Paper — 177
22. Life and Death — 187
23. By the Skin of the Teeth — 199
24. "Buon viaggio!" — 209
    Epilogue — 219

Historical Notes — 223
Acknowledgments — 251
About the Author — 253

A NOTE TO THE READER

This is a work of historical fiction. Fictional characters and events are products of the author's imagination, and any resemblance to any actual persons, living or dead, is entirely coincidental. When real historical people appear as characters and real historical events are described, accuracy is the objective, though occasional liberties may be taken which do not affect the general historicity of the text. An appendix of historical notes will be found at the end of the book, in which fact is separated from fiction and supporting contextual details are sometimes added. Notes are divided by their corresponding chapter, and the reader is encouraged to consult them as each chapter is read. For the sake of authenticity, meters and kilometers are used for measures of lengths instead of feet and miles. Maps of Austria and Vienna are provided at the end of the book.

1

PLANTING SEEDS

On a clear, chilly mid-November day in 1937, Franz Josef Gruber stood on the third-class deck of the SS *Europa* leaning on the handrail as he peered at the crowd of waving spectators on the dock, trying to pick out his parents and younger siblings. He shielded his blue eyes from the bright sun with one hand, squinting while the wind ruffled his blond hair. Failing to find them, he decided to wave anyway. *At least they will think I'm waving at them*, he thought. The individual figures receded into an indistinguishable blur as the ship began moving away from the pier and Joseph, as he was called, wiped a tear away with the back of his hand, feeling a sudden wave of homesickness. He would not see them again for a year.

As two diminutive tugs slowly pushed the massive steamship out into the New York harbor, Joseph could see the Empire State Building in the distance, and just beyond it his favorite city landmark, the Chrysler Building with its Art Deco crown. He shifted his gaze to Ellis Island nearby, where his family had arrived in America nearly twenty years earlier. Although he had been only four years old at the time, Joseph remembered the anxiety he had felt like it was yesterday. Holding tightly to his mother's hand, they had wound their way through endless lines, dragging their bags, filling out forms and getting them stamped. They were poked and prodded, and their eyes, ears, and mouths examined. When the small family finally stood on a New York street corner, his father had spread his arms and proudly announced in their native Viennese dialect, "Mir san jetzt Amerikaner!" *We are now Americans!*

Joseph smiled wistfully at the memory, thinking how little they had known about their new home or the struggles they would experience there. Widespread anti-German prejudice had made the transition more difficult, but then there had been seven good years, which came to a sudden halt with the onset of the Great Depression, followed by seven lean years. The descendant of five generations of clockmakers, Otto Gruber found it hard to sell hand-carved wall clocks during a depression and had to resort to doing odd jobs wherever he could find work, just to put food on the table for his growing family. In addition to Joseph there were now two daughters and another son, and the family budget was stretched to the breaking point.

Otto had been a mechanic in the Austrian army during the war and had become a jack of all trades. Working alongside his father, Joseph learned something about automobile engines, plumbing, electrical wiring, and carpentry, but most of all about building cabinets for clocks. Carving the decorative wood cabinets for the fancy Vienna Regulators was his passion, and he was determined to become the best. He was now on his way to Vienna to work with his Uncle Oskar, Otto's twin brother, a master clockmaker whose business was thriving. With a year of training in Oskar's workshop, Joseph would return with polished skills to boost the family business. The cost of the transatlantic fare had been a real sacrifice for the family, but he was sure it would be worth it.

Moving on its own now, the huge ocean liner steamed past the Statue of Liberty. Joseph contemplated it in silence while the ship passed. Then he spoke aloud, pointing at the torch-bearing icon, "The next time I see you, I'll be a new man. I'm going to make my family proud! Just you wait and see!"

"Excuse me?" A slightly-built old gentleman with a closely-trimmed white mustache and goatee, wearing an overcoat and hat, turned to face him. "Were you to me speaking, young man?" The man spoke with a strong German accent.

"Oh—no sir!" Joseph grinned, blushing slightly. "Just talking to myself—and her!" He pointed again to the towering green figure. "She's really something, isn't she?"

"Absolute!" the elderly man agreed, nodding. "Have you read the poem? 'Mother of Exiles,'" that is what it says. 'Give me your tired, your poor, your huddled masses, yearning to breathe free.'" He heaved a deep sigh, staring at the statue, and placed a hand over his heart. "America has been to my family very good!"

"Why are you going back to Europe, then?" asked Joseph. "Don't you like it here?"

"I came my children und grandchildren to visit," the elderly man smiled. "Now is it time for me to go home—back to Wien, the City of Dreams!"

"I'm going to Vienna, too!" exclaimed Joseph. "I was only four when my family left, so I hardly remember anything about it."

"You will love Wien!" beamed the old man. "Und speak you German?"

"Jo, i kann guad Deutsch red'n." *Yes, I can speak good German.*

The man threw his head back and laughed aloud, clapping his hands in delight. "Wienerisch! Des is a Ohrenschmaus für mi!" *Viennese! That is a treat for my ears!*

Continuing the conversation in the Viennese dialect, he inquired about Joseph's family and his reasons for traveling to Austria. They stood at the railing chatting until the statue disappeared from view and the skyline of New York dropped below the horizon. Then, extending his hand to shake Joseph's, the man bid him farewell, promising to see him again at dinner. "I am called Herr Engelmann," he said with a smile. "Und what is your name, young man?"

"Joseph. Actually, it's Franz Josef Gruber. I was born on the same day the Emperor died, and my parents named me in his honor."

"Ach! Wonderful! You have a very proud name, Joseph! Later will we talk more!" Herr Engelmann headed below deck to his room, leaving Joseph to ponder the unlikely coincidence of having met a fellow Austrian on the ship. He was relieved that Engelmann approved of his use of Wienerisch, remembering with a frown how his high school German teacher had reacted when he first spoke.

Helmut Hartstein was a former German army officer who had marched with Hitler and the NSDAP in the 1923 Munich Beer Hall Putsch, following which he had emigrated to the United States to avoid prosecution. As a German language teacher, he was a demanding taskmaster, inspiring fear in many of his students. When Joseph, a fifteen-year-old high school sophomore and newcomer to the class, opened his mouth and—in Wienerisch—proudly announced that he could already speak German, Hartstein had practically exploded.

"Das is nicht Deutsch!" he had shouted, slamming his palm on the desktop in front of Joseph so forcefully that Joseph had involuntarily jerked back, pale-faced and wide-eyed. "Das ist Müll!" *That is not German! That is rubbish!* He had angrily ordered Joseph to speak only Hochdeutsch, or High German. Thoroughly intimidated, he had obeyed, but at home things were different.

At first he had started avoiding using the Vienna dialect even when speaking with his parents, leading them to ask why. It had led to a confrontation, since it appeared to them that he was putting on airs and disrespecting their family's cultural roots. Joseph had been confused, torn between pleasing his teacher and pleasing his parents. Eventually he had done both, speaking only High German in the classroom, and only Wienerisch at home. This compromise left him feeling uneasy, with a sense that he was being disloyal to both.

It would not have been a difficult choice had not Hartstein begun to warm to Joseph. He rarely smiled or gave encouragement to any of his students, so when he gave Joseph approving nods and barked "Ja!" at his answers to questions, it made him feel proud and boosted his confidence. Hartstein even wrote complimentary notes on Joseph's papers, and detained him after class frequently to give him positive comments. On one occasion he had observed that Joseph, with his blond hair and blue eyes, was "a fine Aryan specimen" who would someday be a valuable member of the German nation, or "Volksreich." This had also been a source of pride for Joseph, who afterward would admire himself in the mirror, wondering what it really meant to be an Aryan.

He had been surprised when, in October following his graduation in 1934, Hartstein had invited Joseph to join him at the annual German Day celebration in Madison Square Garden. He was further surprised at the strong political overtone in the arena, with Nazi swastikas prominently displayed along with American flags. Hundreds of men and women in military-style outfits served as ushers, wearing black pants or skirts, white shirts, and black ties, with Sam Browne belts. The crowd of twenty thousand roared approval at every mention of Hitler's name and cheered lustily at references to the accomplishments of Americans "of German blood."

Afterward, standing outside on the street, Hartstein had fixed his pale blue eyes on Joseph's and, with an upward tilt of his nose, said with a raspy edge to his voice, "Joseph—you may have been born an Austrian, but so was Hitler. Like him, you belong to the *German* race —the greatest race in the history of the world! The sooner you realize that, the sooner you will become a powerful force for progress. Germany needs young men like you—don't delay to commit yourself to the Führer—to Germany!" Surprised, Joseph had mumbled something unintelligible in reply, embarrassed at his own confusion.

Joseph had been deeply troubled by the experience. He attempted to discuss it with his father, but Otto merely shrugged and said it was a matter for Germans and no concern of his. Joseph kept his thoughts to himself after that, but he examined the newspapers at every opportunity for news about developments in Germany.

Soon after that Joseph heard that Hartstein had returned to Germany to rejoin the army. A few months later he received a small parcel in the mail, postmarked Berlin. It contained a used copy of *Mein Kampf*, Hitler's personal and political manifesto. On the title page, Hartstein had written "Sieg Heil!" and "Deutschland Über Alles!" The book was, of course, in German, and like almost all printed matter in Germany it was set in the old Fraktur typeface, which Joseph found very challenging to read.

After struggling through it for weeks he finally concluded that Hitler wanted to destroy communism, Russia, democracy, and Jews. He wasn't sure how all this destruction was going to be "a powerful force for progress" as Hartstein had promised, but he couldn't deny that Germany seemed to be doing very well under Hitler's leadership. Last year's Olympic Games in Berlin had been a great success, and Joseph had been inspired to start working out to build his muscles. He and a friend had split the cost of the famous Charles Atlas "Dynamic-Tension" exercise course, and he rose early every morning to flex and stretch. He was sure he was getting stronger.

Hitler's antisemitism did not surprise or shock Joseph. After all, he often heard derogatory remarks about Italians, Irish, blacks, Jews, and others—including Germans, who had been America's enemy during the war. His own parents seemed fairly cynical about all of those groups. His mother had even complained about Hartstein, frowning that Germans always thought they were better than Austrians. "They think they're better than everyone," his father had laughed. Without putting it into words, Joseph had decided that such prejudices were rather silly and that people should be taken on their own individual merits. His baseball teammates had included Jews, Italians, blacks, and Irish, and he wondered why adults could not get along as well. *Hitler might be doing some good things for Germany,* he thought, *but he's not the Führer for everyone.* Nevertheless, *Mein Kampf* was tucked into his suitcase, with dogeared pages and a few handwritten notes in the margins. He was interested in finding out what his Uncle Oskar thought about it all.

The Atlantic Ocean was rough and stormy during the five-day voyage and the passengers rarely ventured out onto the decks. Consequently, Joseph spent a lot of time with Herr Engelmann. He enjoyed listening to his stories about past times in Vienna, and in turn he talked of his love for carving the wooden clock cabinets. They discovered a chess set in the lounge and spent an hour or more every day playing. Engelmann was an experienced player and demolished

Joseph in their first game, after which he began to offer advice and coaching. "Don't push your pawns out like that—you are exposing your king!" "The pawns are the most important pieces on the board! They control the game!" "Sometimes sacrifices must be made in order to win!" "Anticipate your opponent's next move by studying his last move!" Joseph found it all a bit too much to grasp at once, but Engelmann was patient and calm—not at all like Hartstein—and he found himself looking forward to the time he spent with the old man every day.

When the SS *Europa* reached the German coast, Joseph was astonished to learn that it was yet another hundred kilometers inland on the Elbe River to get to the port of Hamburg. The view along the river was not appealing, being very flat and unremarkable, but Joseph was so tired of looking at the ocean that he didn't care. Once on land again, Engelmann, being the more experienced traveler, led the way as they took a tram to the train station and purchased tickets on a night train to Vienna. It was a few hours until the train's departure, so they stored their suitcases and walked out to the street, looking for a quiet place to eat a late lunch.

In a modest gasthaus nearby they enjoyed a bowl of eel soup and bread rolls. It was a bleak day with overcast skies, and they were glad to be out of the wind. As they gazed out the large window onto the busy street, a man with dangling side curls and a wide-brimmed black hat—obviously an Orthodox Jew—stood waiting at the bus stop with a folded newspaper tucked under his arm. Joseph had seen numerous men dressed in this fashion in New York and paid no attention, dipping his bread roll in the soup.

Suddenly three young men surrounded the Jewish man. They appeared to be about Joseph's age and wore dark pants with boots and khaki shirts with a red armband bearing a black swastika. What followed shocked Joseph. The Nazi youths shouted curses and laughed at the man as they shoved him back and forth between them, sailed his hat and newspaper into the street, and snatched his glasses from his face and stomped the lenses into fragments. And then, most shocking of all—another man walked into the picture. He was small and elderly, with white hair and goatee, and he held out his hands, plainly telling the youths to stop. *That man looks fam—why, that's Herr Engelmann!* Joseph's jaw dropped and he looked across the table to make sure his companion was not there. He had been so focused on the scene outside that he hadn't even noticed his leaving the table. Straining to hear, he could pick up some of what was said outside.

"That is enough! You've had your fun. Leave this man alone."

"Who are you to tell us what to do, old man? Mind your own business!" And one of them cuffed Engelmann on the back of his head, jeering at him. Joseph gripped his chair arms with white knuckles and leaned forward, his breath fogging a circle on the glass.

"There is nothing good about abusing—" began Herr Engelmann, raising his palms in a gesture of peace. Another of the three slapped him in the face with the back of his hand. Engelmann's head jerked and a trickle of blood ran from his nose. He pulled a handkerchief from his pocket and held it to his nose. The three Nazis walked away, still laughing and jeering. As they left, one shoved Engelmann, who would have fallen had not the Jew caught him in his arms. They spoke quietly to each other briefly and patted each other on the shoulder, and then Engelmann went back into the restaurant. Joseph could hardly breathe and felt sick to his stomach as he watched his friend take his seat again.

"That wind is getting colder," Engelmann commented calmly as he dabbed at his nose with the bloody handkerchief. Joseph stared at him, wide-eyed for several seconds before speaking in a hoarse voice.

"Why did you go out there, Herr Engelmann?"

Engelmann lifted his eyes and looked sadly at Joseph. "Why didn't *you*?" he asked quietly.

Joseph literally gasped, and he felt as if all the air had been let out of him. His eyes darted toward the man outside, retrieving his hat and newspaper in the street. A wave of shame swept over him and he licked his dry lips nervously, his face reddening. Old Herr Engelmann was a braver man than he, he realized.

Sensing Joseph's distress, Engelmann smiled at him sympathetically. "Joseph, my friend," he chided gently, "you have to know when to advance your pawns!" Watching Joseph's face fall, he reached across the table to squeeze his arm. "And sometimes you have to make a sacrifice to win the game." Joseph nodded as if he understood.

Engelmann stood. "Now, let's get back to the Bahnhof before it gets any colder out there."

2

SETTLING IN

The locomotive hissed to a stop in a cloud of steam at nine o'clock sharp the next morning. Vienna's Südbahnhof was almost sixty-five years old, and with its classical architecture—replete with rounded arches, columns, pediments, and statues—it was a relic of a by-gone era. Joseph, judging by what he had already seen from the train window, suspected that the entire city was a relic of a by-gone era. The morning light, admitted by the partially-glassed roof some twenty meters above, filtered through the steam, creating a hazy atmosphere.

Joseph stepped down to the platform and waited for Herr Engelmann to join him. He took the older man's suitcase while he descended the steps, using his umbrella as a cane. They walked together along the platform, with Joseph taking care to match his friend's slow pace. They paused at the top of the grand marble stair-case that descended in a two-tiered cascade, flowing down to the lobby floor.

Engelmann set his suitcase down and clapped Joseph on the shoulder. "Joseph, my friend! It has been so good to enjoy your company! You have made it a pleasant trip indeed!"

"I am the one who has enjoyed *your* company, Herr Engelmann!" Joseph replied fervently. "I hope that I will see you again!"

"Of course! That would be wonderful! Come to my bookstore on Mariahilferstrasse—'Buchhandlung-Engelmann.' I am there every day—perhaps we will play a game of chess!"

Joseph promised to visit the bookstore soon, and they descended to the main floor. Herr Engelmann took a side exit to where the taxis waited while Joseph walked out the front door through the ten-meter-high stone arches. *They sure build 'em to last,* he thought, glancing up at the massive façade. Standing on the sidewalk, suitcase in hand, he looked around uncertainly. He had the address of Uncle Oskar's shop and the number of the streetcar to take, but the plaza was so wide and so full of traffic that he could not see where to board the streetcar. He suddenly realized with a sense of panic that he did not have any Austrian schillings to pay the fare. His first thought was to run after Herr Engelmann and borrow some coins, but then he heard his name.

"Joseph? Franz Josef Gruber?" The voice was hesitant and unsure. He turned and saw a young man coming out of the Bahnhof. He appeared to be a teenager and resembled Joseph, with blond hair and blue eyes.

"Yes, I'm Joseph Gruber."

"I'm your cousin, Stephan! Papa sent me to meet you. We must have passed each other in the lobby." They shook hands warmly and embraced. "It wasn't hard to pick you out! With twin brothers for fathers, we look almost like twins ourselves!"

"Yes, we do!" Joseph responded, grinning. "I'm so glad to finally meet you—especially since I don't have any schillings to pay the streetcar fare!"

Stephan laughed. "No problem! I've got passes for both of us. Let's go home!"

It was only twenty minutes to their destination—the "Uhrma-cher-Gruber" shop—owned by Joseph's Uncle Oskar, whose family lived above the shop. They stepped off the red and white streetcar into a spacious plaza and waited for the trolley to leave so that they could cross the street. When the car rolled smoothly away, they stepped off the curb into the street. After two steps Joseph stopped so abruptly that Stephan bumped into him.

"Something wrong?" Stephan asked.

Joseph did not reply. He was staring upward, open-mouthed, at the over one-hundred-meter-high façade of a pale pink Art Deco-style building with a teal cupola and matching teal lettering, "APOL-LO," high above the street. The ornate entrance, flanked by four columns, faced the street corner at an angle, giving it an open, free look. He pointed speechlessly at the building without taking his eyes off it.

Stephan laughed. "That's the Apollo Theater—a movie theater. They can seat fifteen hundred people at once. It's very popular."

Joseph released his breath with an audible "whoosh" and looked at Stephan. "I love Art Deco," he gushed. "I have to see inside that building!"

"We'll go to a movie sometime, then," Stephan promised. "Our shop is right across the street, so you can look at it all you want."

Joseph glanced up at the theater repeatedly as they crossed the street to the Uhrmacher-Gruber shop. *Maybe Vienna isn't really just a relic of a by-gone era*, he thought, with a sense of anticipation. *It's not New York, but maybe there are some interesting things here, too.*

A bell tinkled as they pushed the door open, and Joseph drew in his breath sharply as his eyes quickly scanned the many beautiful and ornate clocks hanging on the walls. There were also mantel clocks on shelves and two massive grandfather clocks towering over everything. The sound of so many clocks running simultaneously filled the room with a rich murmur of soft tick-tocks and intermittent whirring sounds which Joseph found calming and restful. There was just something somehow *patient* about the steady working of a clock that he loved. His father's shop also had clocks on display, but nothing like this. The rich, dark wood cabinets, beautifully painted face plates, and rhythmic swinging of the pendula were for him a multisensory delight. He stood for a moment, taking in the experience. Then he realized that Stephan was waiting for him by a curtained doorway at the back of the shop and hurried over with a sheepish grin.

Behind the curtain was a well-lit workshop, which was as exciting to Joseph as the display room, if not more. A half-dozen clock cabinets lay on large, rough-hewn tables, partially assembled. Wood lathes and vises were mounted on stands, and planers, chisels, and mallets were scattered about. There were cans of oil, varnish, and wood stain, paints and paint brushes, sanding paper, and panes of glass by the square meter, not to mention an assortment of wood blocks and boards waiting to be fashioned into works of art—Joseph inhaled the scents deeply. "This is a real workshop!" he exulted. "This is what heaven must be like!"

"Joseph!" a voice boomed, startling him out of his reverie. "Welcome to Vienna!" Uncle Oskar descended upon him, enveloping him in a tight bear hug, rocking him back and forth, and then clapping him on both shoulders at the same time and shaking him again. "I haven't seen you since you were this high!" He held his hand down to show how little four-year-old Joseph had been. "You look just like Stephan! You are my second son!" And he embraced Joseph emotionally again, with more rocking and shaking. For Joseph it was eerie to see his father's double, and more than a little weird, but he couldn't help but be infected by his uncle's enthusiasm. Laughing, he hugged too. "I freu mi so do zu sein!" he said in his best Wienerisch. *I'm so happy to be here!*

"And you even speak Viennese!" Oskar beamed. "Your father has done well!" Turning to Stephan he said, "Take Joseph upstairs and show him where to put his things. Then we will go see Anna Marie." Turning back to Joseph, he added, "Mama Gruber is out shopping right now—we will have a special dinner tonight in your honor!"

As they climbed the stairs Joseph found that the building had five floors, and that he and Stephan shared a room on the top floor. The second floor was another working area with a drafting table, reference books, clock weights, face plates, and the internal gears of several clockworks. The third floor was the family space with a parlor, kitchen, and dining room. The fourth floor was for the parents, and the fifth was for their two children.

When he had hung up his few clothes in the wardrobe, he walked over to the large window that looked out onto the street below and parted the white, sheer curtain. Across the street the Apollo Theater loomed overhead, seemingly almost close enough to reach out and touch it. Even though they were on the fifth floor the Apollo was much taller, and craning his neck to look upward Joseph still could not see its top.

"Come with me," said Stephan, grinning. "I'll show you something you'll really like!"

Climbing yet another flight of stairs, they emerged onto the roof. The wind was brisk and cold, but Joseph barely noticed. The view of the theater was breathtaking, and Stephan laughed out loud at his exclamations of delight. After a moment he turned and surveyed the area in all directions. "It's quite a view from up here," he said with a nod. "I'm looking forward to seeing more of the city."

"You'll learn your way around pretty quickly," Stephan said. "The transportation system is easy to learn."

Rejoining Uncle Oskar the three went to a coffee house nearby, where Joseph met his cousin Anna Marie, who worked there. Seventeen years old, Anna Marie was bright and outgoing. Like the rest of the family, she was a blue-eyed blonde and had no shortage of young men seeking her attention. She had asked in advance to have the afternoon off so that she and Stephan could show Joseph around the city. The three men sipped coffee at a table, talking and waiting until Anna Marie could leave, and then Oskar returned to the shop while the young cousins headed toward the city center to see the sights.

It was a thoroughly enjoyable afternoon for Joseph. He saw the famous Opera House, the Parliament building, and the huge Hofburg —the palace of the Habsburg emperors which now served as the headquarters of the president and chancellor. There were, of course, several old churches, both Gothic and Baroque styles, which were very impressive. They climbed the steps of the tall spire of St. Stephen's Cathedral —called Stephansdom—for a panoramic view of the city, and Anna

Marie and Stephan pointed out various places of interest. Joseph, being used to the skyscrapers of New York, initially thought the view lacked interest, but then decided that he liked the openness of the many plazas and the light that reached the streets. *I could get used to this,* he thought.

The city's small size compared to New York surprised him. From the center of the old district, it was no more than ten kilometers to the western limits of the city, and even less to the east where the Danube River flowed. In the crystal-clear air he could see a group of low, forested mountains cradling the northern edge of the city, a reminder that Austria was, after all, an Alpine country. They spent only a few minutes in the cathedral spire, as it had no glass in the window openings and the November wind soon had them descending back to the street, pink-cheeked and shivering.

Homeward bound on the streetcar Joseph had a sudden thought. Turning to his cousins, he asked, "Where is Mariahilferstrasse? Is it very far away?"

"Not at all!" said Anna Marie.

"It's just a few minutes' walk from the shop," added Stephan. "Practically next door. Why?"

"I made a friend on the ship—an old man from Vienna. He said he owns a bookstore on Mariahilferstrasse— 'Buchhandlung-Engelmann,' I think he said. I'd like to visit him sometime."

"We know exactly where that is!" exclaimed Anna Marie. "You can walk there in less than five minutes!"

"I've been there," said Stephan. Giving Joseph a raised eyebrow he added, "He's Jewish, you know."

Surprised, Joseph hesitated, furrowing his brow. "Is that a problem?" he asked.

"It is for *him*," Stephan said with a shrug. "Ever since Hitler took over in Germany, we've had more and more Nazis here in Austria. A lot of people are prejudiced against Jews, and it could get worse."

Joseph, standing in the middle of the car, shifted his grip on the leather strap hanging from the ceiling as he absorbed this information. "What do you think about it?" he asked.

Stephan shrugged again. "My best friend was Jewish. His family lived close to us, and we went to school together. They emigrated to America earlier this year because of all the hostility. I hated to see him go."

"Why don't people like them?" Joseph asked. "There were Jews in New York too, but most people didn't care."

"They're just different," frowned Anna Marie. "And there's so many of them! A newspaper in the coffee house said that there are over a hundred thousand Jews in Vienna now. And they usually stick together, which seems standoffish."

"Do you think it's because they aren't Christians?" asked Joseph.

"No, not really," said Stephan, shaking his head. "Even Jews who aren't religious are treated the same way as the others, and even if they don't live in the Jewish neighborhoods. Your friend may be safer than some, but he should be careful."

Joseph described the scene he had witnessed outside the restaurant in Hamburg. "I've never seen anything like that in New York," he concluded. "Are there Nazis like that here too?"

"Not exactly, no," Stephan grinned. "They've been banned in Austria ever since the civil war they started three years ago! Most of them went to Germany, but there are still some around. They don't wear swastikas or Nazi uniforms—at least not yet."

"Civil war? I didn't hear about that!"

"It only lasted a few days, and a few hundred people were killed. Our chancellor was assassinated, and the new one—Schuschnigg—cracked down on them and executed the leaders. Their political party was outlawed."

"I was scared to death!" interjected Anna Marie. "School was closed for a week!"

"I think I do remember hearing something about it now," Joseph scratched his head. "An insurrection. Emergency powers. Not a democracy anymore. Right?"

"Pretty much," agreed Stephan. "We have political parties, but the chancellor runs things."

"What did you mean when you said the Nazis don't wear uniforms or swastikas *yet*? Do you expect that to change?"

Stephan and Anna Marie looked uncomfortably at each other, hesitating. With a sigh Stephan said, "Things are getting tense. Hitler is pushing to unify Germany and Austria. Some Austrians like the idea, but a lot don't. If Hitler gets his way the Nazis will run Austria before long, and judging from what has happened in Germany, the Jews may be in trouble."

They arrived at the Apollo Theatre plaza just then and most of the riders exited the car. The bell tinkled as they entered the shop; Oskar glanced their way and then returned to discussing a fine wall clock with a customer. They quietly passed through the display room and headed up the stairs. Joseph met Mama Gruber on the third floor and got another bear hug and a kiss on both cheeks.

Joseph's mouth was watering as he smelled the delicious aromas emanating from the kitchen, and he could hardly wait for dinner. After a sumptuous meal of goulash, noodles, and cucumber salad they enjoyed steaming hot tea and apple strudel for dessert. Conversation around the table was active and enthusiastic as Joseph was drawn into sharing news about his family in New York, the voyage from America, and what he thought of Vienna so far.

Uncle Oskar then launched into telling Joseph how Vienna had changed during his life. Anna Marie and Stephan's expressions indicated that they had heard all of this before, but they listened, smiled, and contributed details if their papa overlooked something.

"More than half of my life Austria was a monarchy! And an empire! We ruled most of Central and Eastern Europe. The Balkans were ours. But *now*?" He spread his hands expressively. "Now we are a *tiny* country, barely able to survive! Our empire is gone. Our emperor is gone. Even our currency is changed!" He paused for a sip of tea, and Anna Marie prompted him with a question, as if following a script.

"How has the money changed, Papa?"

"When I was a child, we spent silver florins. By the turn of the century, we had changed to gold crowns. And then, in the mid-twenties, we started using schillings, which are neither silver nor gold! *Mein Gott!* Sometimes I don't know how to make change for customers. I can't keep up with what money we're using!" Everyone laughed, including Oskar.

"Right after the Great War Austrians wanted to unite with Germany, but the Allies wouldn't let us. Now, Germany wants to unite with *us*, but we don't want to!"

"Some people do though, Papa," Stephan objected.

"Not as many as you think!" argued Uncle Oskar. "After the uprising in '34, nobody trusts the Nazis anymore. Hitler claims he just wants all Germans to be together, but he only wants to use Austria and its resources. He may have been born in Austria, but Germany can keep their shouting corporal with his little mustache!" Oskar emphasized his disdain with a dismissive wave of his hand. "We don't want him back!"

"But would things really be any different if the Nazis took over Austria?" asked Stephan skeptically. "The government we've got now is pretty much fascist already. A lot of people think it would be good if Hitler did for Austria what he's done for Germany."

Oskar scowled. "The only reason we lost our democratic government is because the Nazis tried to destroy it, and we had to defend ourselves by suppressing them. Hitler destroyed the democratic government in Germany too. He's a dictator, and I don't want that for Austria."

"Wasn't the emperor like a dictator?" asked Anna Marie innocently. "That wasn't a democracy either, was it?"

Oskar stopped with his mouth open and then shut it with a frown. He gave his daughter a severe look but then smiled indulgently. "No, the monarchy was not a democracy either," he said gently. "It is true that Austria has had a democratic government for only a few years in its long history, and we don't have one now, but I don't want the Nazis to run our country. If we're going to have a despot in charge, at least let it be one that cares about us." Joseph remained expressionless but shifted uncomfortably in his chair.

"Let's not argue about politics!" pleaded Mama Gruber. "We have Joseph here! Let's be happy!"

"Yes!" boomed Oskar. "Forgive me! I sometimes get worked up talking about such things. But enough! Let's talk about clocks!"

Mama Gruber groaned loudly, and Anna Marie and Stephan burst out laughing. "No!" they all cried in chorus. Oskar feigned a look of shock at their response.

"I can't wait to get to work in the shop," Joseph said enthusiastically. "I love building the cabinets, and I want to learn everything you can teach me!"

"Yes!" boomed Oskar again, clapping his hands in delight. "Wonderful! We will begin first thing tomorrow morning. Breakfast is at six-thirty, and then we'll get right to work!"

That was the signal for the young folks to head upstairs to bed. It was quite cold on the fifth floor where there was no heat other than a single vent in the hallway floor, and Joseph went to bed with his socks on in addition to his long underwear. He then realized that living across the street from one of the largest movie theaters in Austria was not entirely a good thing—the light and crowd noise were distracting, despite the heavy curtains that were pulled across the window. That night it didn't matter though. He was so tired that he was asleep almost as soon as his head touched the pillow.

3

"NOTHING LASTS FOREVER"

J oseph blew the sawdust away and reached for a finer grade of sandpaper to finish the piece. He had been working on a walnut clock cabinet for three days straight, getting it ready for staining to bring out its beautiful wood grain patterns, and it was now as smooth as silk. The carved crown and foot pieces would then be added to complete another Vienna Regulator wall clock cabinet. The glass panes and clockworks would be the final additions. He was eager to see it assembled, hanging on a wall, and running.

Pausing briefly, he glanced quickly around the workshop. He was not alone—Stephan also worked there, along with white-bearded Herr Schneider, the lederhosen-wearing master carver from Tyrol. Oskar was usually there also, when he was not serving customers in the display room. There was little conversation as each focused intently on their tasks: tracing pencil lines on pieces of wood, cutting the wood, sanding, gluing, assembling, staining, carving, and more. Joseph was familiar with the many steps required to build a clock, but in a four-man workshop, things moved much faster. He found it exciting and looked forward to handling the carving knives and chisels himself.

He picked up the crown piece which Herr Schneider had just

finished carving, and studied it carefully. The chisel marks were still evident in the wood, and he ran his fingers over the faint irregularities to get the feel of Schneider's method before beginning sanding. The master carver noticed this and came over to stand beside Joseph.

"What do you think?" he asked gruffly, his weathered face as expressionless as a piece of carved oak. "Did I do it right?"

Joseph laughed, embarrassed. "It's marvelous! Beautiful! I want to learn to carve like this!"

"Have you ever carved wood before?"

"Yes—my father is Uncle Oskar's twin brother and we have a clock shop in New York. It's just the two of us, and I've been helping him build clocks since I was ten. Papa taught me to carve, but you are the best! I hope you'll teach me a few things too."

Schneider gave a single nod. "Oskar mentioned that you wanted to learn carving. But first you must sand this one as smooth as those other pieces!" His voice was raspy and his face inscrutable, but under the bushy eyebrows his eyes betrayed the pleasure he felt at being asked to share his skills. Joseph was busy with the sandpaper even before the old man turned away.

Oskar gave Joseph and Stephan the afternoon off on Saturday to do some more sightseeing, and they were joined again by Anna Marie. With only about four hours of daylight remaining after lunch, they hurried into the city. Knowing Joseph's love of the Art Deco style they took him to the Austrian national radio center—ORF Funkhaus —where the former chancellor had been assassinated during the 1934 insurrection. He also got to see the Vienna Secession building which housed many artworks of that movement, including some by Gustav Klimt. They spent an hour viewing art in the Belvedere Palace, an art museum established in the mid-1700s, and then headed to the western districts of the city for a brief visit to Schönbrunn Palace, the summer residence of the Habsburgs, famous for its spectacular gardens.

Joseph was very impressed with the size and grandeur of the palaces, and he especially enjoyed seeing all the many works of art from so many time periods and styles. His favorite experience of the day, however, was going to a movie in the Apollo Theater that evening. He could hardly watch the movie for looking at the furnishings and architectural features. Afterward, Stephan and Anna Marie laughed and teased him. They found it amusing that he —a strong and athletic young man who used his hands doing manual work—took such an interest in art, especially in a modern style like Art Deco, rather than something more traditional and masculine.

"You're not seeing the power of these designs," objected Joseph. "Look at the vertical lines, geometric angles, and symmetrical curves. The repeated patterns are like sound waves, or radio waves, and just look at those bold, bright colors! Did you know that Art Deco styles were inspired by the discovery of King Tut's tomb a few years ago? This may be modern art, but it draws on the Egyptian art from more than three thousand years ago!"

"Well!" exclaimed Stephan. "I didn't know you were so serious about it! You really seem to know what you are talking about."

"I want to design wall clocks in Art Deco style," Joseph said with a grin. "And mantle clocks too. I think people will love it, and we could sell a lot of clocks."

"That's a wonderful idea!" Anna Marie beamed. "Nobody else makes clocks like that. You could start something new!"

"I'll have to convince Uncle Oskar and Herr Schneider, though," said Joseph. "They probably won't like the idea, but maybe they'll give it a chance. I'll have to make some drawings and show them how great it would look. I have some ideas, but it will take a lot more work."

They continued talking quietly as they ascended the steps to their fifth-floor bedrooms. When the other two went to their rooms Joseph went to the roof for one last look at the theater. He surveyed the city over the rooftops with its countless lights sparkling in the darkness and dozens of church steeples and cupolas pointing to the sky. *So different from home,* he breathed. Turning his eyes upward to the heavens he murmured, "You can see a lot more stars at night here than in New York." Finally, with his breath forming a cloud of fog, he headed back down into the building. *I think I'm going to like it here,* he smiled to himself.

Church bells could be heard all across the city on Sunday morning as the Gruber family went to Mass at the nearby Mariahil-fekirche, on Mariahilferstrasse. The parish church, almost three hundred years old, was Baroque in style with two spires topped with onion domes, green with age. It was white inside and out, with a large statue of Franz Joseph Haydn, the famous composer, in the small plaza. Other statues adorned the façade of the church and the interior was richly ornamented as well, with an abundance of gold and silver, paintings, and several side altars. The high altar was gorgeous.

As they settled into one of the dark wooden pews Joseph whispered to Stephan, "This is almost beautiful enough to make me forget Art Deco!" Stephan snorted involuntarily, drawing a glare from Uncle Oskar. Before he could whisper a reply, the pipe organ began to play, filling the church with its deep, rich voice. Joseph sat attentively throughout, absorbing the ritual and following along with everyone else in standing or kneeling at the designated times. The service was more formal than what he had experienced at home, lasting about an hour. At the conclusion they filed out with the other congregants into the bright sunshine.

"Papa," asked Anna Marie, "why do they always do the service in Latin? Why not do it in German, so everyone could understand it?"

"Because that's the way it's always been done," Oskar replied.

"But why has it always been done that way?" she pressed.

"Because that's the way it's *supposed* to be done," Oskar replied.

"But why is it supposed—"

"It just *is*," Oskar interrupted brusquely. "It's *church*, and church is in *Latin*. That's the way it's always *been*, and that's the way it will always *be*. If you want to understand it, learn Latin!"

"Maybe they should do it in Wienerisch!" Stephan deadpanned. Oskar stopped walking and turned on him, hands on hips. Stephan quickly held up his hands, grinning. "I was joking! No Wienerisch in church! I know!" Oskar shook his head in exasperation and continued walking.

On the way home Joseph noticed a street sign with the name "Mariahilferstrasse." Seeing it reminded him of Herr Engelmann's bookstore and he made a mental note to go there later in the day. That afternoon he and his cousins set off to walk down Mariahilferstrasse, Vienna's busiest shopping street. It was almost December and Christmas decorations were everywhere, creating an air of excitement which was enhanced by the light snow that was falling.

As they strolled casually along, chatting and window shopping, they came to the bookstore, only three or four blocks from the parish church. The three entered the shop, which was pleasantly quiet in contrast to the crowded avenue outside.

"Good afternoon! Welcome to Buchhandlung-Engelmann," smiled a pretty girl in a shopkeeper's apron. "How may I help you?" She appeared to be about the same age as Anna Marie, and her long, dark hair was pulled back in a loose bun. Her gaze was direct, and the eye contact made Joseph feel strangely awkward.

"Hello," he replied. "I—ah, I am here—ah," he cleared his throat. "I'm here to see Herr Engelmann." Clearing his throat again, he added, "We're friends."

At this an eyebrow rose ever so slightly and the corner of her mouth twitched upward, suggesting that she had her doubts about that. Nevertheless, she turned and called through an open doorway, "Opa! A friend is here to see you!"

Within seconds Herr Engelmann, also wearing a long apron, came bustling through the opening. Upon seeing Joseph, he exclaimed "Joseph! My friend! So good to see you!" Hurrying over he embraced Joseph warmly and shook his hand. Beaming, he turned to the girl and said, "Miriam—this is the friend I met on the ship from New York! He was born here in Vienna and speaks Wienerisch!" Gesturing toward Stephan and Anna Marie he continued, "And these must be your wonderful cousins!"

With introductions and hand-shaking completed, Joseph and Engelmann went on talking as if they were the only ones in the store. Meanwhile Stephan and Anna Marie browsed the displays of books and Miriam made sales to a couple of customers. After a few minutes

Anna Marie called out, "Joseph! You have to see this book! This is the book for you!" She came over to them carrying an oversized book and showed the title: *Art Deco Designs for Today*. It was profusely illustrated with pictures of furniture, radios, clocks, jewelry, ceramics, clothing fashions—anything that could be designed in the Art Deco style. "This is exactly what you need!" she exclaimed enthusiastically.

Flipping quickly through the pages Joseph agreed. "Yes! This would be a big help." Turning to Engelmann he asked, "How much does this cost?"

"For you—nothing!" Engelmann smiled, holding both hands up, palms out. "This will be my gift to you. Welcome to Vienna! I hope you learn to love it as much as I do!"

"I'm sure I will! Thank you—this is very generous of you, Herr Engelmann. I will make great use of this in the clock shop."

"Wonderful! And you must come back often. We will set up a chess board in the back room, drink coffee, and eat rugelach and honey cake!" He walked with them to the door.

"Pleased to meet you, Miriam," Joseph said, nodding in her direction.

"Likewise," she replied with another penetrating gaze and then gave her attention to a customer. This somehow made Joseph feel dissatisfied; he hesitated, and then reluctantly followed his cousins out to the street.

The snow was coming down more heavily, and after walking another couple of blocks they decided to return home. The snow was beginning to accumulate on the side streets, where there was less traffic. "By morning, everything will be white," Stephan predicted.

"I love snow at this time of year," Anna Marie beamed. "It makes it feel so Christmassy!"

"It's the same in New York," Joseph agreed. "It looks so clean at first, but when it turns to slush and ice, it's not so pretty."

"Well, let's just enjoy it while it *is* pretty," she declared. "Nothing lasts forever!"

That struck Joseph as a rather cynical thing for a young girl to say, but he had to admit that it was true. To enjoy good things while they lasted was actually pretty good advice, he decided.

He spent the rest of the afternoon with the family in the parlor, studying the pictures in his new book and sketching ideas for clock designs. Classical music played quietly on the bulky radio console in the corner, interrupted periodically by monotone voices giving news and weather reports. Oskar read the newspaper, occasionally making cryptic comments about items of interest. Mama Gruber knitted a scarf with red and white yarn—the colors of the Austrian flag. Anna Marie and Stephan played a two-handed card game. Joseph found himself relaxing, and realized that he was already feeling quite at home.

At bedtime he ventured once more to the roof to enjoy the view of the snow-covered city. "Nothing lasts forever," he said aloud, as if addressing the city itself. "Enjoy it while it lasts."

4

REALITY

L ife quickly settled into a routine. Each week, Joseph worked in the shop from Monday through Friday and a half-day on Saturday, rotating from one task to another, gaining experience in all aspects of clock making. Saturday afternoons were spent out in the city with Stephan, sometimes joined by Anna Marie. Saturday always ended with a movie in the Apollo, more for the appeal of the building than for the movie itself. Sunday meant going to Mass with the family in the morning and visiting Herr Engelmann's bookstore in the afternoon, usually alone. Joseph was enjoying every minute and was having the time of his life.

The visits to the bookstore became even more interesting when Herr Engelmann asked Joseph to help Miriam to improve her English. "She will emigrate to the United States to be with the rest of our family as soon as the visa is approved," he explained. "I want her to be able to speak English as well as possible when that happens—not half-German, like me."

"How long has she been waiting?"

"Two years."

"Two years!" Joseph exclaimed, astonished. "Why does it take so long?"

"The United States has a quota on immigration from each country," Engelmann explained. "Only about fourteen hundred visas are granted per year from Austria, and it's not easy to get one. They don't even issue all of the visas they could. First, you have to register with the American consulate and get on the waiting list. Then you have to collect the required documents, including identity paperwork, police certificates, exit and transit permissions, and a financial affidavit to prove that you have a sponsor and won't become a burden on the state. Some of these documents have expiration dates, which further complicates things. You also have to have a valid ship ticket to America. And if you don't get your visa by the end of the year, you have to start all over again in January! So, you see," he spread his hands with a sad smile, "it is very hard! But I have faith that she will get her visa—soon, I hope!"

Joseph pondered this new information. "Does she have any family here besides you?"

"Not for long. Her father was a policeman, and he was killed in the insurrection in '34. Her mother is my youngest child. She didn't tell me that she had been diagnosed with cancer because she knew that I wouldn't have gone to America to visit my other children and their families. By the time I returned her condition had worsened, and—" his voice cracked with emotion—"and she isn't expected to live past New Year's Day." He wiped a tear from his eye and sighed. "That's why I want Miriam to go to be with the rest of the family as soon as possible. I don't want her to stay here."

"Will you go with her? You won't stay here by yourself, will you?"

Engelmann shook his head and laughed softly. "I can't leave Vienna! I was born here. I've lived here for seventy-five years, and I will die and be buried here. I will sleep forever in the City of Dreams!"

Joseph felt deflated and sat silently, unable to think of anything to say.

"Forgive me, Joseph! I shouldn't be talking like this!" He patted Joseph's knee and rose from the chair. "Let's find Miriam and tell her the good news that you'll be her new teacher!"

Despite the tragic circumstances Joseph was glad to spend time with Miriam. An hour of English conversation on Sunday afternoons quickly turned into two hours. They talked about every topic imaginable—books, movies, music, art, food, life in America, and more. He asked questions about Jewish life and faith, and learned that her family were non-practicing Jews, though they sometimes went to the local synagogue just to have fellowship with other Jews in the community. She talked about her relatives in the United States, but never spoke of her mother's condition, and Joseph didn't want to ask. He was becoming rather fond of her, but her reserved nature gave him the impression that she did not feel the same way, so he kept his feelings to himself.

Christmas fell on a Saturday that year. Oskar closed the shop at noon on Christmas Eve, and Joseph stayed to finish work on some personal items. He was receiving wages for his work but still couldn't afford to buy gifts for everyone, so he had carved small figures from pieces of scrap wood and then stained or painted them. For Anna Marie, who loved cats, he had carved a reclining black cat with green eyes. Stephan's favorite movie was *King Kong*, so he whittled a rough, fist-sized, savage-looking gorilla with white fangs and yellow eyes. For Oskar and Mama Gruber, he cut a pine board into the outline of Austria and contoured its surface to reflect the topography of the country, with mountains in the west and south and a winding blue line representing the Danube River in the north. He painted the mountains brown with snow-capped peaks, and the valleys green. Dark circles marked the cities, with Vienna the largest, of course. He placed these all on a shelf to finish drying overnight.

He had also made a gift for Miriam, but wasn't quite finished with it. He didn't know if she and Herr Engelmann observed Christmas, and since Saturday was Sabbath to Jews, he decided to deliver her present on Sunday when he made his weekly visit. She had confessed to a love of castles, so he had fashioned a small oak tower with turrets and an arched, gated entrance. He etched grooves in the walls to represent stonework and shuttered windows. Rather than paint it, he had stained it an antique ochre to give it a medieval look. He was rather proud of his efforts and hoped they would all be pleased.

Christmas Day was family time. Gifts were exchanged in the morning. Joseph's carvings were received with compliments, and he was surprised to discover that the red and white scarf was for him. Anna Marie and Stephan gave him mezzanine level tickets to a movie at the Apollo, and Uncle Oskar gave him a new set of professional wood chisels, all of which pleased Joseph to no end.

Dinner at noon was a special treat, with a steaming pot of beef and vegetable stew, dumplings, and a mixed fruit dish. For dessert there was a chocolate cake with five thin layers, separated by even thinner layers of custard and raspberry jam. The men all praised the meal effusively, and Mama Gruber and Anna Marie beamed with pride. In the afternoon the three cousins took a long walk, going past the parish church and down Mariahilferstrasse to enjoy the decorations again. The fresh snow gave everything a clean, pristine look, and the cold bite in the air made Joseph glad for his new scarf.

The idyllic mood of the Christmas season evaporated with Joseph's Sunday afternoon visit to the bookstore. He sensed that something was amiss as soon as he entered the store. Miriam was not there, and Herr Engelmann was agitated and distracted. Concerned, Joseph asked, "What's the matter? Is something wrong?"

Engelmann sighed. "My daughter has been in the hospital for three days now. They don't expect her to live much longer. Miriam is with her, and I'm going to close the store early today and join them."

"I'm so sorry," Joseph said quietly. "Is there anything I can do?"

"Thank you, but no. We knew this was coming, but it's still hard to accept. Her loss will be devastating to us, and it makes it even more important for Miriam to get that visa." He smiled sadly and clasped both of Joseph's hands. "She will need you now, more than ever," he said emphatically. "Your being an American somehow gives her hope that she will get there, eventually. It gives her something to hold onto. Thank you for coming!"

Joseph mumbled a dull response about being happy to help. Picking up a pencil from the counter he jotted down a number. "This is the telephone number for Uncle Oskar's shop. Call me if there's anything I can do." They shook hands sincerely, and he left.

Outside on the sidewalk it felt colder than before, the wind more penetrating, the Christmas decorations along the street less cheery, and the passersby less friendly. Shoving his hands into the pockets of his coat he felt the carving he had brought to give to Miriam. He glanced back at the store, thinking that he might go back in and leave it for her, but Herr Engelmann had already hung the "Closed" sign on the door and turned off the lights. He walked slowly away. Taking a roundabout route home, he passed Mariahilfekirche, pausing in front to contemplate its beauty.

"'Mary's help,'" he whispered. "That's your name. Do you help Jews too?" On impulse, he walked into the church. A few others were scattered inside, sitting in the pews, heads bowed. He moved slowly and quietly down the nave, just past the ornate pulpit on the left wall, and stepped into a chapel on the right side, nearest the high altar. Dropping a schilling into the box he lit a candle, crossed himself, and knelt to pray.

He stayed for most of an hour, praying and meditating. It occurred to him, even as he sought Divine intervention on Miriam's behalf, that he would miss her terribly if she went to America. Anna Marie's words came back to him: "Nothing lasts forever! Enjoy it while it lasts!" *So true,* he thought bitterly, *but it's not an easy thing to do.* Then it occurred to him that if Miriam emigrated to America to be with her family, she would be in New York. Suddenly he felt much better—not quite *happy*, but definitely more optimistic. After another quick prayer he crossed himself again and headed for the exit.

On Tuesday Oskar approached Joseph in the workshop and handed him a slip of paper. With a look of fatherly concern he said, "Your friend, Herr Engelmann, just called. His daughter has passed away and the funeral will be tomorrow. You are invited to attend." The location of the synagogue and the time of the service were written on the slip. "You may leave to go, if you wish."

"Thank you, Uncle Oskar. I appreciate it. I won't be gone long."

The service the next morning was brief. About two dozen black-clad mourners were present. Joseph stood at the back of the room and followed the procession to the cemetery. After the grave was filled, he expected the group to disperse, but instead they all returned to the synagogue for a special meal. Called the "meal of condolence," each item on the menu possessed symbolic significance: bread, hard-boiled eggs, and lentils. Tea and wine were served also.

Herr Engelmann introduced Joseph to some of his friends who were curious about his presence as an American and a non-Jew. While he was chatting with them Miriam suddenly appeared at his side and thanked him for coming. Her face looked drawn and tired and her eyes sad and red from crying. Joseph wished mightily that he could say something to assuage her grief, but after stammering a few words of sympathy, feeling out of place he said his good-byes and departed.

It was the first funeral Joseph had ever attended, and it had a sobering effect on him. In fact, it was the first time he had been in a cemetery and he found the sight of so many graves and tombstones disturbing. He had never had to contemplate the reality and the inevitability of death, and it gave new significance to Anna Marie's words: "Nothing lasts forever! Enjoy it while it lasts!"

He wondered what it was like to lose both parents before the age of twenty and to be left with no immediate family other than an aged grandfather. These thoughts made him miss his own family even more keenly, and a wave of homesickness unexpectedly swelled within him. That night he reread the letters he had received from them, imagining that he could hear their voices and laughter. He then stayed up late writing a lengthy letter home, expressing his love for them and his desire to be home again. Joseph was left with a renewed determination to make his year in Vienna worthwhile and to acquire all the knowledge and skills possible before returning home. More than ever, he felt a sense of mission, and redoubled his efforts to make the most of the time.

5

PORTENTS

The next two months passed quickly for Joseph. Every day in the workshop, under the expert tutelage of Herr Schneider he learned more about the techniques of using the various gouges, chisels, and knives to create intricate carvings and designs. Uncle Oskar assigned him all of the different tasks involved in building a clock cabinet, personally supervising his progress. He was pleased to see that his skills were improving rapidly.

Anna Marie and Stephan introduced Joseph to the beautiful Amalienbad public swimming pool. It was a half-hour's ride on streetcars but well worth the trip because the interior was fabulously Art Deco—especially the thermal pool, which was ringed with tall, Egyptian-style columns. Joseph was almost beside himself with excitement trying to see everything at once, much to the amusement of his two cousins. While they swam, he sketched the exotic columns, intending to incorporate them into his Art Deco clock design.

His Sunday afternoons with Miriam and Herr Engelmann were something he looked forward to each week. He still found her direct eye contact a bit unsettling, but her quiet modesty was endearing. She was very intelligent and advanced quickly in her English proficiency. He showed her his clock sketches and found her to be quite knowledgeable about art. Her suggestions led him to modify his plans in several aspects, and he came to place a high value on her opinions.

He also valued Herr Engelmann's comments on the political developments taking place in Austria—and there were new developments almost every day. Tension was rising and everyone was speculating about what Germany was going to do—or rather, about what Adolf Hitler was going to do.

On the first Sunday in March, while they played a game of chess, Joseph asked, "Do you think Germany will annex Austria?"

Engelmann frowned. "Hitler has said for many years that this was his goal. Since his earliest days in politics, he has preached the doctrine of a 'Greater Germany,' to include all ethnic German-speakers. So, to answer your question—I think it is only a matter of time. Sooner or later, he intends to make Austria part of Germany. In fact, he's already set it in motion."

"How so?"

"Just last month the police raided the Vienna headquarters of the Austrian Nazi Party and seized an arsenal of weapons. They were planning an overthrow of the government. And just a couple of weeks ago Hitler bullied Schuschnigg into appointing Nazis into his cabinet. Assassinations continue on a regular basis—hundreds since the 1934 revolt. Austria is hanging by a thread."

"Will Austria allow this, or will Austria fight for its independence?"

Engelmann paused, studying the board. Moving his knight he said quietly, "Check." Joseph blinked, and spent a long minute examining the position.

"That's checkmate, isn't it?" he asked finally.

"No, you have a way of escape," Engelmann said, "but it will cost you your queen."

Joseph grunted and twisted in his chair, hesitant to lose his most valuable piece. "If I give up my queen to stop checkmate," he grimaced, "I will surely lose the game before long."

"This is the same as the position of Austria," Engelmann nodded.

"She is in a very difficult situation and can escape Hitler's clutches for now only if she is willing to use every resource at her disposal. However, the final outcome may be inevitable."

Joseph continued staring glumly at the chess board. "Is it really so hopeless?"

Engelmann shrugged. "Austria is not able to stand up to a powerful state like Germany. Without support from Britain and France she cannot prevail, and I don't expect those countries to risk anything for Austria."

"Why not?"

"Have they denied Hitler anything yet? They said nothing when German soldiers marched into the Rhineland two years ago. Did they object when he absorbed the Saarland? Or when he rearmed his military? In addition to that, Germany has been allowed to stop making reparations payments. All those things were strictly forbidden by the Treaty of Versailles, and he violated all of them. The very heart of the post-war treaty has been ripped out.

"We thought that Italy might help us," he added, "but then Mussolini and Hitler signed an alliance pact and became friends, so that's out too."

Joseph sat quietly for a few minutes, looking at the board. "Uncle Oskar said that after the end of the war Austria wanted to unify with Germany, but the Allies wouldn't allow it. Is that right?"

"Perhaps. The post-war government in Vienna did propose a unification and the Allies did reject it, but it's not clear what the Austrian people thought of the idea. It seems that public sentiment has waxed and waned over the last two decades, and it's no clearer today than it was then."

"What do *you* think?"

"I think the majority oppose it, but those who want change are always louder than those who want the status quo, and the loudest voices may dominate."

"I meant, what do you personally think about the *unification*?"

Engelmann frowned again. "I oppose it, of course. I fear that it will go very hard on Jews here if Germany takes power. Jews have faced increasing persecution and discrimination under Hitler's rule —you know about the Nuremberg Laws, don't you?"

"I've heard of them. What are they?"

"In these laws the Nazis define who is a Jew and who isn't. If you are a Jew, you aren't allowed to be a citizen, vote, own a radio or telephone, practice medicine, or even just buy chocolate!"

Joseph shook his head in disbelief. "You and Miriam are non-practicing Jews, though. You wouldn't be affected by laws like that, would you?"

"Oh, yes!" he nodded vigorously. "According to the Nazis, Jewishness has nothing to do with your religious faith. It's all about your ancestors! And Jews are not allowed to marry non-Jews or to have romantic relationships with them. It defiles the German blood! Aryan blood must be kept pure! As if there actually were such a thing!" He pretended to spit on the floor.

"What makes it even more ridiculous is that your grandparents are considered to be Jewish if they participated in the Jewish community, attended synagogue and such. They could all four be gentile converts, but you are said to have 'Jewish blood' and belong to the 'Jewish race' even if they were actually Germans to the tenth generation!"

Joseph slowly and reluctantly picked up his queen piece and moved it to the square occupied by the black knight, and removed the knight from the board. Engelmann took the queen and replaced it with his bishop. Joseph sighed and scratched his head.

"By the way," Engelmann smiled mischievously, "do you know what Hitler's father's surname was?"

"I assume it was 'Hitler,'" Joseph said. "What else would it be?"

"Schicklgruber!" Engelmann laughed out loud and rapped the table with his knuckles. "He changed his name a few years before his son was born. Can you imagine how things might be different if he hadn't?" He laughed again. "Picture this: Nazi Stormtroopers goosestepping down the avenue with their swastikas and helmets, shouting 'Heil Schicklgruber!'" The old man giggled uncontrollably, weakly waving his arm in an imitation of Hitler giving the Nazi salute. Joseph couldn't help laughing too.

"Even funnier is this," Engelmann continued. "Schicklgruber was an illegitimate child and no one seems to know who his father was. Hitler never talks about his family history, but there are rumors that he might be a quarter Jewish!"

"No!" Joseph exclaimed in shock.

"Not that it matters. Even if it were true, according to the Nuremberg Laws he would not actually be Jewish. But then, neither would Jesus."

"Jesus was Jewish?" Joseph asked, confused. He had never thought about Jesus being Jewish.

"Did you think Mary was a *Roman*?" Engelmann laughed again. "Of course she was Jewish! But according to the Nuremberg Laws, to be Jewish you need at least three Jewish grandparents, and if Jesus was born of a virgin as Christians believe, then he had only two. And Hitler would have only one, so he's in the clear and so is Jesus. Convenient, wouldn't you say?"

"Very!" Joseph agreed, and pushed a pawn forward to attack the black bishop.

"You're giving me a free pawn?" Engelmann gave Joseph a disapproving look as he took the pawn with the bishop.

"Actually, I just wanted the bishop out of the way," Joseph smiled. He moved his rook across the board to Engelmann's back row, passing through the square previously occupied by the bishop. Setting it down with a thump he announced, "Checkmate!"

Engelmann stared at the board in amazement and then clapped his hands in delight. "Beautiful! You seized victory from the ashes of defeat!" Rising to his feet he reached across the table and shook Joseph's hand with both of his. "If only Austria could be so valiant!"

As they walked toward the front door of the bookstore, Engelmann said, "Just a minute! I have something you should read!" Reaching under the sales counter he produced two books and handed them to Joseph. "This is a two-volume biography of Adolf Hitler, written a year or two ago by a German journalist. It's the best source of information about his life and early years in politics. I just finished reading it myself. When you're done, bring it back and I'll put it out for sale."

Joseph stepped out onto the sidewalk just as a company of Austrian Nazis marched past in the street. They wore brown shirts with swastika bands on their sleeves, without coats despite the cold. Stomping loudly, out of step and apparently fueled by alcohol, they raised their arms in Nazi salutes, shouting Hitler's name and singing discordantly, "Deutschland Über Alles." He stood and watched them pass with a sick feeling in his stomach. *Some fine Aryan specimens these fellows are,* he thought sarcastically. *A bunch of drunken Schicklgrubers!* Tugging his cloth cap tightly in place and turning up his collar to the icy wind, he hurried home.

6

ANSCHLUSS!

The next week was an emotional roller coaster for all Austrians. Hitler demanded that the Austrian chancellor, Schuschnigg, resign and turn over control of the government to his Austrian Nazi supporters. Instead, on Wednesday as the Austrian Nazi Party rioted in the streets, Schuschnigg announced that a national plebiscite would be held on Sunday so that the people could choose whether to be annexed by Germany or not. There was immediately a great show of support for the government from both the socialist and conservative parties, promising to work together to defend Austria's sovereignty.

Uncle Oskar was confident that the people would vote for independence and not for annexation. "We'll show that little corporal he can't push us around!" he grinned. "That Schicklgruber bastard may be an Austrian by birth, but Germany can keep him!" Joseph had shared the story about Hitler's father and Oskar thought it was hilarious, though he was apparently confused about which one was the illegitimate child.

The situation intensified as the day of the plebiscite approached. On Friday, Hitler again demanded that Schuschnigg resign and threatened to invade Austria if he didn't. That evening the Gruber family sat anxiously in their parlor listening to the radio news report. The German army was said to be massing along the Austrian border in preparation to invade.

"They did that in '34 also," Uncle Oskar scowled. "But they didn't invade *then*. Hitler is bluffing again! Schuschnigg won't fall for it! Hitler will back down—he knows better than to cross that line!" His confidence was infectious, and Joseph and the others began to relax and feel more optimistic. However, within a couple of hours the crackling radio speaker was filled with the voice of Chancellor Schuschnigg, who in a brief speech announced the shocking news that he had called off the plebiscite and submitted his resignation, giving in to Hitler's demands in order to stave off an invasion and bloodshed. "We have yielded to force," he said, and concluded the speech with the words, spoken in a sad, trembling voice: "God protect Austria!" The speech was followed by the playing of the national anthem.

The Grubers sat in silence, staring at the square wooden box in disbelief. After the national anthem was completed, the program went off the air and only faint static came out of the felt-covered speaker. Uncle Oskar got up and walked slowly across the green carpet and turned it off. The total silence in the room was almost unnerving and Joseph squirmed uncomfortably in his chair. Without saying a word Oskar went up the stairs to his bedroom, and Mama Gruber followed, wringing her hands.

"What's going to happen now?" asked Anna Marie uneasily. "Does this mean that the Germans won't invade?"

"I don't see why they would," Stephan replied. "Hitler got what he wanted. Austrian Nazis will run the government now, and they will do whatever he tells them. It's not exactly independence, but maybe it's better than being annexed and ceasing to exist at all!"

Anna Marie looked at Joseph. "What do *you* think will happen, Joseph? Do you think they will invade?"

Joseph hesitated, and then answered. "I agree with Stephan that there's no reason now for an invasion, but I'm not sure there won't be. Hitler isn't one to let things alone. If he thinks he can get away with it, he'll probably do it, and I think the question is not whether there is a reason *to* invade, but is there a reason *not* to invade? I'm afraid that the answer to that question is—'No.'" They exchanged concerned looks and Joseph added, "It won't surprise me if Hitler comes to Vienna by the end of the month and brings soldiers with him. If he does, the question is, will Austrians resist?" They contemplated this quietly for a moment and then, without anyone offering an answer to the question, headed upstairs to bed.

The next morning as the family sat down to eat breakfast, Uncle Oskar turned on the radio—something he never did at breakfast. "Just want to see what is happening," he said apologetically. Joseph poured himself a cup of hot tea and layered his buttered bread roll with cheese and wurst. He was about to take a bite when the announcer's excited voice suddenly broke into the music program: "At dawn this morning, the German Army crossed the border into Austria! German tanks, armored cars, trucks, and other mechanized transport are heading toward Linz!"

Mama Gruber screamed and dropped her cup and saucer with a loud clatter. Covering her face with her apron she ran from the room, sobbing. Oskar, ashen-faced, folded his napkin and went to console her. Anna Marie looked at Joseph wide-eyed. "You were right, but off by about three weeks!" Joseph dropped his head and shrugged. There were no other sounds for a few minutes other than those of eating utensils and tea cups. Eating was an excuse for not talking, and they were all too stunned to carry on a conversation.

The radio continued to reveal the day's developments. Reinhard Heydrich and Heinrich Himmler, of the Nazi SS, had arrived by airplane from Berlin at the Vienna airport early that morning. Schuschnigg had been arrested. The Austrian Nazi Party had taken control of the Rathaus—city hall—and the national parliament building on the Ringstrasse. The Viennese were advised to avoid the city center and stay off the main streets. Finally, Stephan reached over and turned the radio off. The silence was welcome.

Uncle Oskar closed the shop for the day. The three cousins walked to Mariahilferstrasse and stood in front of the church, next to the Haydn statue. A large swastika banner was draped over the façade of the church, and Nazi flags fluttered from streetlamp posts. Joseph shivered in the cold wind—or was it from nerves?

They were startled by loud, harsh voices and metallic banging sounds. Turning, they saw Nazi-uniformed men roughly shoving three men in business suits into the back of an unmarked truck and then slamming the doors shut. The truck drove away with a roar and a cloud of dark smoke. As the truck left, they saw that it had been parked in front of the Social Democratic Party's offices—a left-wing party that opposed unification with Germany.

Two blocks away they found a man lying in an alley beside a garbage can, his head and face covered in blood. They helped him to his feet, supporting him as he swayed and almost fell. It was evident that he was Jewish. His side curls had been cut off and his right hand had been badly broken, with fragments of bone protruding through the skin.

"What happened to you?" Anna Marie asked, horrified.

"Nazis," he mumbled, and spat blood. "I was just walking along the street and they attacked me. Four of them. I thought they were going to kill me!"

"Where do you live?" Stephan asked. "We'll help you get back home."

He could walk only with assistance, so they helped him to his doorway and rang the bell. A woman carrying a baby on her hip opened the door and uttered a cry of horror at the sight of her husband. He staggered inside, and the door closed behind him. The three walked slowly away.

Joseph had a sick feeling in his stomach. He was suddenly afraid for Herr Engelmann and Miriam and hurried to the bookstore. The front door was locked and it was dark inside. Shielding his eyes with both hands to peer through the plate-glass display window, he saw nothing out of order. He stepped back to the curb and looked up at the apartment windows. The curtains were pulled shut. Turning to his cousins who had trailed behind him, he said, "No sign of any trouble here. I hope they are alright."

"Maybe you can telephone them from the shop?" suggested Stephan.

"Good idea!" agreed Joseph. "Let's go home. This is all very—" he hesitated, unable to think of a word that expressed his feelings.

"Horrible," Anna Marie offered. "And frightening." Joseph and Stephan nodded agreement. She squeezed her way between them as they walked and took the arm of each, holding on tightly all the way back. Back in the shop, Joseph telephoned the bookstore but did not get an answer. He was uneasy the rest of the day and slept fitfully that night.

The next morning was Sunday, March 13, and the radio informed them that Adolf Hitler would be arriving in Vienna later that day. There would, of course, be no plebiscite. The Führer, the announcer said, would be staying at the Hotel Imperial on the Ringstrasse not far from the Opera House. Joseph remembered reading somewhere how Hitler had shoveled snow on the sidewalk in front of that hotel as a penniless young man, and that returning to it as a conquering hero was a dream of his. *Well*, thought Joseph glumly, *I guess he can cross that one off his list.*

At the Mariahilfekirche the pews were full of people. Joseph had never seen so many in attendance. He could hear sniffling sounds and sensed a pervading malaise of dread and sadness. The organ's deep chords did nothing to lighten the mood. However, the soft light filtering through the stained-glass windows gave the interior a mystical glow, and the high ceiling with its rounded arches seemed to invite the presence of the Divine. Joseph began to feel himself transported into a spiritual realm, away from the crisis taking place outside.

The sermon was about faith and perseverance through hardships, and Joseph, encouraged, realized that this was the right path to follow. He lifted his eyes and fixed them on the priest standing in the elevated pulpit. At the conclusion the priest dramatically raised his hands high and declared loudly and defiantly, "Our Führer is Christ!" The congregation spontaneously responded with a cry in unison, "Our Führer is Christ!" The sadness and despair that Joseph had felt at the beginning of the service was miraculously dispelled, and the atmosphere was now energized. Everyone else seemed to feel the same way. People were standing up straighter, looking each other in the eye and shaking hands.

Filing out into the sunshine, it felt like a new day. The air was cold, but the sun was bright and the sky cloudless. Joseph inhaled deeply, feeling invigorated by the chill. The Grubers mingled with the other congregants for a few minutes before heading home. Walking back to the shop, Joseph was so preoccupied with his thoughts that he didn't even look at the Apollo Theater. While Mama Gruber was preparing lunch he called Herr Engelmann again, but still there was no answer. He was worried.

After lunch he walked over to the bookstore and found it locked and dark. Having anticipated this, he pulled from his pocket a folded piece of paper and slipped it under the door. The note asked Engelmann to call Uhrmacher-Gruber as soon as possible and let Joseph know how he and Miriam were doing. Returning to the shop, he spent the afternoon working on a personal project in the workroom, planing and smoothing wood for a clock cabinet. Late that afternoon, just before he was about to go upstairs for dinner, the telephone rang. It was Herr Engelmann.

"Herr Engelmann! I've been trying to get in touch with you since yesterday! Are you alright?"

"Hello, Joseph." His voice was tired and dull. "Miriam and I are safe—for now. Thank you for your concern."

"Yesterday my cousins and I found a Jewish man who had been badly beaten by Nazis. I was afraid that you might have—" Joseph stopped, hesitant to speak the unspeakable.

"No, we have not been harmed, but others have not been so lucky. I don't know how long we will be spared. We spent yesterday and today standing in line at the United States consulate but did not get to talk to anyone." He sighed heavily. "It is more important than ever that Miriam get her visa to emigrate. Unfortunately, now there are so many applicants that it is almost impossible to get anything done."

"Is there anything I can do to help? Perhaps if I go to the

consulate with her, as an American, I might be able to help her get an interview!"

Engelmann hesitated before responding. "I doubt that would make a difference, Joseph, but at this point—" he hesitated again. "At this point, I'm willing to try anything."

"I'll be there first thing tomorrow morning, then," Joseph promised. "I'm sure Uncle Oskar will give me the morning off. We can be at the consulate by eight o'clock."

"Eight o'clock will be too late," Engelmann averred. "By then there will be a line of hundreds, maybe more. Can you be here at six? The streetcars will have begun running, and you can make it to the consulate before seven."

"Of course! Six it is. I'll see you then!" Joseph hung up the telephone feeling anxious but also relieved that there was at least something he could do to help.

7

DESPERATION

The next morning Joseph rose early and slipped downstairs in the dark apartment. He was surprised to see Mama Gruber in the kitchen already. "I didn't want you to leave without breakfast!" she said, putting a plate of toasted bread and cheese and a mug of hot tea on the table. As he gratefully sat down, she put a hand on his shoulder. "I hope you can do something to help your friends," she frowned. "This is all so wrong." Joseph thanked her, wolfed down the food, and hurried out the door.

Miriam was waiting, wearing a long black coat with a fur collar, a fur cap, and gloves. She held a large, fat envelope in front of her, containing a sheaf of visa application documents. Her cheeks were pink in the frosty air, and Joseph found himself thinking how pretty she was. They walked briskly to the streetcar stop and sat side by side on the trolley. The Ringstrasse, the main traffic artery of the central city, was lined with Nazi banners. German military vehicles were omnipresent, and as they passed the Hofburg they noticed a significant number of German soldiers in the plaza.

"I wonder what's going on?" Joseph remarked. "Is something happening?"

"I heard that Hitler is going to make a speech here," Miriam replied. "They are probably his security force, getting ready for it."

After a half-hour's ride they disembarked near the United States consulate. It was not yet seven o'clock but there was already a line of a couple hundred people stretching down the sidewalk. Joseph walked past the line to the front door, with Miriam following. He showed his U.S. passport to the officer at the door. "I'm an American citizen," he said. "I'd like to discuss some personal matters with the ambassador, please."

"There's no ambassador here," the officer frowned. "The consul can help you with whatever you need, though."

"Consul," repeated Joseph with a nod. "That's what I meant."

"Go to the front desk and tell them what you want and they'll give you an appointment," said the officer, opening the door.

The room was crowded with lines of people at a long counter of windows, talking through the speak holes to staffers, sliding papers back and forth through the tray. The air was filled with the busy murmur of anxious voices, punctuated every few seconds by the sound of an ink stamp or stapler. The staff member at the front desk was engaged in conversation with an older man in a suit. When Joseph approached the older man turned and asked, "How may we help you, sir?"

Joseph introduced himself and Miriam and showed his passport again. "I'd like to talk to the consul, please. I have some personal matters—"

"I'm the Chargé d'Affaires," the man interrupted, not unkindly. "John Cooper Wiley." He extended his hand. "I'm the one you want to speak to. What is your business?"

"We need an immigration visa. My friend here has been applying for one for two years and has all her paperwork in order but can't get an appointment to talk to anyone about it. I thought that maybe I could help her get an appointment. Can you help us with that?"

Wiley grunted and crossed his arms, rubbing his chin and frowning as he studied them. The staff member behind the desk said firmly, "She needs to go back outside and get in line. It may take a while, but she'll eventually get—"

Wiley waved his hand dismissively, cleared his throat, and interrupted again. "Mr. Thomas, my assistant, will talk to you. I can't guarantee anything, Mr. Gruber, but he can look into your friend's case." Turning to the desk he asked, "When is Roger available?"

With a surprised look, the staffer hurriedly consulted his appointment calendar on the desk. "Actually, Mr. Wiley, he is free right now for a few minutes."

"Good! Tell him they are coming up." Wiley turned to Joseph and Miriam. "Go up the stairs, turn left, and knock on the second door." Extending his hand he added, "Good luck!"

"Thank you, sir!" Joseph exclaimed. "That's very kind of you!" Miriam added her thanks, and they headed upstairs. As they reached the second floor, she squeezed Joseph's arm.

"I'm so scared, I can hardly talk," she whispered. "I can't believe this is actually happening!"

"Have faith!" Joseph said quietly. "Don't be afraid."

The voice inside bid them enter. It was a small office, furnished with rather worn blue carpet, red curtains, and dark wood furniture. Roger Thomas appeared to be about thirty years old with thinning brown hair, horn-rimmed glasses, and a rumpled suit and tie. A partially-eaten bread roll stuffed with cheese was on a plate on his desk, and he slurped a swallow of coffee before motioning for them to sit. He glanced quickly at his wristwatch, cleared his throat, and introduced himself.

"Roger Thomas, assistant Chargé. How may I help you, Mr. Gruber?"

"Actually, it's my friend who needs your help," Joseph began, tendering his passport yet again. "I'm an American citizen, but she is an Austrian. She has relatives in America and wants to emigrate as soon as possible."

"I see." He glanced over the passport and returned it.

"She has all of her paperwork—" Joseph began, but Thomas raised his hand for silence.

"Let her speak for herself," he said bluntly. Turning to Miriam he said, "Sprechen Sie English, Fräulein?" *Do you speak English, miss?*

"Yes sir," she replied in perfect English. "I speak English."

"Tell me about yourself, then."

Miriam told briefly how all of her relatives except for her mother and grandfather had emigrated to America over the past few years, and now that her mother had passed away, she wanted to go join them.

"What about your father?"

"He was a policeman, and was killed in the uprising in '34." She dropped her head, wincing at the pain of the memory.

"How old are you?"

"Seventeen, sir."

"Have you finished high school?"

"I will graduate this June, sir."

"Do you have any work skills?"

"I work in my grandfather's bookstore and keep his accounts."

"Have you obtained the necessary application documents?"

"Yes sir." She handed him the large, thick envelope, along with her Austrian passport.

He opened the envelope and pulled out the papers. He thumbed through them casually and then returned them to the envelope and placed it on his desk. Taking a pencil, he copied her name—Miriam Bauer—from her passport onto the envelope and then added it to a stack of a dozen similar envelopes.

"You are going to America and leave your grandfather here alone?" he asked skeptically.

"He wants me to go, and I am begging him to come with me," Miriam almost whispered, "but he insists on staying. Vienna is his home."

Thomas contemplated her for a moment. "Are you Jewish, Miss Bauer?"

"My mother was Jewish. My father was half-Jewish."

"And your grandfather?"

"Jewish, sir."

"He should reconsider staying here. It's going to be rough for Jews."

"It's already rough for Jews, sir."

"So I hear." He made a face as he concentrated, apparently making a reluctant decision. "Miss Bauer, I'm going to push your application forward."

"Oh, thank you!" she almost sobbed, covering her face with her hands. Joseph put his hand on her shoulder supportively.

"Don't thank me yet!" Thomas protested. "There are rules and regulations that must be followed, and that takes time. We will have to verify all of the information on your application, confirm the status of your relatives in America and their ability and willingness to sponsor your immigration so that you won't become a burden to the state. There are health records to be provided, also. I can't estimate when this will all be completed, or whether your application will be approved, but we will do the best we can." Handing her a business card he added, "You can call this number to check on your status. Now, I am late for an appointment."

They all stood up and Miriam stepped forward to clasp Thomas's hands in gratitude. Joseph shook his hand also. "I couldn't help noticing your lamp there," Joseph remarked, pointing to an Art Deco desk lamp. It was brilliantly colorful with its lamp shade mosaic of stained glass.

"Yes, it's a Tiffany!" beamed Thomas, suddenly warm and personable. "Cost me a month's salary!"

"I love Art Deco also," Joseph nodded. "And Klimt!" He gestured toward a framed print of Gustav Klimt's *The Woman in Gold* hanging on the side wall of the office.

"*The Woman in Gold!*" exclaimed Thomas. "I love Klimt's work! So beautiful!"

"I knew her," Miriam said simply. The men both stared at her.

"What do you mean, *you knew her*?" asked Thomas in astonishment.

"The woman in the painting—her name was Adele Bloch-Bauer. We were related somehow. I was only about four years old when she died, but I remember visiting the family. The painting was hanging over the fireplace in their parlor. I always thought it was so pretty, with the gold leaf shining." The men's stares were making her uncomfortable. Blushing, she shrugged, "That's not the only painting Klimt made of her, you know."

"Why haven't you told me this before?" Joseph gasped, putting his hands to his head as if in pain.

"You didn't ask," she said flatly, and went to the door. "Thank you, Mr. Thomas. I am eternally grateful!" She opened the door and exited the room. Joseph gave his head a vigorous shake, as if trying to clear his mind.

"Jeepers creepers!" he exclaimed.

"I second that," Thomas grinned.

Joseph hurried after Miriam, catching up to her on the stairs. Back on the sidewalk they paused, taking deep breaths of the cold air. As they walked toward the streetcar stop he said, "I think the line is twice as long as when we got here."

"Yes, it is," she agreed. "I feel sorry for all of them. I almost feel guilty for having gotten in ahead of them, but I'm so grateful for your help."

"Let's walk for a while," he suggested. "Uncle Oskar said I could have half the day off, so let's not be in a hurry." Miriam liked that idea and they strolled for blocks, chatting, laughing, and enjoying each other's company.

They became quiet, however, when they reached the Hofburg. A large multitude was rapidly filling the spacious Heldenplatz, packing in toward the Hofburg palace where a large Nazi swastika banner was draped from a balcony overlooking the vast square. Martial music was being played from somewhere near the front of the crowd, and some boys were climbing onto the equestrian statues for a better view. The two stood just inside the massive gates and surveyed the scene in silence.

A deafening roar went up from the crowd. Joseph could now see figures on the balcony, but not clearly. He saw one extend his arm in a Nazi salute, and the multitude responded again with a roar, shouting "Sieg Heil!" It took several minutes to calm the audience, and when it was quiet enough, Hitler began speaking. "As Führer and Chancellor of the German Nation and the Reich, I report before history the entry of my homeland into the German Reich." The crowd exploded with cheering again and did so several more times during the speech.

Joseph and Miriam exchanged concerned looks, shaking their heads at the shocking display of adulation. After a few minutes they had had all they could stomach, and they slipped out through the gates and resumed walking along the Ringstrasse. Catching a streetcar at the next stop they were soon back at Mariahilferstrasse. It was a mostly quiet ride with only sporadic conversation, as each was immersed in their own thoughts.

Herr Engelmann was overjoyed at hearing the news Miriam shared about her visa application, and he embraced Joseph warmly with tears in his eyes. However, when they described to him what they had seen at the Heldenplatz, he seemed to wilt. "I had hoped that the Austrian people would stand up for themselves and for their country," he said sadly, shaking his head. "Apparently that was too much to ask."

"Will you and Miriam be in any danger?" Joseph asked. "Is there anything I can do to help?"

Herr Engelmann hesitated, and then glanced about as if to see if anyone was listening, even though no one else was in the store. "There is one thing that you can do for us, Joseph! I hate to ask it, after you have been so much help already—" He hesitated again, biting his lip.

"Whatever you ask, I'm ready to do it!" Joseph declared boldly.

"Thank you, Joseph!" Engelmann nodded. "Wait here." He hurried into the back room, reappearing in a few seconds carrying a small, plain wooden box. He carefully placed the box on the sales counter as if it contained something fragile. Putting both hands on the lid, he fixed his gaze on Joseph as if looking into his soul. Joseph began to feel a bit uneasy.

"I expect that the Jews of Austria are going to suffer abuse at the hands of the Nazis," Engelmann said slowly. "I hope that I am wrong, but I have heard from friends in Germany about what they have experienced, and I don't expect it to be better here. So, I am preparing for the worst." He shrugged and gestured helplessly, and Miriam put her hand on his arm.

"I want you to take this box home with you, Joseph," he continued. "Keep it safe for me—for *us*," he put his hand on Miriam's. "It contains everything that's of value to me." He opened the box and Joseph's eyes widened. It contained stacks of bills, but not Austrian schillings. They were German Reichmarks. There were other items in the box also.

"Now that Austria belongs to Germany, our money will change. A friend of mine in a bank has warned me to get all of our savings exchanged into German marks and hide them. I am keeping enough to cover our expenses for now, and hopefully we will sell enough books to help make ends meet. Put this somewhere safe."

"Yes sir," Joseph mumbled, stunned. "What are those other things?"

"Just some personal treasures—my wife's and my parents' wedding rings, some old photographs, my father's pocket watch, and my grandfather's tobacco pipe. I don't want the Nazis to take them. Make sure Miriam gets to America with these things, and if for some reason she doesn't—" he stopped short and gave her a look that was almost frightened—"just make sure our family in America gets them."

"Opa!" Miriam gasped, clutching his arm with both hands and then impulsively embracing him. They held each other tightly and he stroked her hair, murmuring words of comfort.

Joseph felt sick to his stomach and angry at the same time. "Don't worry, Herr Engelmann," he vowed. "I'll take good care of your things, and I'll make sure Miriam gets to America—and you too, if you'll go."

Herr Engelmann shook his head ever so slightly with a sad smile. "Thank you, Joseph. You're a good young man!" The two of them turned and, still holding onto each other, walked into the back room. Joseph stood for a moment alone, contemplating the box, and then with a sigh picked it up and left the store.

8

CLOSING JAWS

"Papa, are you and Mama going to vote in the plebiscite tomorrow?" Anna Marie asked innocently at breakfast. It was a Saturday in early April, almost a month after the annexation, and Hitler had ordered a referendum to allow the people to express their approval or disapproval.

"No," Oskar replied bluntly, chewing a bite of dark bread and cheese. "No point in it. The whole Reich is voting, and even if everyone in Austria voted against it, we'd be outnumbered by the German voters."

"Herr Schneider says it isn't going to be a secret ballot," offered Stephan. "If you vote 'No' it will be obvious, and you don't want the Nazis coming after you!"

"Jews and Gypsies aren't allowed to vote," added Joseph quietly. "And several thousand socialists and communists have been arrested, so I think it's obvious how it's going to turn out."

"We'll just mind our own business," said Oskar. "We need to finish those clocks to take to Salzburg by the end of next week, so let's focus on doing our work."

Downstairs in the workshop, Joseph hung his blue work apron around his neck and tied the strings behind his back. "What do you want me to do while you finish the crown piece for this Regulator?" he asked Herr Schneider.

"*You* finish the crown piece," replied the bearded Alpine master gruffly. "You're ready." Joseph looked at him in surprise. "Use the small v-gouge," he added. "And don't mess it up!" He reached into the front pocket of his lederhosen and handed Joseph the tool, and then walked away to work on another clock.

Joseph took a deep breath and ran his fingers slowly over the surface of the wood, almost caressing it. Placing the edge of the tool on the wood like a surgeon with a scalpel, he gently began incising the grooves. Occasionally blowing tiny chips and slivers away, he focused so intently on his work for the next hour that he did not hear Schneider approach. He was a bit startled when the master leaned in for a closer look and studied Joseph's work for several seconds. Joseph waited, holding his breath nervously. Schneider stood up. "I knew you were ready," was all he said, and returned to the other table without looking back.

Joseph caught Stephan's eye across the room and they both grinned with delight. Stephan gave him a thumbs up signal, and Joseph resumed carving with renewed energy and confidence. Before he knew it, it was lunch time. Since it was Saturday the shop closed at noon, and they were free for the rest of the day. Stephan went to the coffee shop to get Anna Marie and Joseph went to the bookstore to get Miriam. The four were going swimming at the Amalienbad pool.

Joseph sat beside Miriam on the streetcar. "Have you heard anything yet about your visa?" he asked.

"I called the consulate last week," she replied, "and they said it was too soon to have any news. I'm to call again next month."

"Have you talked to your Opa about going with you?"

"He won't go. He says it would take too long to do the paperwork and he doesn't want me to have to wait for him. Besides, Vienna is his home. He doesn't want to leave."

"I'll talk to him again tomorrow afternoon. We've got to change his mind," Joseph said grimly. "Bad things are happening, and I'm afraid for him—and for you."

"I'm afraid too," she shuddered. "We know people who've been arrested and taken away. Others have been abused on the street. Some have lost their businesses and belongings. One of my teachers was fired for being Jewish. It's just awful!"

"Have either of you been mistreated?"

"No, we've been lucky so far. But every time I leave home, I'm afraid. And Opa is afraid *for* me. We can't go on living like this." Miriam's fear showed in her eyes and it made Joseph feel rage rising in his heart. He was determined that he would not let anything happen to her.

The Amalienbad pool was an enchanting place for Joseph. Miriam had never visited before and was stunned by its beauty. The two-story galleries emphasized the height of the interior space, and the glass ceiling high overhead, arched like an airplane hangar, let soft light fall onto the aqua blue-green pool. Miriam gasped in delight when Joseph pointed out the ornate columns around the thermal pool. "That's part of the inspiration for my clock design," he grinned. "Isn't that something!" She agreed that it was.

Joseph took a few minutes to make a quick sketch of some details in the thermal pool before joining the other three in swimming. He donned his swim trunks and, pausing to flex his muscles in the mirror, went out to the pool. Miriam, wearing a blue swimsuit, was standing in the shallow end of the pool with her hair pinned on top of her head to stay dry. As he walked toward her, two young men swam up and confronted her. They were lean and dark-haired with unfriendly expressions, and stood too close for propriety.

"You look Jewish to me," one said, sneering. "Are you *Jewish*, girl?"

"Mind your own business!" Miriam replied firmly, but with a fearful glance as she stepped backward.

"You *are* Jewish!" accused the other, curling his upper lip. He stepped forward and reached toward her with his hand. "Not afraid of getting *wet* are you, Jew-girl?"

"Pfoten weg!" Joseph snapped in Wienerisch. *Get your paws off!*

Their surprised eyes went up to his muscular figure standing on the deck of the pool looking down at them. "Who do you think you are?" jeered one of them, attempting to sound bold even as he dropped his hand.

Ignoring the question Joseph continued, "Leave her alone! She's my friend, and no concern of yours."

"You like Jew-girls, Tarzan?" Grinning evilly at his companion, he tried to take the offensive.

"You don't look very Aryan yourselves," parried Joseph. "In fact, you both look like foreigners, to me. Maybe we should have a policeman check *your* papers."

They blinked in surprise and shot each other an uncertain look. They hadn't expected to be challenged. "*You* mind your own business," bluffed one, lamely. Turning back to the pool he added, "We came here to swim, not to argue with the likes of you!" The two swam away and Joseph sat on the edge of the pool, dangling his feet in the water.

Before he could speak, Miriam said, "I want to leave. I don't want to swim anymore." She held her hands above the water as she hurried to the steps.

"They won't bother you anymore," Joseph promised. "I'll stay close and make sure no one—"

"I'm cold," she insisted, sounding almost angry. "I want to go home!"

"Alright," he consented quickly. "We'll leave right away. I just need to tell Stephan and Anna Marie."

Within a few minutes they walked out of the natatorium and boarded the streetcar. They sat quietly together at first, and after a while Miriam spoke. "I'm sorry I spoiled your afternoon. I wish I hadn't come."

"It's their fault—not yours."

"You know, you could get in a lot of trouble sticking up for a Jew like that." She gave Joseph a quick, nervous, sideways look.

"Well, you know," he replied with a wink, "you're only three-fourths Jewish!"

"The law says that's enough to make me a Jew, and I am."

Joseph's mind suddenly flashed back to a scene in Hamburg

several months ago, and he recalled a vision of Herr Engelmann intervening on behalf of a Jewish man being mistreated by two Nazis. "Your Opa told me once, 'You have to know when to advance your pawns.'" He smiled and shrugged. "I may not be a knight in shining armor, but I can advance my pawns. If trouble comes, it comes."

She put her hand on his and fixed him with her characteristic, direct gaze. "Thank you, Joseph. Opa was right—you are a good man."

Joseph swallowed hard and suddenly felt very uncomfortable. On impulse he pulled out his sketchbook and flipped it open to his clock designs. "This is how I was planning to use the design of those columns around the thermal pool. I'm trying to figure out how to incorporate the vivid colors. Paint doesn't seem to be sharp enough. What do you think?"

She studied him for a few seconds with an amused smile. "Perhaps you should try enamel paint. Several layers of it would create a polished, bright effect, sort of like Klimt did with *The Woman in Gold*."

He stared at her wide-eyed. "Enamel! I never thought of that! That is a *fantastic* idea! Thank you!" He threw his arm around her shoulders and gave her a crushing hug. "Now I'm *really* excited! I can't wait to get to work!" For the remainder of the journey home, they talked about his clock design, with heads close together over his sketchbook. They were so engaged in the conversation that they almost forgot to exit the streetcar at their stop.

Upon entering the bookstore, they found Herr Engelmann unusually quiet and somber. "Opa, is something the matter?" Miriam asked.

He made a wincing face and hesitated, clearly reluctant to answer. They waited and finally with a sigh, he said, "Bad news, I'm afraid, my dear. Since Austria is no longer an independent country, all foreign embassies are being closed. It's not clear exactly what that means, but you may not be able to get your visa here in Vienna anymore. You might have to go to Berlin."

Joseph felt as if he'd been punched in the stomach. He could only stare in shock. Miriam's reaction was more visible—she let out an involuntary cry of dismay, her hands going to her mouth. "No!" she cried. "No! They can't do that!" And she ran past them into the back room sobbing loudly.

"I can't believe it!" Joseph gasped. His knees suddenly weak, he leaned against the sales counter for support. "Surely the consulate will still help with visas? What about all those people standing in line every day? They've got to do something for them!"

"I don't know," Engelmann said tiredly, shaking his head. "I just don't know." Giving Joseph an apologetic look, he added, "I have to go to Miriam. She needs me." And he followed her through the curtain.

Joseph stood on the sidewalk in the chilly April breeze for a long moment. Across the street was a small jewelry store which was owned by a Jew. There was a notice taped to the display window, and Joseph walked over to investigate. His eyebrows lifted in surprise as he read that the business had been "Aryanized," or taken over by non-Jewish ownership. Curious, he peered through the glass. The dark interior was in disarray and some of the display cases appeared to be damaged. Glancing about, he saw a policeman strolling in his direction. Vienna policemen now wore the Nazi swastika armband and carried pistols on their side.

"Good afternoon, officer," he said pleasantly. "Can you tell me what happened to this store? Did the owner sell his business?"

"*Sell!*" The policeman snorted contemptuously. "It was *taken* from him, like other Jew-owned businesses all over Vienna. He committed suicide, which is just as well, since he would have been deported anyway." Seeing Joseph's expression of surprise he added, "Things are different now. Jews aren't going to have it so easy anymore! They'll get what's coming to them!" Clicking his heels and extending a stiff arm, he barked, "Heil Hitler!" He then looked expectantly at Joseph, waiting for his response.

Joseph nodded thoughtfully and said, "Thank you, officer! You've been most helpful." As he walked away the officer repeated his "Heil Hitler!" even louder. Joseph ignored him and continued to walk, leaving the policeman glaring after him. At a third "Heil Hitler!"— this time with a commanding tone—Joseph, without turning around, made a feeble wave of his arm and took a few steps mimicking Charlie Chaplin's famous penguin walk. While crossing the street at the next corner he saw that the officer was following him, and he began to feel nervous.

Reaching the Mariahilfekirche, he ducked inside and found a seat in one of the side chapels. He lit a candle and crossed himself, and sitting down, he bent forward, resting his elbows on his knees. He found that he had a lot to pray about. While praying for Herr Engelmann and Miriam, a sudden inspiration came to him. He sat up abruptly with a grunt. *Would this work? Could Herr Engelmann's store really be protected from Aryanization?* He became excited that his idea might actually work. Looking up at the statue of the Virgin Mary he breathed, "Thank you! I knew you'd come through!" He hurried out of the church and ran back to the shop, looking for Uncle Oskar.

"WHATEVER IT TAKES!"

By working into the evenings they had managed to complete the clock order on time. Six Vienna Regulators and eight mantle clocks were now carefully wrapped and loaded into the back of Oskar's small van for delivery to Salzburg. The whole family was going—it was a welcome escape from the city, and besides, both Stephan and Anna Marie had April birthdays, so it was a celebration excursion. Joseph was particularly pleased that Uncle Oskar had agreed to allow Miriam to join them. She and Anna Marie had become good friends and would share a room in the Pension. This was Joseph's first opportunity to travel outside Vienna since his arrival five months earlier and he was eager to see the countryside and the famous castle in Salzburg.

The van did not have seats for all six of the party so the women and Stephan took the train while Joseph, who had experience driving on the right side of the road—something new in Austria since the Anschluss—rode in the van with Uncle Oskar. In fact, Oskar asked Joseph to take the wheel as soon as they were outside the city, and he proceeded to drive all the way to Salzburg. They departed shortly after sun-up and drove carefully along the two-lane roads, stopping occasionally to check on their fragile, valuable cargo.

Their route took them westward through St. Pölten, Melk, and Steyr, and along the shores of the beautiful lakes Attersee and Mondsee. The scenery became more dramatic and Alpine as they travelled, and Joseph was transfixed by the magnificent views of the mountains and the picturesque villages with their onion-dome church spires. Oskar hadn't been to Salzburg in several years and he was also enjoying the scenery as he relaxed in the passenger seat with a bottle of beer.

"You know, Joseph," Oskar said, gesturing with his beer bottle, "that was a really smart idea you had, to have Herr Engelmann sell his bookstore to me. That could save his life!"

"Yes," Joseph agreed. "Even though it wasn't for full price, he would have gotten nothing if the Nazis had confiscated it. Hopefully someday he will be able to buy it back from you at the same price." The thick stack of German marks was now in the wooden box under Joseph's bed, with the family treasures of Herr Engelmann.

"Of course," Oskar nodded, and belched. "As long as he pays the taxes, everything should work out just fine. Glad to—watch out for that pothole!" Expelling his breath with a loud "Whew!" he added, "That was a close one!"

After another kilometer Oskar turned to Joseph with a furrowed brow. "It surprised me that Engelmann was willing to do it, though. The store was worth at least three times what I paid him." He paused reflectively and added, "He seemed to trust me quite a lot."

"He trusts *me*, and I trust *you* to treat him fairly," Joseph replied. "Like you said, if the Nazis seize it, he won't get anything. This way, hopefully they won't take it and he can get it back later. I'm sure he would do the same for you if the shoe was on the other foot."

Oskar grunted. "Maybe so. Seemed like a nice fellow."

They reached Salzburg in the early afternoon and delivered the clocks. The purchaser was a business which sold expensive furnishings, located on the busy main street in central Salzburg. They hung the cabinets on the wall in the display area and assembled the clockworks, pendulums and weights. Once all of the clocks were running and chiming properly, Oskar collected the payment of almost three thousand Reichmarks.

Returning to the van he elbowed Joseph with a grin. "That covers what I paid for the bookstore and then some!" When they reached the Pension the rest of the family were already there. Oskar gave Joseph and Stephan each a hundred marks as a bonus for the big sale. "I'll give Schneider his bonus when we get back," he beamed. "This is a good ending to a good week!" Joseph had to agree—it did feel like things were looking up, at least a bit.

Even Miriam seemed to be in a good mood. The four youngsters walked up to the castle, Hohensalzburg, after supper. The massive fortress, begun in the eleventh century, was fabulous to behold, especially in the moonlight. They stood at the parapet looking down on the myriad lights of the city and the winding Salzach River. The backdrop of snow-capped mountains gave the scene a fairy-tale quality, and Joseph couldn't get enough. They strolled about for an hour taking in the view from different directions, and then it was time to go back down to the city.

The next day was Sunday and the family went to Mass in the Salzburg cathedral, known as the Salzburger Dom. The cathedral was more than three hundred years old and featured twin towers with a large, soaring cupola over the apse. The cavernous interior was ornately baroque, richly ornamented, and very *big*. The nave was a hundred meters long, leading to the high altar with its painted altarpiece, statues, and marble columns.

After the service Joseph asked Miriam, "What did you think?"

She looked perplexed. "Do you understand Latin?"

"No, that's just the way it's been done for almost two thousand years."

"Interesting," was all she said.

Slightly annoyed, Joseph pressed, "What do you mean, 'interesting'?"

"Well, Jewish synagogue services are in Hebrew, but Jews learn Hebrew in school. We understand what is being read from the Torah, the prayers, and sermons. It just seems strange to me that Catholics don't understand what is being said in the worship services."

"I agree!" Anna Marie chimed in, having overheard the conversation. "I think they ought to use German, not some ancient language that nobody understands!"

"Or require everyone to learn Latin in school," suggested Miriam. "Being able to understand what the priest is saying seems pretty important to me."

"That's too much trouble when they could just speak the language that everyone already knows," countered Anna Marie. "It's not like Latin is some magical language we have to use so that God will understand. He understands German, and Hebrew too!"

"Better not let Uncle Oskar hear you say that," warned Joseph. "He wouldn't like it a bit!"

"Wouldn't like what?" asked Oskar over his shoulder. Anna Marie burst out laughing and clapped her hands in merriment.

"It's nothing, Papa!" she giggled. "We're just talking about overthrowing the government and restoring the monarchy! But don't tell anyone!"

They all laughed, and Oskar then said seriously, "Be careful about saying such things in public! The Nazis don't seem to have a sense of humor."

"Don't talk about Nazis!" objected Mama Gruber. "This is supposed to be a vacation. We're here to enjoy ourselves!" They all agreed to talk about more pleasant topics, and chatted and laughed as they roamed the picturesque city center for an hour before deciding on a place to eat lunch.

The waiter took their orders, and Joseph noticed that he gave Miriam a hard, squinting stare before disappearing into the kitchen. A moment later the corpulent owner of the restaurant came to their table, clearing his throat ostentatiously. "I beg your pardon, honored guests," he intoned, "but is it true that you have a Jew in your party?" All eyes involuntarily focused on Miriam, who turned pale and froze. There was a second of stunned silence, broken by Joseph.

"Do you ask that of every guest with dark hair?" he challenged. "Or can you read a person's ancestry just by looking at them?"

"One judges by appearances," he insisted, jutting his chin out with jowls vibrating. "These days, one can't be too careful!"

"Well, if you must know," Joseph confided in a lowered voice, "she is actually a Gypsy and is going to steal you blind, and probably kidnap a child too."

"Joseph!" Miriam gasped, wide-eyed. "You're awful!"

Joseph laughed and patted her hand. "Just teasing!" he smiled. Turning to the restauranteur, he said in a more demanding tone, "Are you going to serve our food, or should we go somewhere else to eat?"

"No, no," he demurred quickly, "No problem! I was just—"

"Thank you," Joseph interrupted brusquely. "Your hospitality is appreciated."

The man looked at Oskar, who only shrugged. "Guten appetit!" *Good appetite!* He bowed quickly and backed away, returning to the kitchen.

"I didn't know you were so assertive, Joseph!" said Oskar. "Maybe I should let you negotiate our next clock sale!"

"I'll get you a good deal!" Joseph grinned. The others laughed and nodded, and returned to their conversations, but it wasn't the same. Miriam was especially quiet and did not have much appetite when the food arrived. Mama Gruber noticed this and after several worried glances at Miriam, finally spoke.

"Miriam! Don't let that stupid man upset you! You are part of our family now and anyone who insults you, insults us. We are all together, my dear!"

Miriam was so touched that a tear trickled down her cheek. "Thank you, Mama Gruber!" she smiled as she brushed away the tear. "That means a lot!" She seemed to feel better after that, and even laughed at one of Oskar's jokes. The atmosphere returned to normal and they even ordered dessert to finish the meal.

The restauranteur extended his arm and bid them a gruff "Heil Hitler!" as they departed, glaring angrily when they did not return the gesture. Heading out to see the sights for the afternoon, Oskar and Mama Gruber led the way followed by the two girls, who hooked arms and talked and giggled continuously. Joseph and Stephan brought up the rear.

"Swastikas are everywhere now," Stephan commented, with a critical look at the numerous flags and banners visible down the street. "I wonder where that comes from—did they just make it up?"

"I've been reading a biography of Hitler—Herr Engelmann loaned it to me," Joseph replied. "It's two volumes and hundreds of pages. The author claims that the swastika is a symbol used by the Mongolians and Chinese. It would be funny if the Supreme Race borrowed its main symbol from a non-Aryan culture in the Far East, wouldn't it?" They both laughed.

"And what about the Nazi salute that everyone is constantly making?" Stephan continued. "That's from the Roman Empire, isn't it?"

"Yes, but the Nazis got it from Mussolini and the Italian fascists. They're not Aryans, either!" They laughed again. "The Schicklgruber crowd strikes me as a bunch of ignorant hypocrites!" he added. "If Aryans are supposed to be blond and blue-eyed, what does that say about Hitler, Göring, Goebbels, and the rest of the top Nazis? Not a blue-eyed blond in the lot of them."

"I never thought of that!" Stephan exclaimed. "That's funny!"

"Yeah," Joseph scowled, turning serious, "but there's nothing funny about what they are doing to Jews and others they don't like. People who are law-abiding, tax-paying citizens shouldn't be beaten in the streets, arrested and sent to detention camps, and robbed of their property. That's why it's important that Miriam and Herr Engelmann get out of here before it's too late."

"What do you mean, 'before it's too late?'"

"I don't know, but I can't believe that things are going to get *better* for them. And if it gets *worse*—" he hesitated, shaking his head. "I don't want to find out what that would mean."

That thought ended the conversation and they walked in silence for several blocks. Joseph found himself watching Miriam as she chatted and laughed so cheerfully with Anna Marie. *How can she be so carefree, considering the dark cloud that is hanging over her? She's got to be scared out of her mind.* With a frown he unconsciously flexed his muscles. *I'm not going to let anything happen to her or Herr Engelmann,* he vowed. *Whatever I have to do to protect them, I'll do it.* Herr Engelmann's words suddenly came back to his mind: "Sometimes you have to make a sacrifice to win the game!" He took a deep breath and repeated grimly to himself, *Whatever it takes!*

10

STORM CLOUDS

Joseph had not been back in Vienna a week when he witnessed something so shocking that it filled him with horror and dread. It was Saturday evening and he and Miriam had gone to a movie at the Apollo Theater. She wore a scarf over her hair to reduce the chance that she would be recognized as Jewish, removing it only when the theater lights went down for the movie to begin.

The movie was *The Adventures of Robin Hood*, starring Errol Flynn. Joseph thought that the story resonated with the situation in Austria —a cruel tyrant taking over the government and abusing the people. He silently cheered on the hero, Robin Hood, as he fought back against the evil oppressors. He also thought that the name of Robin's beloved Maid Marian was interestingly similar to Miriam's name, and this made him feel even more strongly identified with the story. He reached in the dark and touched her hand, and she immediately laced her fingers with his and squeezed. After that it was a struggle for Joseph to stay focused on the movie.

The actors' voices were dubbed in German, which was typical for foreign language movies. Even though Joseph was used to this by now, he still found it amusing to hear German words coming from the mouths of American actors. He leaned over and whispered into

Miriam's ear, "They ought to be speaking Wienerisch!" She giggled out loud, drawing a "Shhh!" from behind. When the movie ended at about ten o'clock, they reluctantly joined the crowd as it exited slowly to the street, still holding hands.

The crowd thinned as people departed in various directions. The pavement glistened under the streetlamps and there was an almost transparent fog in the air, creating an ethereal glow. Their unhurried footsteps echoed hollowly between the buildings lining the street, and they turned onto Mariahilferstrasse, only a couple of blocks from the bookstore. That's when it happened.

First, they heard the sound of many feet marching and loud voices shouting and chanting. Then, a large contingent of brown-shirted Nazi Stormtroopers suddenly began pouring out from a side street, and they stepped back into the shadows against a wall, with Miriam shielded behind Joseph. Numbering perhaps five hundred strong, the roar of their voices thundered down the avenue, bouncing off the buildings and echoing in deafening fashion. The mob was so raucous, Joseph could not understand the chants, but picked out the words "Jew," "Führer," and "blood."

As the marchers turned down the street and began to pass them, Joseph and Miriam saw that the mob had a victim in its grasp. A young woman was being dragged by her arms, jerked and roughed up as they went. Her head had been shorn of all hair, and two blond braids were dangling from a sign hung around her neck. Something like white paint had been smeared on her head and ran down her face, she was missing a shoe, and her blouse was torn open, exposing her undergarments. As they passed under the light of a streetlamp, Joseph saw what was written on the sign: "I offered myself to a Jew." And then, like a boisterous ocean wave, the mob passed and was gone. The noise of their tramping boots and the shouting and chanting gradually faded as they progressed down the street toward the city center.

Joseph and Miriam continued to stand in the shadows until it was quiet again. He realized then that Miriam was shaking like a leaf in the wind and put his arm protectively around her shoulders. Without speaking a word they hurried to the bookstore—which now bore the name "Buchhandlung-Gruber"—where she fumbled in her small purse for the door key, dropping the key in the process. Joseph picked it up and unlocked the door. "Good night," he said softly, but she could not speak. She stepped quickly inside and turned the bolt. She looked at him through the door with a stricken face, and put her palm against the glass. Joseph placed his hand opposite hers, and then she was gone into the darkness.

In a daze, Joseph walked slowly home, stopping more than once to stare in disbelief in the direction taken by the Stormtroopers. As the significance of what he had seen began to sink in, he realized that he too was in danger. *That girl was not Jewish!* he thought. *She was blond, like me! But because of her relationship with a Jew, she was being publicly humiliated, maybe even injured. Even Aryans are being attacked now! If they had seen us standing there, we might have been dragged down the street too.* He had thought that Miriam was the one in danger and that he should protect her and Herr Engelmann, but *now*—now he realized that he also could suffer the wrath of the Nazis. He began to understand the fear and insecurity that Miriam felt.

Upon reaching Uhrmacher-Gruber he knew he would not be able to sleep, so rather than go upstairs immediately, he went into the workshop and spent an hour working on his clock project. It was starting to take shape, and he was pleased at his progress. After sanding a piece of the cabinet box for almost an hour, he ran his finger over it. *Smooth as glass!* he smiled. *The world has never seen a clock as beautiful as this will be! Rich people will want to buy it, but it won't be for sale!* He ran his eyes and fingers lovingly over the pieces of wood, nodding in satisfaction. Finally, at midnight, feeling calm and composed, he tip-toed up to bed.

He returned to the bookstore on Sunday afternoon for his visit with Herr Engelmann. Miriam had told him about the scene from the night before, and Engelmann was despondent and gloomy. He took so long to make a move on the chess board that Joseph thought he had forgotten whose turn it was, and he then made a disastrous move which spelled immediate defeat. Realizing his mistake, Engelmann tipped his king over, resigning from the game. With a sad smile he reached across to shake Joseph's hand.

"You're very worried, aren't you?" asked Joseph sympathetically.

Engelmann sighed. "Things keep getting worse," he said, shaking his head. "I try to be optimistic for Miriam's sake, but—" He could only gesture helplessly.

"Have you learned any more about the consulate—whether you can still get visas there?"

"No. They don't know, either. I called a couple of days ago and they were still waiting for instructions from Washington. Everything seems to have come to a complete halt, and no one knows when—or whether—things will get back to normal."

"I'll go back over there this week and talk to Roger Thomas again," Joseph said. "Miriam should go, too. I think he liked us. Did you know that she knew the woman in Klimt's *The Woman in Gold*? Thomas has a print of it on his office wall!"

Engelmann smiled wryly. "Yes, Joseph, I did know that! We were related, you know." Joseph, realizing that he had asked a dumb question, closed his eyes and groaned. Engelmann laughed. "It's good that he likes Klimt. Maybe he'll work something out for her. However, I suggest that you wait a couple of weeks before visiting him. We don't want him to feel that we are harassing him."

Joseph reluctantly agreed to wait and went out to the front room where Miriam, in her blue clerk's apron, was straightening books and displays and running a feather duster over the shelves. He pretended to browse through a stack of books on a table while actually watching her out of the corner of his eye. As a result, he accidentally dropped a heavy book on the floor with an explosive sound, making her jump and whirl around.

"Joseph!" she glared, pointing the feather duster at him in threatening fashion. "I just straightened that table! Don't you go messing it up!"

"Sorry!" he grinned sheepishly. "It slipped."

Her mouth twitched as she struggled to look angry. Jutting her chin out, she marched over to him and tickled his face with the feather duster. They both laughed, and he pretended to sneeze. "Gesundheit!" she smiled. *Health!*

"By the way," she continued, "have you finished that biography of our dear Führer? I'd like to get it back in the display window in case some Stormtroopers come by with money to spend."

"That might not be a good idea," Joseph frowned. "The author doesn't think too highly of 'our dear Führer.' In fact, he's pretty critical."

"That's probably why he wrote it in Switzerland," commented Herr Engelmann, who had just entered the room. "I've learned that Heiden had to leave Germany after the Nazis took power, and they have burned all of his books that they can find. We should probably get rid of them. It wouldn't do to have them found here."

"I'd like to keep them, if you don't mind," Joseph offered. "I'll pay you. They're very interesting, and I may read them again."

"Please do keep them!" exclaimed Engelmann. "Consider it a gift!"

Joseph insisted that he would pay for the books, and Herr Engelmann insisted that he not. They argued good naturedly back and forth until Miriam swatted Joseph's face again with the feather duster. "Take the books, Joseph!" she ordered. "It's rude to refuse a gift!"

While Joseph sputtered, rubbing his eyes, Herr Engelmann laughed. "It's settled then!" He made a mock bow to Miriam. "The queen of the bookstore must be obeyed!"

"That's right," she nodded, holding up the feather duster like a scepter. "It's settled!"

"It's settled!" Joseph conceded, raising his hands in surrender. Then suddenly, in alarm, he asked, "What time is it?"

Engelmann produced a silver pocket watch and flipped the cover open. "It's almost six o'clock."

"I must be getting home," Joseph grimaced. "Mama Gruber doesn't like it when anyone is late for supper!" He shook Engelmann's hand and thanked him for the books, and gave Miriam an affectionate pat on the shoulder. She flicked his nose with the feather duster again and made a face. He grinned and ran all the way to

Uhrmacher-Gruber, arriving just in time to take his seat with the family.

"Abendbrot"—literally "evening bread"—at the Gruber household usually consisted of sliced bread with cold cuts and cheeses, accompanied by wine, mineral water, and hot tea for anyone who wanted it. There was always a tasty dessert, such as apfelstrudel or topfenstrudel. Uncle Oskar liked to have the radio tuned to a station that played waltzes and other popular music, with the volume turned down to a relaxing level.

They finished the meal and remained at the table, talking and sipping their drinks. The music stopped and the announcer began to summarize the day's news. The NSDAP—the Nazi Party—controlled the radio stations and the news broadcasts, so all of the news was presented from that viewpoint. The announcer explained that ethnic Germans in the Sudeten region of Czechoslovakia were being mistreated. The Sudeten Nazi Party was demanding full autonomy from the Czech government and was receiving support from Berlin. Hitler called for justice for those "of German blood," and threatened to intervene if necessary. Tensions were rising.

"Mark my words," said Oskar grimly, "Czechoslovakia will meet the same fate as Austria before the year is out!"

"Surely not!" protested Mama Gruber. "The Czechs aren't even German! There is no way they will let Hitler take over their whole country! I'm sure the British and French would object."

"Austria was just a warm-up," Oskar insisted. "The Sudetenland is next, and I don't believe he will stop there. The British and French don't care about Czechoslovakia. He will gobble it up like a cat with a mouse, and no one will stop him." He looked around the table with his eyes spitting fire. "Mark my words!" he said again. "It will take a war to stop him!"

"Have any of you read his book, *Mein Kampf*?" asked Joseph. None of them had. "I was given a copy. In it, Hitler says he plans to destroy Russia and take back all of the land Germany won in the war—land that was taken away in the Treaty of Versailles. I didn't believe it when

I read it, but now I do. He intends to have a war with Russia and is moving east for that purpose."

"We need to emigrate to America right away!" exclaimed Anna Marie in alarm.

"I don't think that will be necessary," Oskar disagreed. "Hitler isn't stupid enough to start a war with Russia. Czechoslovakia, maybe, but not *Russia*!" Anna Marie started to object, but Oskar held up his hand for silence, cocking his head toward the radio. "Shhh! *The Blue Danube*! My favorite!" The familiar strains of the Strauss waltz came floating from the speaker, and Oskar closed his eyes and smiled, waving his hand as if directing an orchestra. Joseph and his cousins, perceiving that the conversation was over, quietly exited the room, heading upstairs.

All three went up to the roof. Although it was late April, the temperatures were still quite chilly. The sun was setting behind the Apollo Theater to the west, bathing the sky with a pinkish-orange glow. To the east they could see the spires of several churches, including Stephansdom in the distance, a couple of kilometers away.

"It's so pretty up here," Anna Marie said, pulling her sweater tighter around her. "I love sunsets!" After a moment she asked, "Joseph—do you really think there will be a war with Russia?"

"I think Hitler wants it," he replied, "and unless something stops him, I think he will probably get it." Turning to Stephan, he continued, "If it happens, you will probably be forced to join the army, and may get sent to Russia to fight for Germany."

"No!" she cried in distress. "Stephan—you must emigrate to America! Go with Joseph when he goes back home! I insist! Promise me you will go with Joseph!"

"Don't get so upset," Stephan demurred. "I agree with Papa. Hitler won't be so stupid as to start a war with Russia. I don't think there's anything to worry about." Focusing a glare on Joseph, he added, "You shouldn't be saying things like that and upsetting the family. You don't know what will happen any more than we do."

"True," Joseph admitted. "I'm sorry for upsetting you. I'll keep my thoughts to myself from now on, and hope and pray that things do work out all right."

They enjoyed the sunset until it was dark and the temperature dropped a few more degrees, and then went down to their rooms. Joseph read for an hour in the Heiden biography, finally finishing the second volume. He pulled his suitcase from under the bed and opened Herr Engelmann's box, which was buried under some clothes. Taking a few Reichsmarks he had saved in a sock, he added them to the box. *Sorry, Herr Engelmann,* he shrugged. *I really do have to pay you for the books, feather duster or no feather duster. But thank you, anyway.*

As he was about to close the suitcase, he noticed the corner of a book protruding from under a shirt. He pulled it out—it was his worn copy of *Mein Kampf.* He opened it and stared blankly at Herr Hartstein's inscription on the title page for several seconds. He hadn't even seen the book since leaving New York, and it looked strangely foreign to him now—an artefact from a different time, a different life. *I'll be throwing this in the trash,* he thought. *I don't want anyone to know I have it!* He replaced the book under the shirt, vowing to rid himself of it at his next opportunity, closed the suitcase, and pushed it back under the bed. Lying in the darkness he listened to Stephan's slow, rhythmic breathing for a long time before drifting off to sleep.

11

NO SMILES

"I have brought Doctor Tischer's clock," Joseph said to the woman at the window. "It's running properly now." He carefully unslung his knapsack and set it on the parquet floor of the office. The Napoleon-style mantel clock was wrapped in a wool blanket, its gong jangling slightly as he lifted it up to the counter. "Where would you like me to put it?" She pointed to a shelf across the room and went to fetch the doctor.

Joseph opened the convex glass door on the front of the clock and wound the spring with the key. Tischer came into the room, a stethoscope hanging around his neck. "Heil Hitler!" he saluted, extending his arm. Ignoring him, Joseph pushed the minute hand of the clock around the face until the clock began striking the hour, and continued until the clock was set to the correct time.

"We had to replace the spring and one of the winding gears," Joseph explained. "It should work perfectly now." He handed the invoice to the doctor, who stared at him intently before handing the bill to the woman at the window.

"Pay him!" he said abruptly, and went to the interior door. Pausing, he looked back at Joseph again, frowning, before returning to his patient. Two women sitting in the waiting room also frowned as they stared at Joseph. They averted their gaze when he returned the stare. Joseph pocketed the money, shouldered the knapsack, and hurried down the stairs to where Miriam waited inside the door to the street.

"It's only been two months since the Anschluss and I'm already sick and tired of all this saluting and 'Heil Hitler' all the time," he groused. "People are so stupid."

"You should probably do it anyway," she said. "You could get into trouble, and it could cost your uncle some business. Nobody cares if you really mean it or not."

"I don't know," he scowled. "It seems like cowardice to fake it."

"You know the old saying," she smiled—"Better a live dog than a dead lion."

"I don't like that saying!" he glared. "But I get your point. I'll think about it." She tucked her hand in his arm and they walked across Heiligenstädterstrasse to the Würstelstand Leo. "I saw an advertisement for this place in the newspaper," Joseph said more cheerfully. "It's the oldest würstelstand in Vienna—started ten years ago. Let's try it!"

They took their würstel and buns loaded with sauerkraut and mustard and stepped around the wagon to eat standing at a small pedestal table. Joseph grunted with pleasure as he bit into the hot, juicy frank and chewed with kraut dangling from his lips. Halfway through, he noticed that Miriam was not eating, but was examining hers with an expression of distaste. "What's the matter?" he asked. "Something wrong?"

"Joseph." she said in a tone that suggested disapproval. "Have you forgotten that I'm Jewish? I don't eat sausage."

He froze. "But I thought you were a non-practicing Jew!"

"True, but I still observe Jewish dietary traditions. I don't think I can eat this."

"I didn't know. I'm sorry. We'll find something else for you to eat."

Just then there was a commotion in the plaza behind them. They turned to find that a gang of a half-dozen Stormtroopers were roughing up a middle-aged woman in an expensive coat with a fur collar. There were several other people crowding around to watch as they forced her onto her knees next to a bucket and threw a small bristle brush in front of her. "You filthy Jew!" one of them sneered. "Get busy cleaning that dog sh-t off the street!"

"And hurry up!" added another one. "Or you'll be getting a bath!" The crowd of onlookers hooted and laughed, adding their insults. It became clear what he meant by a bath when he unbuttoned the front of his pants and began to urinate on the woman. The crowd cheered and clapped as she sobbed and scrubbed the brown stains with the brush, dipping it into the bucket of acid, burning her fingers in the process.

Suddenly the Stormtrooper who was urinating was shoved roughly, and losing his balance, sprawled on the pavement. Everyone turned to stare at Joseph. "What the hell do you think you're doing?" demanded the one who seemed to be the leader. "Are you a Jew-lover?"

"I'm a decent human being," snarled Joseph. "Unlike *you*. If you want to have fun with someone, try me instead." He knelt beside the woman, taking the brush from her hand and dipping it in the bucket. Glaring at them, he added, "You might want to think twice before you pee on someone who has a pail of acid." They blinked and stepped back, unsure what to do.

"Hey! I think we've got another one over here!" Everyone turned to see a grinning Stormtrooper standing beside Miriam. "I swear she's a Jew too! Let's give her a brush and a bath!"

"Idiot! Have you ever seen a Jew eat *würstel*?" Miriam asked icily, holding up her sausage bun. "No Jew would eat schweinfleisch!" She proceeded to take a bite and chew vigorously. With her mouth full of würstel, and sauerkraut tendrils hanging down her chin, she glared at him and sneered, "If anyone here needs a bath, it's *you*! Get away from me—and stop raising your arm like that!" She waved her hand in front of her nose as if smelling something unpleasant.

There were a couple of seconds of shocked silence, and then someone in the crowd laughed out loud, and others began laughing also. Red in the face and scowling, the Stormtrooper stepped away from Miriam. "My mistake! *Guten appetit!*" He turned to walk away, but then turned back to her and extended his arm and cried, "Heil Hitler!"

Miriam raised her würstel bun in desultory fashion and, with her mouth so full her words could hardly be understood, replied with what could pass for the expected salute. The Stormtrooper hesitated, but then accepted it as satisfactory. The leader pointed to Joseph and said in a threatening tone, "You're lucky today, *mench*. Don't interfere again or it won't go so easy with you!" He grabbed the pail and brush and the group left to seek another victim elsewhere.

The crowd quickly dispersed and the Jewish woman, humiliated, hurried away without speaking. Joseph walked slowly over to Miriam, meeting her eye contact questioningly. "Why did you do that?" he asked, almost in a whisper.

She swallowed the food and washed it down with a drink from the bottle of fizzy mineral water. "Suppose I hadn't," she said calmly. "Suppose they had forced me down on my knees and peed on me. What would you have done?"

"I would have beaten them to a bloody pulp!" he rasped, his voice failing him.

"All six of them at once?"

"Yes." He stared at her for a long moment and then heaved a deep breath. "You did that to protect me."

"Yes." She paused, and then added, "I didn't particularly want to get peed on, either." Joseph could only stare, speechless. She examined the sausage bun with a critical eye. "You know, this is actually pretty good!" she commented, and took another bite. "Don't tell Opa."

"That took a lot of guts." The voice spoke German with an American accent. Joseph and Miriam whirled about and found themselves facing a man wearing a suit and tie, standing by the side of the würstelstand with his paper-wrapped lunch in hand.

"Roger Thomas!" exclaimed Joseph and Miriam in unison. The executive assistant from the U.S. consulate made a quick bow.

"You're the one who knew *The Woman in Gold!*" he smiled, nodding to Miriam. "Miriam Bauer. And you're Joseph—but I can't remember your last name."

"Gruber—but it doesn't matter about me. Miriam is the one who needs the visa."

"Yes, I know. I wish I had better news for you," Thomas said apologetically, "but the wheels of government turn slowly—*very* slowly, unfortunately. We're still sorting out how the Anschluss will affect our operations here."

"You saw just now how it is for Jews here in Vienna," Miriam said, gesturing toward the wet stain on the street behind them. "It is awful, and getting worse all the time. It isn't safe for us to be on the street."

"Believe me, we're doing what we can," he said earnestly. "Remember, the antisemitic laws in Germany were developed gradually over the five years since Hitler came to power, but here in Austria it has all happened at once, and the sudden change is shocking."

"Very shocking," Miriam murmured. "I never dreamed it would be so terrible."

"I'll be returning home to New York in November," said Joseph. "Would it be possible for Miriam to get her visa by then? That way, she could travel with me."

Thomas shrugged helplessly. "Walk with me to the consulate," he said. "Let's talk." He ate his würstel and kraut while they walked. They switched into English while strolling along, and he was again impressed with Miriam's facility with the language. "I had forgotten that you speak English so well, Miriam! You must have a very good teacher!"

"I do, indeed!" she laughed, patting Joseph's arm. "He's been helping me for six months now." They went on discussing the crisis facing the Jews in Vienna, and the Nazi Party program in general. Thomas was skeptical that Hitler would attempt to seize Czechoslovakia, and held out hope that even the Sudetenland could be saved from his clutches. A war with Russia was out of the question, he insisted.

"Have you read *Mein Kampf*?" asked Joseph. "Russia is Hitler's main target. He wants to regain all the land Germany lost at the end of the war."

Thomas waved his hand dismissively. "He wrote that book while he was in prison fifteen years ago! I don't think anything he said then should be taken seriously today."

"I hope you're right," Joseph said doubtfully. He didn't agree with Thomas but kept his thoughts to himself as they approached the consulate. The line of visa applicants stretched down the block and around the corner. The sight filled Joseph with a feeling of despair and desperation. Surely the U.S. government would expedite the paperwork and rescue these forlorn, helpless people! He had a foreboding sense that time was running out.

Thomas again promised to do everything he could to push Miriam's application along, and he bade them a cheery farewell as he turned to go into the consulate. They hurried on down the street without speaking, past the thousands of eyes watching them. Fearful eyes. Hopeful eyes. Sad eyes. No smiles.

12

"IM HEIL'GEN LAND TIROL"

Joseph shoved his suitcase under the wooden bench of the third-class compartment and took a seat by the window. *Third class doesn't even get padded seats? Really?* He sighed. *My rear end is going to be sore by the time we get there, for sure.* He looked out at the station platform and waved to Miriam, who waved back and smiled. Three weeks away from Vienna—away from Miriam—was not a pleasant prospect. He dreaded the separation, but at the same time he was excited to get to go to the fabled mountains of Tyrol with Herr Schneider. His brief exposure to the beauty of the Alps during the trip to Salzburg had only whetted his appetite for more.

It was Schneider's habit to take a few weeks of vacation in June each year to visit his family in the village of Alpbach. It was also a professional trip for the master woodcarver, since he would be entering a piece in the regional woodcarving competition held annually in Innsbruck. He had won first place several times over the years, and had confided to Joseph that this would be his last time to participate. His bulky leather rucksack under the bench held his carving and little else—the aged mountaineer wore only lederhosen and white woolen shirts.

Schneider had invited Joseph to go along, after first getting Uncle

Oskar's permission. Oskar had been delighted—"This will be a great opportunity for you to expand your woodworking repertoire, Joseph! You can't get that kind of experience here in Vienna!" He had practically ordered Joseph to make the trip.

Schneider was not particularly talkative—a man of few words. He sat motionless with eyes closed, head bobbing slightly, apparently asleep. The half dozen other travelers in the compartment were similarly stoic, so it was a quiet ride for the first two hours as the train headed west toward Salzburg. This suited Joseph just fine as he enjoyed watching the landscape gradually change from gently rolling hills to increasingly rugged foothills, and then mountains. Views of the Danube River and then the lakes near Salzburg were captivating and commanded his admiration. But that was only the beginning.

From Salzburg the train turned southward, and the scenery was absolutely breathtaking. The train wound its way high above the valley floor, providing splendid panoramas of snow-capped peaks above and rivers and villages below, interrupted by occasional tunnels. Needle spires of Tyrolean churches replaced the Turkish-inspired onion turrets of the eastern provinces, signaling a distinctly different cultural environment. Joseph was glued to the window, transfixed by the incredible vistas and picturesque settings. After passing through Zell am See and Kitzbühel, he finally settled back in his seat, surprised at how exhausted he was from such prolonged concentration and excitement.

He glanced at Herr Schneider for the first time in more than an hour and saw his blue eyes twinkle beneath the bushy eyebrows. "This is so beautiful!" Joseph gushed. "I've never seen anything as incredible as this! It's like I've died and gone to heaven!"

"Tyrol *is* heaven!" exclaimed Schneider, slapping his knee with a bony hand. "When you are high up in the mountains, you are closest to God!"

"I believe it," nodded Joseph. "I don't know why you left this to go to Vienna!"

Schneider shrugged and the twinkle faded from his eyes. "I thought I had to pursue my career," he said sadly, pausing before adding, "and there were other reasons why I had to leave." He gave his head a quick shake as if trying to dislodge unpleasant memories. "It was a long time ago. Not worth talking about." Joseph would have liked to hear more, but he respected the older man's reticence and did not ask.

"When we get to Wörgl, we must change to a local train," Schneider said a few minutes later. "This train goes on to Innsbruck, and doesn't stop in Brixlegg—it's too small." As Joseph soon learned, the small, local train was pulled by an old steam engine which huffed and puffed patiently alongside the Inn River, visiting every hamlet along the way. It was only fifteen kilometers to Brixlegg, but thanks to frequent stops it took more than thirty minutes.

"So, this is where you're from?" asked Joseph, looking around with interest.

"No, I'm from Alpbach, a little village south of here. The train doesn't go there—we'll have to take the bus." They sat on a bench at the bus stop for an hour, eating ice cream and waiting for the next departure. Mountains loomed across the Inn, and the cloudless blue sky only reinforced Joseph's impression that Tyrol was a piece of heaven on earth.

"There are some things about Tyrol that you should know," Schneider said in a serious tone of voice. "I know that you and your uncle's family do not support the Nazi Party, but be aware that the Nazis are quite popular here, and be careful what you say."

"Why would the people of Tyrol support Hitler?" asked Joseph in surprise. "Are they antisemitic?"

"No more than anybody else," replied Schneider. "There aren't many Jews in Tyrol, and most Tyroleans have never seen a Jew. I hadn't, until I went to Vienna. It's not about Jews—it's about land."

"Tyrol's land?"

"Yes, but it's complicated," explained Schneider, clearing his throat and appearing somewhat agitated. "Tyrol has always defended its land against foreigners who invaded us. Our hero is Andreas Hofer, who led the fight against Napoleon and the French a hundred and thirty years ago. He won several battles until he was betrayed by a neighbor, captured, and executed by a firing squad. To this day, we still celebrate his memory and sing an anthem in his honor.

"After the end of the Great War, however, Tyrol was divided and the southern portion was given to the Italians. Italy was an ally of the Austrians at the beginning of the war, but they switched sides. The Allies promised to give South Tyrol to them if they would fight against us. So, just as Andrea Hofer was betrayed by a neighbor, Tyrol was betrayed by an ally and neighbor. When the war ended, Italy claimed the land that had always belonged to us, even though almost everyone there speaks German.

"The American President Wilson talked a lot about national self-determination, and we hoped this meant that South Tyroleans would be allowed to rejoin their brothers and be Austrians again, but that did not happen. We were ignored at the Versailles Conference. Betrayed again!

"Hitler talks a lot about uniting all Germans—'Pan-Germanism,' he calls it. That's the reason for Germany annexing Austria, and now he's trying to annex the Sudetenland from Czechoslovakia for the same reason—German-speakers live there. We hoped that Pan-Germanism would lead to Tyrol being reunited again, but—no! In return for Mussolini giving his approval to the Austrian Anschluss, Hitler has agreed to let Italy keep the South Tyrol! Betrayed again!"

Joseph frowned, perplexed. "If Hitler didn't deliver on his promise to reunite all German-speakers, why do Tyroleans still support him?"

Schneider spread his hands in helpless frustration. "They feel they have no choice! The history of our land is one of repeated betrayals by those who pretended to be our friends. There is no one we can turn to for justice! Vienna is no use anymore. We can't fight Germany or Italy. No one speaks up for Tyrol! But all this disappointment has only made us stronger. It forces us to rely on each other. It is Tyrol against the world, and someday we will prevail!"

His fists clenched and eyes flashing, Schneider glared at Joseph for long seconds, and finally relaxed. The twinkle came back into his eyes and he patted Joseph's knee. "So, you see, Joseph," he smiled, seeming a bit embarrassed by his display of emotion, "you should know some things about Tyrol!" He laughed shortly. "Here comes the bus!"

The red and white bus, filled to capacity with twelve passengers, sputtered out of Wörgl, heading south. The driver was clearly in no hurry, which Joseph didn't mind since it allowed him more opportunity to observe the countryside. As they left the town behind, the road immediately began to climb up the mountain valley, the Alpbachthal. Stone and brick walls bordered the road most of the way, with stout nets hanging from the looming rock face to control avalanches and rock slides. Joseph's ears popped each time he swallowed.

Using mostly the lower gears, the bus laboriously climbed onward. It stopped twice at a couple of tiny clusters of buildings hardly deserving of the name "village," whereupon a few riders exited each time. It continued for a few further tight turns and switchbacks, and by the time the bus finally stopped in Alpbach, there were only four passengers left on board.

"So, *this* is where you are from?" Joseph remarked as they stood with their bags beside a white church with a tall, tapering, green needle spire. The bus belched a cloud of smelly black smoke as it resumed its journey, and they both waved it away distastefully as they stepped back to the curb.

"No," said Schneider. "My family's house is up that way," pointing toward a dirt road that disappeared up the mountainside into the shadows of the fir trees. "My son will be here at five o'clock with a cart." He pointed to the clock face on the side of the church tower. "We have an hour to wait. Let's go inside and sit down." He led the way into the church building, and they sat in a sturdy but ornately carved wooden pew in the back.

The interior of the parish church was a wild riot of color, unlike anything Joseph had ever seen. Statues, icons, frescoes, altars—no space was left unused. Red, green, white, and a great deal of gold glistened from all sides. Marble columns, ribbed barrel-vaulted ceiling, stained glass—Joseph was experiencing sensory overload, and after a few minutes he had to bow forward and focus his eyes on the floor.

This is even more elaborate than the Mariahilfekirche, he thought in amazement.

They were the only ones in the church—or so Joseph thought, until someone began practicing on the organ for tomorrow's Mass. They sat silently, listening to the music with closed eyes until a hand tapped Schneider on the shoulder from behind. He promptly stood and motioned for Joseph to follow. Outside in the cool air and bright sunshine, Joseph felt reinvigorated. Schneider introduced him to his son, Peter, who welcomed Joseph with a powerful handshake. Like his father, Peter wore a bushy beard, though his was mixed black and gray.

Joseph climbed into the back of the cart with the bags, while Schneider rode on the seat with his son. A shaggy brown horse drew the cart as they headed up the steepest gradient of the day. Joseph had to brace his feet against the back of the cart and hold on to the sides to keep from falling out. They bumped and rocked their way up the mountain path ducking the overhanging limbs of fir trees, and finally reached their destination—a typical Tyrolean farmhouse, with masses of red geraniums flowing over balconies on two levels. Smoke wafted upward from a chimney, and chickens clucked and pecked in the grass. Through a window he saw a woman filling a pail from a manual water pump, looking up to wave and smile. Two dogs came barking, wagging their tails excitedly. A voice from inside the house cried, " Der Opa ist do!" and three small children burst out the door, shrieking with joy. Joseph decided he was going to like it here.

After a delicious supper of Tyroler Groestl—Joseph's first encounter with the popular Tyrolean dish—and the children had been put to bed, Herr Schneider motioned for Joseph to follow him outside. Peter and his wife joined them, along with their son and his wife. Peter's mother-in-law remained in the house with the children. The group began walking a footpath up the mountain, reaching the summit in about a half-hour. Daylight was slowly fading; it would not be dark until about nine o'clock at this time of year. Above the tree line they had a gorgeous panoramic view of the surrounding peaks, painted in the brilliant colors of the setting sun. Joseph was entranced by the spectacular Alpine beauty and assumed that the reason for the trek up the mountain was to enjoy the view—but he was wrong.

"Let me explain what you are about to see," Schneider said. "In the old days, it was difficult to communicate from one valley to another, so fires were lit on the mountain tops in times of emergency. When invaders attacked, for example, the Landsturm would be mobilized in this way. Do you remember that I told you about the French invasion, and how Andreas Hofer led the Tyrolean forces to repel them?"

"Yes," said Joseph. "They won the battle against Napoleon."

"But we didn't really expect to win," explained Schneider. "On the eve of the battle, the people prayed and entrusted the outcome to the sacred heart of Jesus, and we lit fires on the mountains in the shape of a heart and a cross. When we won the battle, we gave the credit to God. Ever since then, on the eve of the Sacred Heart of Jesus Sunday —which is tomorrow—we always light the fires again to celebrate the victory. It is very important to us Tyroleans."

"Is that what all these branches are for?" Joseph asked, looking over his shoulder at what appeared to be a scattering of brush in the meadow.

"Yes, and you'll see fires on all those mountains around us too. It's a sign of the faith of Tyrol, and our trust in God to deliver us."

"Is that why it says 'Im heil'gen Land Tirol' over the door at your house?"

"Yes—very observant, Joseph! Our land is sacred to us! That's also why we *must* be reunited with the Südtirol! Tyrol can *never* be divided!" Schneider's walrus mustache and long beard shook with his vehemence.

Suddenly, pointing up at the darkening sky he almost shouted, "I see stars! It's time!" Turning, he waved at the other four of the party who were already positioned around the brush piles. Joseph saw brief flares of light as they struck matches, and then the flames began to spread steadily. Joseph realized then that the branches and brush were not piled randomly, but arranged in a design. Within a few minutes it became clear that it depicted a heart overlaid with a cross.

"Beautiful!" he exclaimed. When he turned back around to look across the valley at the other mountain peaks, the sight took his breath. Hearts and crosses of flames blazed out of the darkness as far as he could see. He gasped. "That's—that's—that's *unbelievable!*" he finally managed to sputter.

"That's the sacred heart of Jesus!" nodded Schneider with satisfaction. "Tyroleans have been doing this for generations. It's who we are." All of them sat on the ground and gazed in silence at the fires until midnight. By then Joseph's eyes were so heavy he could hardly keep them open. Their fire having burned itself out, they began the descent back to the farmhouse, aided by flashlights.

The next morning the entire family trekked down to the village and attended Mass at the parish church. Afterward they chatted with friends and townspeople in the small plaza for a while, something Joseph found almost impossible due to the strong dialect spoken by all the Tyroleans. Even Schneider's family was difficult to understand, and if not for Schneider's help, conversation would have been futile. Joseph could do little more than shake hands, smile, and make simple responses, such as "Danke!" and "Bitte!"

"I believe you are Opa Schneider's young friend from Vienna, yes?" Joseph turned to see the parish priest extending his hand. Relieved to be able to speak standard German with someone, he grasped the proffered hand.

"Yes! Well, actually I'm an American, but I'm visiting my relatives in Vienna."

"An American! That's interesting! I've never met an American before. What do you think of Tyrol?"

"It's the most beautiful place I've ever been!" Joseph declared enthusiastically. "Why, last night on the mountain, the burning hearts and crosses were incredible!"

"Go back again tonight and you'll see a different kind of fire on the mountains," the priest commented wryly. Giving Joseph a quick look, he asked, "Are you a Nazi supporter?"

Joseph glanced about to see if anyone was listening, and answered in a lowered voice, "No, I'm not. Are you?"

The priest hesitated and also looked around before answering. "No," he said quietly. "I was serving a parish in Bavaria, and when the Nazis came into power five years ago, I requested to be reassigned. Now, unfortunately, it seems the Nazis have caught up with me and there's nowhere else to go."

"What did you mean, that I would see a different kind of fire on the mountains tonight?"

"Swastikas. The Nazis are popular here and their supporters light fires in the shape of swastikas, just like they lit fires last night for Jesus. I find it almost sacrilegious. You can see them burning in the mountains all around the village at night—it's very disturbing."

"Yes, I think it would be very disturbing," Joseph agreed. "Oh—sorry!—I have to go! The Schneiders are leaving now. Maybe we can talk more next Sunday?"

"Excellent! I would like that very much!" They shook hands again, and the priest went about greeting other parishioners as Joseph joined the family for the hike back up the trail.

That afternoon Schneider took Joseph to his workshop behind the farmhouse. It was well-equipped with woodworking tools of all kinds, including vises, saws, chisels, and a hand-operated lathe. He pulled his carving from the rucksack, put it on the heavy table, and removed its protecting blanket. It was an eagle, perched on a mountain crag with wings partially spread as if about to take flight. Its beak was open in mid-scream, and the powerful talons curled around the rough surface of the rock face. The eagle depicted raw power and defiance, and Joseph imagined that he could see its eyes flashing and hear its battle cry. It was carved from oak and needed sanding and staining to be complete.

"Herr Schneider!" marveled Joseph, in awe. "That is fantastic! I've never seen such a beautiful carving! It's a *masterpiece!*"

"Thank you," replied Schneider modestly. "I'm proud of it, myself. But it still needs some work." The competition was exclusively for wildlife carvings, he explained, and all pieces had to be submitted by the end of the week. "While I'm finishing it—" he paused and reached under the table. Setting a gnarled hickory stump on the table, he continued, "See what you can do with this! Maybe you can enter a piece, also." The stump was irregular and twisted, standing about two feet high and a foot wide.

Joseph studied it for a minute, letting the wood speak to him. Cocking his head to one side, he asked, "Can the carvings be of *any* wildlife?"

"Anything at all."

Joseph grinned. "I have an idea! I'd like to give it a try!"

Schneider gestured toward the tools scattered about. "Get started! You don't have much time."

They worked assiduously all week but set aside time each day for hiking the mountain paths and playing with the children. Joseph gradually developed an ear for the Tyrolean dialect and was able to converse with the family more successfully. One evening at supper, he asked why the dialect was so different from Austrian German. Peter replied, "It's the isolation. Until recently, the people in the high valleys had no easy way to interact with outsiders. In fact, each village has its own dialect, and villagers at one end of the valley sometimes can't understand those from the other end of the valley! The road from Brixlegg to Alpbach was built only about ten years ago. Radio helps—although reception is sometimes bad. We hear Hochdeutsch and learn to speak like that. So, if you think our dialect is hard to understand *now*—" he grinned. "It's a lot better than it used to be!"

"Of course, the Hochdeutsch on the radio all comes from Germany, so you know what *that* means," frowned Peter's mother-in-law. "Nothing but 'Sieg Heil' and Nazi propaganda all the time!" An uncomfortable silence followed, with the family members giving each other uneasy looks. The quiet was broken by one of the children.

"I don't like Hochdeutsch," piped up Rudi, the four-year-old. "I like Tyroler Marend!" Everyone burst out laughing, and he beamed proudly at his own cleverness. Marend, Joseph had learned, was the traditional mountaineer afternoon snack, usually consisting of bread, cheese, and sausage.

"I like Marend too!" he assured Rudi with a smile. "It's the best!"

"What kind of animal carving are you making for the competition?" asked Frau Schneider, Peter's wife, changing the subject.

Joseph smiled secretively. "It's very American," he hinted, "but you'll have to wait another day or two to see it!"

On Friday afternoon the unveiling of the sculptures took place. The family filed into the workshop and gathered around the big table. Joseph lifted the blanket from his work, and after a moment of shocked silence they all burst into laughter. Joseph was not offended —in fact, it was the reaction he had expected. Exploiting the twisted contours of the gnarled stump, he had created a squatting, menacing gorilla, behind which rose the Art Deco façade of the Chrysler Building with its graduated arches. The gorilla was almost as tall as the skyscraper, with his burly arm draped around it, reminiscent of the famous King Kong. The smoothness of the building and its clear finish contrasted strongly with the rough surface of the ape's body and its dark reddish stain.

"I told you it was American!" he grinned. "Very New York!"

"That's very creative," Herr Schneider observed. "You did a remarkable job of using the natural shape of the wood. It's not likely to win first prize, but I'm impressed." Joseph swelled with pride— coming from his mentor this was high praise indeed.

When the eagle sculpture was uncovered, the reaction was very different. Joseph joined in the ooh's and ah's of admiration. Schneider had chosen a deep yellow stain for the eagle, giving it a golden hue which accentuated the wood grain. The cliff face was only a little darker, but enough to provide some contrast and focus the viewer's eyes on the eagle. It was truly magnificent. As Joseph walked around to see it from all angles, he noticed a smooth medallion carved into the back, with an inscription. Leaning in close, he read the words aloud: "Im heil'gen Land Tirol."

Turning to Schneider, he smiled. "It's perfect."

.   .   .

The next two weeks passed too quickly for Joseph, but finally it was time to leave. Peter took them in the cart back down to Alpbach where they caught the bus to Brixlegg, and then took the diminutive steamer to Wörgl, where they boarded the express train for Vienna. Schneider's "Tirol Adler" remained on the fireplace mantel at the farmhouse, with its first-place ribbon. At Wörgl, while waiting for their train, they ate the lunch of bread, cheese, and bacon which the women had packed for them. Joseph couldn't help but notice that Schneider had hardly spoken a word since they left the house.

"It's hard to leave this place, isn't it?" he asked sympathetically. Schneider only grunted his assent and continued chewing slowly.

After a long pause, he said quietly, "It's not just the place, it's the family. When you're my age, you don't have much time left to enjoy them." Joseph remained respectfully silent as Schneider looked up at the mountains across the river. "I say this every year when I visit, but this time I really mean it—it's time to come home."

Joseph blinked and stared. "Do you mean you're leaving Vienna? For good?"

"Don't say anything to Oskar. Let me tell him myself. I'll work for him through the end of the year, but after New Year's, I'm coming home to stay."

Joseph was speechless for a moment. He groped for words, and finally managed, "I don't blame you a bit. I'd do the same thing." He scratched his head and added hesitantly, "I don't mean to be nosey, but why did you leave in the first place? I mean, Vienna has a lot to offer, but Tyrol is heaven on earth."

Schneider was silent for so long that Joseph feared he had offended him by asking the question. He was about to apologize when the old man spoke. "I killed a man—several men, actually. It was fifteen years ago. They were Italians, but it was still wrong." Those last words lacked conviction, Joseph thought, but he said nothing.

"The war was over, but with Italy claiming the South Tyrol as their land, tensions were high and violence was breaking out all over. A group of us went over the Brenner Pass to support our brothers.

Some Tyroleans blew up a power station, and the Italian army was chasing them back toward the north. I shot the tire of a military truck and it went off the road into a deep gorge, killing a dozen Italian soldiers. I only meant to stop the truck and help our people escape—I felt terrible. Anyway, that's why I left Tyrol and went to Vienna. I didn't return for several years, but it seems safe to go home now."

He turned to look at Joseph. "You're the first person I've told in fifteen years." There was a question in his eyes as he raised a bushy eyebrow.

"Herr Schneider! Your secret's safe with me. I won't say a word to anyone."

"I knew I could trust you, Joseph. I knew that you would understand that some things are so important that drastic action is required. I suspect that before long, my friend, you may find yourself in a similar situation. Consider the cost, but do what your heart tells you is right."

The train arrived then and they gathered their things and boarded for the long ride to Vienna. Joseph, reflecting on Schneider's last words, couldn't help but recall Herr Engelmann's dictum: Sometimes you have to make a sacrifice to win the game. *Consider the cost,* he repeated to himself, *and do what your heart tells you is right.* As he settled down onto the wooden third-class seat, he had a sense that he was leaving heaven and returning to hell.

13

"I WILL, WITH GOD'S HELP!"

"Check!" announced Joseph confidently, placing his black knight down with an authoritative thump. His pulse quickened in anticipation of a win.

Engelmann nodded approvingly. "Very nice move, Joseph!" he murmured, and moved his king to safety.

"Checkmate!" Joseph declared triumphantly, advancing his queen and taking a white pawn from the board. He extended his hand toward Engelmann with a proud grin.

"Not so fast there, my friend!" he demurred, and moved his own queen to interpose.

Joseph grunted in surprise. "I didn't see that," he admitted. After studying the position for a long moment, he retreated his queen. "I guess I didn't plan that as well as I thought."

"Check," Engelmann said casually, as if commenting on the weather. His knight now attacked both the black king and queen. Joseph slapped his forehead with the palm of his hand.

"I'm forked!" he moaned. "You did it to me again!" Laying his king on its side, he extended his hand again, this time conceding defeat rather than claiming a victory.

"You are a good player, Joseph, but a little impetuous. Premature attacks usually turn out badly." They began resetting the pieces on the board and Engelmann continued, "Chess is like life, in some ways, you know. Timing is everything. Even a good plan will fail if the timing is wrong."

"How do you know when the timing is right?" Joseph asked. "Is it just trial and error?"

"That's a good question! Experience helps, but mainly you just have to examine the situation carefully and don't overlook anything. The details matter. You must look at every piece on the chessboard, and consider all of the factors and variables in a life situation. Then you just have to trust your own judgment and go forward with confidence and determination.

"For example," he continued, "the move that cost you this game was not the check with the knight or the queen. It was when you retreated the queen to a square that allowed me to fork you. When your attack was repulsed, you let your concentration slip and you didn't choose the next move carefully. Even moves in retreat must be made with care—no, *especially* moves in retreat! A retreating move is really the first move of the next attack!"

"I see," Joseph nodded thoughtfully. "Always think of the next attack. I'll remember that!"

Miriam stuck her head into the room. "Are you ready to go?" Joseph looked at her, startled. "Did you forget that we're going to the zoo today?" she asked accusingly.

"No! I'm ready right now!" He hastily rose from the table and, with a quick wave to Herr Engelmann, hurried out the front door behind her. Hooking arms, they walked briskly to the tram stop.

The zoo at Schönbrunn was no more than a twenty-minute ride away on the streetcar, and in mid-summer was open past six o'clock. Because it was one of the few attractions open on Sundays, it was always crowded, which meant that Miriam was less likely to encounter harassment. Just inside the entrance was a würstelstand. Joseph gestured toward it with his thumb. "Maybe you should carry a würstel around with you and eat it if we run into some Nazis."

"That's not a bad idea," she agreed. "Are you buying?"

Joseph looked at her quickly to see if she was joking. She was not. "Sure, I'll buy." He purchased a würstel for each of them, loaded with mustard and sauerkraut. She took a bite as they walked away, and Joseph remarked, "You'd better not eat all of it. Save something for an emergency!"

She laughed with her mouth full and wiped mustard from her chin. "I'll try to control myself! These things are good, though."

"I can't get over the fact that you actually eat würstel!"

Miriam walked several steps before responding. "I've been doing a lot of thinking about what it means to be a Jew. I'm not ashamed of being Jewish—not at all—but I've decided that whether I eat something or not doesn't define who I am. What difference does it really make, anyway?"

"Besides," she continued, "my family have not been practicing Jews for a couple of generations. It seems to me we've already abandoned the most important parts of being Jewish, so why should I care about eating würstel, or anything else?"

"I can't argue with you about that," conceded Joseph. "It does seem like a small thing to me, but then, I'm not Jewish."

She stopped, würstel in hand, in front of the ornate eighteenth-century pavilion in the center of outwardly radiating footpaths, crowded with strolling couples and families. "But I *am* Jewish, Joseph," she looked at him with her direct eye contact that always fascinated him. "Or am I? What does it really *mean* to be Jewish? Is it how a man cuts his hair and beard? Is it about being circumcised? Is it about what you eat? Is it just lighting candles at Hanukkah?"

She shook her head slowly. "No, it can't be those things. It has to be a matter of the heart and mind. It's what you believe—it's your faith." She looked at him even more intensely. "Do you agree? Is that what being a Jew is about? Is it what being a Christian is about?"

Joseph wasn't prepared for such a serious discussion. He cleared his throat and considered taking a bite of his würstel to delay answering. "Yes, I agree. Religious faith is about more than external things like that. It has to be what's inside." He then quickly took a big bite and chewed slowly in case she had more questions.

"So, I've been thinking," she mused. "If I don't go to synagogue but once or twice a year, and if I don't believe in the Jewish scriptures, and don't do the external things—am I really Jewish at all?"

Joseph regretted having taken such a large bite now. He chewed fast and swallowed hard. "That's a good question," he managed to say, and swallowed again. "You've really given this some thought, haven't you?" She glared, hand on hip, pointing at him with the bun as if to say *Just answer the question!* Clearing his throat again, he added, "Yes, I agree. You aren't really Jewish on the inside—but the law says you are Jewish because of your ancestry. That's all that matters to the Nazis."

She was quiet as they walked around the pavilion, and Joseph began to fear he'd offended her. When they reached the other side of the ring, she stopped and faced him. "I've decided to be baptized," she said simply. He stared, speechless. "The Anglican Christ Church is baptizing Jews and giving them a baptismal certificate," she explained. "They say it helps in getting visas— exit visas to leave Germany and also to get into other countries."

"That's good," was all that Joseph could say. "I hope it helps."

"Will you come to my baptism? It's tomorrow morning."

"*Tomorrow!*" He was taken aback, but recovered quickly. "Absolutely! Of course! I'll come to the bookstore and we can go together."

She beamed. "Thank you, Joseph! I knew I could count on you." She hooked her arm through his and resumed eating her würstel as they strolled the paths, admiring the exotic animals.

"Does your Opa know about this?" he asked.

"I'm going to tell him tonight. I hope he will come tomorrow, also."

"Will you be attending services at the Anglican church?"

"Yes. It could help with my visa if I'm actually going to Christian church services, and it might look odd if my baptismal certificate is from the Anglicans and I don't attend there. Besides, I'd rather go where I can understand the language."

"Oh."

She gave him a quizzical look. "You know I'm not a Christian in beliefs any more than I'm a Jew, right? This is political, and it's about helping me get to America. That's all."

"Yeah, I guess so." He hesitated, and then asked, "What *do* you believe?"

"Why do I have to believe *anything*?" she asked in an exasperated tone. "I wasn't brought up believing in things like you were. I just believe in living life from day to day and being a good person. When you die, it's over and done—just like these animals here. This is all we have, so we should enjoy it while it lasts. Nothing lasts forever!"

Joseph blinked. Those were Anna Marie's exact words, months ago. Somehow, he found them extremely unsatisfying and disturbing. However, not wanting to argue, he put his arm around her shoulders and gave her a hug. "Let's go see the elephants," he suggested.

The next morning both Miriam and Herr Engelmann emerged from the bookstore, leaving a "Closed" sign on the door. The three made their way to Christ Church, which was attached to the British embassy, just beyond the lovely Belvedere Palace. The Neo-Gothic building appeared to be older than it was, being only about sixty years old. The interior was the least ornate church building Joseph had ever seen. There were narrow stained glass windows behind the pulpit, but there was no gold, and no statues, paintings, racks of candles, or other ornamentation such as he was used to seeing. The walls were smooth and white—very plain. Even the synagogue where Miriam's mother's funeral was held had been more elaborate than this.

There were about a hundred other people present, almost filling the small sanctuary. They all took seats in the pews, and after a few minutes, a clergyman went to the front and addressed the group. He wore a white robe with a green stole draped around his neck, hanging down to his knees.

"Good morning!" he greeted them cheerfully in English, and then added, "*Guten Morgen!*" He introduced himself as Reverend Hugh Grimes, and explained that before the baptisms there would be some religious instruction. Another group of converts would be coming in the afternoon, he said, so assistants passed out catechism booklets to

everyone, and the instruction began immediately. Joseph and Engelmann had not expected three hours of religious lecture, but they sat
patiently, listening. Joseph noted that Miriam also listened attentively
and scrutinized the catechism booklet closely. *She seems to be taking
this seriously,* he thought.

Just before noon, the group was directed to line up at the
baptismal font. As each person stepped up, Grimes asked them,
"Will you renounce the devil and all his works, and the vain things
of the world, and serve Christ, loving your neighbor as yourself?"
Each candidate had been directed to reply, "I will, with God's help."
Upon receiving that answer, Grimes had them bend over the font,
and he poured a small pitcher of water over their heads. As the
person stepped away from the font, they received a certificate and a
prayer book, and then exited the building a new Christian and an
Anglican.

Miriam handed her prayer book and certificate to Joseph, and
bent over to squeeze water out of her hair, leaving a small, wet circle
on the sidewalk. Engelmann reached out his hand, and Joseph let
him take the prayer book. He took the certificate from the book and
studied it for a moment, and opened the prayer book and read the
title page. When Miriam stood up, he handed it to her with a sad
expression on his face. "Let's go home," he said gently. He turned and
slowly led the way up the sidewalk, and it seemed to Joseph that he
looked older and more tired than before.

The trip back to the bookstore began as a normal, quiet ride on a
streetcar. However, when they changed lines at Karlsplatz, before the
tram left the station two brown-shirted Stormtroopers boarded the
car brandishing batons. "All Jews get off!" they demanded loudly.
They repeated this as they walked down the aisle, glaring at the
seated passengers on each side. Herr Engelmann moved to stand,
preparing to exit the car, but Joseph put a restraining hand on his
shoulder.

"I won't let them put you off," Joseph whispered. "Just stay
seated."

"No!" he replied forcefully. "I won't let you put yourself in harm's way on my account. I'm getting off." When Joseph did not relent, he added intensely, *"Please!"*

Reluctantly Joseph stepped into the aisle and let Engelmann out of the seat. One of the Stormtroopers reached out with his baton to poke him, saying, "Jew! Get out! No Jews in the car!" Joseph stepped between the two, however, and the baton jabbed him in the back instead of Herr Engelmann. "Move out of the way, *mench!*" the Nazi snapped, poking Joseph again. "Step lively!"

Joseph set his jaw and resisted the urge to turn and confront the bully, but he followed Herr Engelmann slowly enough that the elderly man was able to reach the street safely without being pushed. Frustrated, the Nazi cursed and struck the door frame with his baton, making a sharp cracking noise next to Joseph's head. Joseph stepped casually down to the street and gave only a quick glance over his shoulder as he walked away. The Stormtrooper stood in the doorway with anger distorting his face as the folding doors closed and the streetcar began to move.

He and Herr Engelmann watched the string of cars moved jerkily down the street. "Where's Miriam?" asked Engelmann.

Joseph looked around. "I don't see her," he replied. "I don't think she got off."

Engelmann sighed. "No reason that she should—she's not Jewish." Joseph sensed the resignation in his face and in his voice. *This must be really hard for him,* he thought. *I wish she had gotten off the streetcar—it would have meant a lot to her Opa.*

It was a long walk to the bookstore, and the mid-day heat was uncomfortably warm. They walked for a while, and paused to rest in the shade of a tree. There was a bench nearby, but a sign attached to it said "No Jews allowed." Just as they were about to continue walking, Miriam emerged from the crowd of passersby and stood in front of them, looking rather annoyed. "You and that Nazi had the door blocked and I couldn't get off," she said, giving Joseph a penetrating look. "I had to ride to the next stop and walk back." Her hair was still damp, and she blew a bead of perspiration from her upper lip and wiped her mouth with the back of her hand. "It's hot today."

"Yes, it is," Herr Engelmann smiled. He squeezed her arm. "Let's go home."

14

POWDER KEG

After months of planning, drawing, and revising his design, Joseph was finally ready to begin cutting the wood for his Art Deco Regulator. The basic shapes for the cabinet box were simple—square blocks for the floor and top, joined with slender vertical posts. The rear panel would have to be painted before installation, there was much carving to do before the front post columns were ready for painting, and the door would have to be edged and styled. The decorative crown and base would, of course, be the *pièce de resistance,* requiring the most skillful carving and finishing. He had decided to use white oak for its strength and durability.

There was also the matter of the clockworks, the pendulum, the clock face, and the glass. Joseph had spent most of his saved wages to purchase the best quality from the top craftsmen. The glass was to be beveled and etched with his design, and the clock face would have to be custom painted. Uncle Oskar agreed to make the pendulum for free. All that remained was the expensive enamel paint and lacquer to give the finished product a glassy, brilliant shine.

Uhrmacher-Gruber had just delivered another order of several clocks to a customer in Prague and the workload eased for a few days, allowing Joseph to devote several hours a day to his own project. He worked obsessively into the evenings and on weekends, and would be satisfied with nothing short of perfection. By the end of August, the cabinet box was completely assembled along with the door, the rear panel was ready for painting, and he was making good progress on the columns. He decided that it was time to take a break from the work for a few days to renew his focus and energy before taking on the most challenging part of the project.

Thus, on the first Saturday in September, Joseph and Stephan attended a football game— soccer, as Joseph called it—in the stadium at the Prater park. One of the teams was Admira Vienna, and the other was Schalke, from Berlin. There was bad blood between these two teams due to a contested outcome in a game the previous year, and the stadium was filled with fifty thousand loud, raucous fans of the Vienna team. Joseph and Stephan joined in the hooting and yelling, enjoying themselves immensely.

The teams battled furiously into the second half with a tie score, and the crowd was becoming restive. Actually, it was getting ugly. A growling sound rippled through the stadium. Angry fans stomped their feet and shook their fists, shouting at the referee. The referee was a German—and he was the same referee who had officiated at the contested game the previous year. He had incensed the crowd by disallowing a goal by the Vienna team that the fans thought should have counted. It was getting late in the game, with only a few minutes left on the clock.

"Austrians really love their football, don't they?" Joseph said into the ear of Stephan. Stephan nodded as he shook his fist in the air and shouted, "The ref is blind!" Joseph grinned. *This is like a Red Sox and Yankees game,* he thought. However, he soon realized that it was much more than that. Since the Anschluss Austrian sport teams had been taken over by the German sports federations, and many Austrians felt that their teams had been discriminated against. They didn't seem to mind that Jewish teams, players, and coaches had been disqualified from competing, but when the German-controlled media ignored allegations of unfair treatment of the Austrian teams, tempers flared.

On the field the Vienna team skillfully advanced the ball with short passes and intricate teamwork. The spectators roared their approval, and when one of the star players drilled the ball toward the corner of the goal, glancing off the crossbar and appearing to cross the line before being bobbled and caught by the defender, the stadium exploded with deafening cheers. However, the referee waved his hands over his head and pointed toward the opposite goal, indicating that the ball now belonged to the defending team —no goal, again. The angry roar of the crowd made the previous cheering pale into insignificance. Joseph put his hands over his ears and feared that the stadium would collapse from the vibrations.

One of the Vienna players ran up to the referee to protest the ruling, pointing to the goal and motioning that the ball had crossed the line. The referee pulled the yellow card from his pocket and held it up—a penalty on the protesting player. When the Vienna player continued his objection, the referee exchanged the yellow card for a red one and ejected the player from the game. The anger of the crowd bordered on insanity, and the avalanche of sound did not abate until the clock expired and the game was over—with a tie score of 1-1.

Joseph and Stephan were swept along as the fans surged forward like a tidal wave. They stormed the field, chasing the German players and referee, who ran for their lives. They made it to the team bus but the mob attacked the bus, throwing beer bottles and rocks, breaking windows and rocking the bus back and forth until the driver managed to get it moving. Policemen who tried to control the crowd were beaten and trampled. Tires were slashed on the Vienna Nazi leader's car and the swastika flags were ripped from the car, along with those which decorated the stadium and field. The riot had turned from a sports protest into a political demonstration against the German regime.

"We better get out of here!" Joseph shouted to Stephan, who threw one more beer bottle before turning to follow Joseph. They ran from the stadium into the Prater park and kept running until they were a safe distance away. They could hear the sound of approaching sirens. *There must be at least a dozen of them*, thought Joseph. *Half the police force must be coming. Definitely not Red Sox and Yankees. This is crazy!*

"That was fun!" exclaimed Stephan. "We showed those Prussians! Lousy Piefke!"

"I thought Austrians were happy about the Anschluss," remarked Joseph as they walked toward a streetcar stop. "Why do they dislike the Germans so much?"

"It's not so much about the *Anschluss*," replied Stephan. "That seems to be pretty well accepted. It's the Germans' attitude of superiority towards us. They think Austrians are careless, lazy, and sloppy. We think they are arrogant, stiff, and regimented. What is absolutely intolerable is when they cheat to win a football game! We aren't going to sit still and take *that*!" He raised a fist in threatening fashion. "Next time we won't be so easy on them!"

"After today there may not *be* a 'next time,'" Joseph commented drily. "The Nazis won't take this lightly."

"This is just the beginning," vowed Stephan. "We won't be pushed around!"

"We're going to be late," Joseph observed. "The girls will be waiting." They got on board the streetcar and stood, holding onto the hanging leather straps. They were to meet Anna Marie and Miriam at Stephansdom, where a Catholic youth rally was taking place. By the time they reached Stephansplatz at the cathedral they had cooled down, both physically and emotionally, and greeted the girls with smiles.

Upon entering the cathedral Joseph was stunned—the place was absolutely packed with young people. It was a sea of humanity. The four of them hooked arms to keep from being separated and wormed their way forward until they were next to the carved-stone pulpit on one of the massive columns. They were still a long way from the main altar, but at least they could see down the nave to the front. The gothic arches of the roof seemed to reach to the heavens, and the stained-glass windows let soft light flood into the huge interior.

Stephansdom was larger than the Salzburg cathedral, and although Joseph had been inside before, the presence of thousands of people made it seem even larger. He looked up over his shoulder at the organ pipes and was studying the beautiful rose window when someone began singing, and the massed youth joined in with full voice. The explosion of sound reverberated inside the vault so loudly that Joseph, startled, let out a gasp of surprise. Miriam was startled also, and grabbed Joseph's hand with both of hers. *This is louder than the football stadium*, Joseph thought in amazement. Several songs were sung—some of them simple children's songs about Jesus. He was not familiar with all of them, but knew a few well enough to sing along. Miriam even joined in on the refrains after a verse or two. It was impossible not to participate—one felt such a part of the all-consuming experience that it permeated one's body and spirit.

After several songs there was suddenly a perfect silence—so quiet that Joseph felt the hairs on the back of his neck begin to stand up. A man in red vestments stood in front of the altar. When he spoke, his voice carried to every corner and it seemed to Joseph that it was almost supernaturally clear and distinct. His name was Cardinal Innitzer, he said, and he talked in a calm voice about the Christian's responsibility to government, to obey the laws, and respect and pray for the leaders of the country. However, just as Joseph was concluding that the message was about submitting to the Nazi regime, the cardinal's voice changed, rising to a higher pitch and volume.

"But our obedience to the government is not total, nor is it unconditional!" Innitzer cried. "There is a higher law than the law of the state, and that is the law of God! When the apostles Peter and John were ordered to stop speaking of Jesus, they replied 'We must obey God rather than men!'" The assembled throng gave a spontaneous shout of approval which echoed for some seconds before the cardinal could continue. "Jesus himself said that we should give to Caesar what is Caesar's, and to God what is God's!" Another deafening shout left Joseph's ears ringing. With both hands held high, Innitzer shouted, "We must have faith in the Führer—and our only Führer is Jesus Christ!" The explosive response of the crowd surpassed all the preceding in sheer volume and duration. It seemed to Joseph that his entire body was vibrating.

The singing resumed, this time with even more passion and energy than before. When, after an hour, the young people finally made their way out of the cathedral into the fading daylight, Joseph was exhausted. He stood with Miriam in the plaza with crowds of youth streaming past, bumping into them, many still singing. He glanced down at her and, noticing tear tracks on her cheeks, draped his arm protectively across her shoulders. When Stephan and Anna Marie joined them, they walked together up Kärntnerstrasse to the Ring, where they boarded a streetcar home. They were all emotionally drained and talked little along the way.

Joseph walked Miriam to the bookstore and saw her safely inside, and then turned toward home. That evening, sitting in the family room, they described the events of the day in tones of awe. The rest of the family was shocked at what had transpired at the football game, and the rally at Stephansdom seemed to underscore the growing discontent felt by many.

"I don't think it's safe for you to be in those kinds of settings," worried Mama Gruber. "The Nazis aren't going to let that go on, and it could get ugly."

"Did you see the Hitler Youth outside the cathedral as we were leaving?" asked Anna Marie. "They didn't look too happy!"

"Hitler Youth?" Joseph and Stephan replied in unison.

"Yes—there were ten or fifteen of them standing across the street. I guess there were too many of us for them to do anything, but they sure were glaring at all of us."

"Maybe they should have come inside and joined in the singing," suggested Stephan. "Might do them some good!"

"I don't think they would have appreciated what Cardinal Innitzer said," Joseph shook his head. "Their only Führer is Hitler, not Jesus."

"I don't want any of you participating in any more of those rallies," ordered Uncle Oskar, giving them a stern look. "Your mother is right—it isn't safe. We don't want you getting hurt or arrested. You could disappear like a lot of other people have done, and we'd never know what happened to you." They objected but he was adamant, and they eventually acquiesced.

The rest of the evening was spent quietly. Mama Gruber knitted a shawl for an elderly friend and Oskar read the newspaper and listened to Strauss on the radio. Joseph wrote a letter to his parents and then played a card game with his cousins.

Upon retiring he went up to the roof for a few minutes of solitude. He looked in the direction of Engelmann's bookstore, and for the first time frowned at the Apollo Theater, which blocked his line of sight. He realized somewhat uncomfortably that Miriam had lately begun to occupy his mind more and more. *You're really great*, he said silently to the looming spire towering over him, *but you can't compare to her. I don't like you coming between us.* He was startled by his own thoughts and said out loud, "Did you really mean that, Joseph?" *Did I really mean that?* he echoed mentally. *Yeah, I did,* a reply came from somewhere inside. *Miriam is worth ten of any building—make that a hundred —a thousand times more. Even the Chrysler Building? Yes, even that. Don't be ridiculous!* What this really meant, he grasped, was that she meant more to him than his love for Art Deco, for wood carving, for clock making—for the things he had thought were most important to him until now. She came first now, and he didn't want to allow anything to come between them. *She may not feel the same way,* he thought, *but it doesn't matter. Somehow—whatever it takes—I'm going to get her to America—and Herr Engelmann too, if he will come. This place is a powder keg, and the Nazis have struck a match.*

15

THE BELLY OF THE BEAST

Stephan ran his fingers over the rough surface of a wooden sculpture on a shelf in the workshop, shaking his head in disbelief. "I still can't believe you carved this in only one week!" he marveled.

"It still needs a lot of work before it's finished," grinned Joseph. "It caused quite a stir in Innsbruck!" They both laughed at that. "You should have seen Herr Schneider's piece! It was fantastic—took first prize!"

"We're sure going to miss him when he goes home. Papa is worried that he won't be able to find anyone to replace him, and with you leaving also, we're going to be short-handed."

"Maybe you should all just get on the boat and come with me! I'm sure we can find plenty of work for you to do in New York!"

"I'd like that, but Papa would never hear of it. We'll be staying here, for better or worse."

"Well," said Joseph, squeezing Stephan's shoulder, "you can keep King Kong. I know you'll take good care of him, and maybe you can put some finishing touches on him."

"Are you serious?" Stephan was incredulous. "You aren't going to take it with you?"

"Won't fit in my suitcase," Joseph shrugged. "Besides, I know how much you liked the movie—and this will be something for you to remember me by. Consider it an early Christmas gift!" Stephan gripped Joseph's hand and laughed in delight, clapping him on the shoulder.

"I accept!" he exclaimed. "He'll have a place of honor in my bedroom!"

"Enough of that fraternizing!" boomed Uncle Oskar with mock severity. He donned his workshop apron, tying it behind his back. "I've got a job for the two of you. Pack up that Regulator we just finished and deliver it to the customer—here's the address—Prinz-Eugen-Strasse, near the Belvedere Palace." He tossed the keys to the van to Joseph. "Hurry back! We've got lots of work to do! Be careful!"

"I will!" Joseph promised, surprised and gratified that Uncle Oskar trusted him to drive in the city. He had not done any driving other than the two road trips to Salzburg and Prague, and he was excited to drive in Vienna. "Let's get going!" he grinned at Stephan.

Preparing the clock for transport was a multi-step process. The two heavy brass weights were wrapped securely in crumpled newspaper and bundled into a leather shoulder bag, while the carved headpiece was wrapped and placed in a cardboard box. The pendulum was removed and the interior of the cabinet gently stuffed with a soft blanket—crocheted by Mama Gruber—to keep everything in place. The entire cabinet was then wrapped in another blanket and placed in a sturdy cardboard box, which was then taped shut. There being only one clock in the back of the van it was necessary to brace the box with boards and wood blocks from the workshop to make sure it didn't slide around during the trip. Finally, they were ready to go.

Joseph navigated very carefully, using side streets to avoid traffic. Stephan rolled down his window rested his arm on the frame. "That's a strange clock there," he said, gesturing back toward it with his thumb. "Never heard of anyone wanting one in those colors."

"Yeah," Joseph agreed, peering left and right as he came to an intersection. "Black cabinet with a blood-red back panel. And those two yellow lightning-bolts on the headpiece look ridiculous."

Stephan laughed. "I can't wait to see what kind of idiot would want a clock like that! It belongs in a circus!"

It wasn't far to the address, and after a drive of about fifteen minutes Joseph parked at the curb in front of an impressive three-story mansion set back from the street behind a high wrought-iron fence. They got out of the van and surveyed the imposing structure. The architecture was excessively ornate French Baroque, and the iron grill was interspersed with stone columns. The courtyard visible beyond was paved, and at least two automobiles could be seen. A soldier stood at the fortress-like gate with a rifle slung over his shoulder.

"You can't park here!" he barked. "This is a 'No Parking' zone."

"We're delivering a clock," Joseph replied, pointing to the green lettering "Uhrmacher-Gruber" on the side of the gray van. "We're—"

"I don't care what you're delivering," snapped the soldier menacingly. "Take it around to the back before I have you arrested!"

"Certainly! I'll be happy to," Joseph nodded, and produced a piece of paper from his jacket pocket. "Can you tell me where we will find —" he hesitated as he scanned the invoice—"this is for Obersturm-bannführer Adolf Eichmann. Where might we find him?"

The soldier's face went pale and he blinked twice. "Eichmann? Let me see that!" He snatched the paper and scrutinized it almost comically. "Eichmann!" he repeated, as if in disbelief. He returned the paper and said abruptly, "Bring it in here. Park over there to the right. You'll find him on the third floor." He proceeded to open the gates wide and motion them to enter. Joseph and Stephan got back in the van and drove slowly into the courtyard.

As the gates closed behind them Stephan looked at Joseph with raised eyebrows. "Eichmann must be a pretty important person!"

"Apparently so," Joseph nodded. "But he has no taste in clocks!" They both snickered and elbowed each other in merriment. He parked the van under a shade tree and turned off the motor. Stephan draped the bag with the weights over one shoulder and another bag with some tools over the other, and carried the box with the head-piece while Joseph carefully cradled the larger box.

They were admitted into the entrance hall by another soldier who pointed them toward an enormous marble staircase. The walls were hung with tapestries, mirrors, and paintings, and a heavy crystal chandelier hung on a chain from the ceiling high above. Joseph recognized that the exotic parquet floor was made with rare hard-woods, and his first thought was that he wished he could get wood like that to make clocks. As they ascended the staircase they were passed by several military officers wearing the black uniforms of the Nazi Schutzstaffel, or SS, who ignored them. Joseph could tell by their accents that they were German, and not Austrian.

The two climbed the next flight to the third floor and found it buzzing with activity. More men in black military uniforms were hurrying about, their boot heels clicking sharply on the expensive floors, talking loudly—they all sounded angry, Joseph thought—and telephones were ringing and typewriters rattling. It all seemed a bit chaotic, and he wasn't sure how to proceed. Stepping over to a man seated behind a desk he cleared his throat. No response. He cleared his throat again. No response again. He cleared his throat a third time, more loudly. The man looked up with irritation. "Is there some-thing wrong with your throat, *mench*?" he snapped.

"Eichmann." Joseph replied coolly with a raised eyebrow, as if giving an order.

The man glared, but there was an uncertainty in his eyes that told Joseph that he had the upper hand. "What about Obersturmbann-führer Eichmann?"

"We are delivering the clock he purchased from Uhrmacher-Gruber. He wants it today."

"Set it down and I'll see that he gets it." The man returned to shuffling papers on the desk.

"That won't do," Joseph said calmly. "Obersturmbannführer Eich-mann wouldn't like that. We have to set up the clock, assemble it, hang it on the wall, and get it to running properly. Show us to his office, please."

The man's face reddened and his upper lip began to curl, but then he shoved his chair back with a screeching sound and stood up. "Very well—but be quick about it! I won't have you dawdling about like peasants!" With boot heels clicking, he marched briskly toward the back of the room, imperiously motioning them to follow. In an interior office he whirled and snapped, "Do your work quickly and be out of here!" He started to leave, but Joseph stopped him with a question.

"Which wall does Obersturmbannführer Eichmann want the clock on? If we put it on the wrong wall, Obersturmbannführer Eichmann will not be happy." The SS officer's nostrils flared and his lips tightened—he was obviously struggling to control his temper. He literally stamped his foot in frustration.

"I'll find out," he hissed through clenched jaws and went heel-clicking at high speed through the outer office, papers wafting off desks in his wake.

They put their boxes and bags down on the floor and waited for his return. "Do you think you might manage to say 'Obersturmbann-führer Eichmann' a few more times, just so they know who we're talking about?" Stephan smirked.

"I think we found the magic words to get things done around here," Joseph grinned. He looked around the room. "This place is a disaster. I thought Germans were supposed to be organized and tidy." There were boxes overflowing with folders and papers, stacks of books on the floor while the bookshelves stood empty, framed pictures leaning against the wall, and a large desk littered with papers, a lamp, telephone, ashtray with several cigarette stubs, a military hat with a skull emblem above the band, and a pair of soft leather gloves. "Mama Gruber would have a fit if she saw this place."

"Looks like he's just moved in and hasn't put his things away yet," observed Stephan. "At least I hope that's it." They chatted casually for a few minutes until they heard the sound of approaching boot heels. They stood slouching, hands in pockets, expecting the familiar officer to arrive but were surprised at the appearance of someone else.

The black-clad man who entered the office had a rather sharp, angular face. His nose was long and narrow, his lips thin and straight, eyes little more than slits. His receding hairline gave him a high fore-head which gave the impression of intelligence, but Joseph found the overall effect to be one of cold calculation. He instantly distrusted and feared the man.

"Heil Hitler!" The SS officer raised his arm stiffly and clicked his heels.

"Heil Hitler!" responded both Joseph and Stephan. "We brought the clock for Obersturmbannführer Eichmann," Joseph added quickly.

"I am Eichmann," the man said curtly. He immediately began surveying the room. "This wall. Put the clock here." He pointed to a place on the wall behind the door.

"Excuse me, Herr Obersturmbannführer," said Joseph politely, "but it's not good to put a clock on a wall with a door. The vibrations from opening and closing it can throw off the clock's balance, and it won't keep correct time." He then pointed to the wall directly facing the desk. "How about that wall? The clock will be more stable there, and more visible too."

"No!" snapped Eichmann coldly. "That's where the picture of the Führer must go!"

"Then perhaps this wall?" Joseph indicated the wall across from the door. "You won't be able to see it very well from your desk, but you'll get a good look at it when you come in the door. If it's on the wall *behind* the door you'll never really see it."

Eichmann's eyes narrowed as he stared intensely at Joseph for a long moment. Joseph thought that his eyes looked evil—as if he were contemplating an outburst, or even physical violence. But then, suddenly, the look changed to one of detached indifference. His lips twitched slightly and he gave an almost imperceptible nod. "Very well. Hang it on that wall." Without another word he spun about and went clicking out the door.

Joseph and Stephan looked at each other and each let out his breath with a low whistle. "I bet nobody else around here has ever disagreed with him before," Stephan said softly.

"Obersturmbannführer Eichmann is not a man to be trifled

with," Joseph agreed. "Let's get that clock hung and get out of here." With a measuring tape they marked the center of the wall and then drilled a hole, into which they screwed a sturdy bolt. They fitted the carved headpiece onto the cabinet and hung the cabinet on the bolt, followed by attaching the pendulum and the brass weights. With a winding key Joseph drew the weights up just below the clock face and, giving the pendulum a slight push, started it running. It ran for about a half-minute and stopped. They shifted the base of the clock to one side by a tiny amount and restarted it. Again, it ran briefly and stopped. It took several tries, each followed by a miniscule adjustment to the hang, and finally it ran without stopping. Joseph advanced the minute hand of the clock, pausing for it to strike the half-hour and hour, until it showed the correct time. They stepped back to admire their work and were startled to hear applause from the doorway. Turning, they were surprised to see a cluster of black-clad SS officers beaming at them.

"Beautiful!"

"Wunderschön!"

"Magnificent!"

Joseph and Stephan bowed gallantly and received another round of applause. Joseph realized with a start what the colors of the clock meant. *How stupid of me not to see that before now,* he thought. The glossy black cabinet, the bold red back panel, and the yellow-gold lightning bolts—not actually lightning bolts, but the stylized letters 'SS'—they were the colors of the German flag. He realized, with a sinking feeling in his stomach, that they had built a Nazi clock for Eichmann!

The group in the doorway parted suddenly and Eichmann stepped back into his office. He stared coldly at the clock for several seconds, his expression never changing. Then, gradually, a smile spread across his bony face and he raised his hands and clapped slowly and softly. "Perfect! Tell Uhrmacher-Gruber that I am very pleased." Walking to his desk he opened the center drawer and took out an envelope. He handed it to Joseph without a word and then stopped at the door and barked to the other officers, "Back to work!" Instantly they were alone in the office.

Joseph peeked into the envelope and saw a handful of German mark notes. "Looks like more than he owed," he murmured. "I guess he really likes it." They quickly collected their tools, blankets, bags, and boxes and were ready to depart. Just as they were about to exit the doorway a lean figure in a crisp black uniform blocked their path.

"Excuse us, please," Joseph said. However, the man did not move. He stood stiffly, hands behind his back in a military stance, his eyes fixed unwaveringly on Joseph who frowned and took a step backward.

"Franz Josef Gruber." The hard voice was strangely familiar. Joseph's eyes narrowed as he looked closely at the face in front of him. Recognition dawned upon him and his mouth gaped open.

"Herr Hartstein!"

"*Obersturmführer* Hartstein," he glared. Clicking his heels and making a stiff-armed salute, he cried, "Sieg Heil!"

16

TEMPUS FUGIT

"Sieg Heil!" Joseph and Stephan responded dutifully, but with their hands and arms full of their bags, boxes, and gear, they could not very well offer the requisite salute. Without thinking Joseph blurted out in Wienerisch, "I hob docht, ihr seid's nach Deutschland g'reist!" *I thought you had gone to Germany!*

Hartstein winced as if in pain. "Did I not teach you better, Joseph? I thought I told you to never speak in Wienerisch again!"

"Y-yes," Joseph stammered, "but—but we're in Vienna now!"

"That's no excuse!" snapped Hartstein. "Hochdeutsch! Immer Hochdeutsch!" *Always High German!* Looking at Stephan he continued, "And who is this?"

"I'm Stephan Gruber—Joseph's cousin."

"You look like brothers—perfect Aryan specimens." He said it as if appraising a horse or automobile. "And why are you both not in the Hitler Youth, or S.A.?"

Motioning with his head Joseph indicated the clock on the wall behind them. "We have jobs, Herr—I mean, Obersturmführer Hartstein. We built this clock and have just now installed it for Obersturmbannführer Eichmann."

"I see," Hartstein said as he looked admiringly at the clock. "Very nice. Very nice indeed. So that's your van parked in the courtyard—Uhrmacher-Gruber." He was silent for a few seconds as he studied the clock, nodding, and then asked abruptly, "Why are you in Vienna, Herr Gruber? Visiting relatives?"

"Yes, *mein Herr*, and making clocks," Joseph replied as he set his boxes on the floor. They were getting heavy and it didn't appear that Hartstein was going to let them leave anytime soon. "I'll be going home to New York in a few weeks." Clearing his throat, he asked again, "And may I ask, *mein Herr*, what brings *you* to Vienna?"

Hartstein pursed his lips and hesitated, eyeing Joseph coolly, deciding whether to answer. "As you can see, I am an officer in the SS. Obersturmbannführer Eichmann is my commanding officer here at the Central Agency for Jewish Emigration. We are expediting the departures of Vienna's Jewish population. There is much to do."

Joseph knit his brows with a confused expression. "I thought the Jews were having difficulty getting visas to leave. Is the SS actually helping them to emigrate from Austria?"

"Of course, we are helping," he smirked evilly. "Nothing could be easier for a Jew than to leave Germany—there is no Austria any more, you know," he added with a raised eyebrow and a frown. "They can leave anytime they wish—they just can't take anything with them."

"But if they leave with nothing," Joseph objected, "other countries won't let them in. They would be burdens on the state, and they won't be able to emigrate at all!"

"That's not our problem," said Hartstein matter-of-factly. "But even in those cases we still assist them in leaving. We assemble them at the Aspangbahnhof and send them to relocation centers elsewhere. It is a well-organized operation—a model of efficiency—and Obersturmbannführer Eichmann is a genius. Vienna will soon be free of Jews." He smiled a cruel smile. "So, you see? We are taking care of the problem. No need to worry about anything."

"Yes, I see," echoed Joseph. "Very efficient! Taking care of the problem."

Just then Eichmann reappeared in the doorway. "I have another job for Uhrmacher-Gruber," he snapped as if giving an order. "The large clock on the wall inside the Aspangbahnhof has stopped running and we need to get it fixed right away. My secretary will give you the work order. Fix the clock immediately and send me the bill. Heil Hitler!" He spun about and was clicking away before they could even return the salute.

Joseph looked at Hartstein and shrugged. "I guess we'd better get going. He wants it done immediately, so—" He bent and picked up the boxes. "Good to see you again, Herr—I mean, Obersturmführer Hartstein."

Hartstein clicked his heels and presented the stiff-armed salute. "Heil Hitler!" he barked.

"Sieg Heil!" returned both Grubers and followed him through the outer office, stopping to pick up the new work order from the secretary, who was the same man who had escorted them to Eichmann's office.

As he folded the paper and put it in his jacket pocket, Joseph casually asked the secretary, "This is a very beautiful building. What was it before the SS moved in?"

The grouchy officer appeared about to ignore him, but a one-sided grin came over his face and he couldn't resist answering. "It was a Rothschild palace! They ran off to England right after the Anschluss—some of the first Jews to leave! Nice of them to leave it for us!" He gave a raspy laugh and finished with a dismissive wave of his hand.

Back in the van Joseph and Stephan looked at each other with wide eyes as they expelled deep breaths of relief. "I couldn't wait to get out of there!" Stephan exclaimed. "Those are some really scary people!" Joseph cranked the engine and Stephan added, "Did you know that was an SS clock we were making? I had no idea!"

"Neither did I. I felt pretty stupid when I realized it. I'm going to wash my hands for ten minutes when we get back to the shop."

Uncle Oskar looked at the new work order and frowned. "I'm not familiar with the interior of the Aspangbahnhof," he said, scratching his head. "I suspect that a large clock on the wall will probably be electric, but let's go take a look and see." As they loaded the van with tools they included an assortment of electrical fuses which Oskar kept for use at the shop, just in case they were needed. Over lunch, Joseph and Stephan related their experience at the SS headquarters. Oskar was quite surprised to learn that their customer was the Nazi SS office in Vienna and that the clock had been designed to reflect the Nazi colors and insignia.

"I'd rather not have known that," scowled Herr Schneider, who had carved the headpiece with the two jagged lightning bolts. "But it makes sense—it was the ugliest clock I've ever carved." Then, with a sideways look at Joseph, he added, "But at least there wasn't a gorilla on it!" Joseph promptly choked on his sandwich and had a coughing fit while the others laughed loudly.

"So, the Rothschilds got out, did they?" remarked Oskar when it was quiet again. "Can't say that I blame them. Better to leave by your own choice than to be deported by the Nazis. No telling where they're sending people."

"I'm sure it's nowhere they would want to go," Stephan said, shaking his head. "They call it 'emigration,' but you're right—it's not really by choice, and it's not to a place of their choosing. It sounds almost like they're being arrested and sent to jail."

"Stephan, did you notice the skull emblem on Eichmann's hatband?" asked Joseph. "Skulls mean death, don't they? I wonder what that's about."

"Yes, and why do they all wear black? They seem to be obsessed with death." Stephan shook his head and rolled his eyes. "I don't want to go back there—too much heel-clicking and sieg-heiling for me."

After lunch all but Schneider went to the train station to inspect the clock. The building stretched an entire city block long, with three-storied, cubical blockhouses anchoring each end. Between the two blockhouses was the passenger hall, more than a hundred meters long with a high, arched ceiling. Its classical façade featured columns and pediments, and tall, rounded windows. Joseph found the overall effect to be ponderous and overdone.

Inside the airy passenger hall there were at least five hundred people milling about aimlessly, carrying suitcases and looking lost.

Despite the warmth of the mid-September afternoon, most wore overcoats and hats. Some towed small children by the hand. There were several soldiers standing at the street doors and exits to the train platforms, and Joseph noticed a few wearing the black SS uniforms.

Oskar looked quickly about and pointed to one end of the hall where a large clock graced one of the stark white end-walls. Black Roman numerals were fixed to the wall in a large circle and the clock hands—two and three meters long—extended from a central hub situated almost ten meters above the floor. The hands declared the time to be half-past eight. "We need to find the man in charge of maintenance," he said, raising his voice to be heard over the hubbub of noise echoing in the cavernous space. "We're going to need a ladder."

While Oskar was in the office showing the work order and inquiring about a ladder, Joseph and Stephan waited in the hall with the toolbox. Joseph watched the forlorn travelers shuffling tiredly about and after a few minutes he approached one of them, an elderly man who reminded him of Herr Engelmann.

"Grüss Gott," he nodded pleasantly, thumbs hooked casually in his pants pockets. *Greet God.*

"Grüss Gott," the old man replied, eyeing him suspiciously. "Are you one of them?"

"One of who—the Nazis? No, I'm not one of them." Silence followed. Joseph shifted uncomfortably. "When does your train leave?" he asked curiously.

The old man looked at the clock on the far wall. "At eight-thirty," he replied drily.

"Where are you going?" Joseph persisted.

"Why do you care about that?" He did not seem irritated at the question. His tone implied that no one cared. "Besides, I don't know. They haven't told us."

"Do you have a visa?"

"You don't need a visa to be deported," he said tersely and with a spark in his eyes. "You don't need a ticket to ride the train to nowhere. You don't need a license to be unemployed." He paused, his shoulders slumped and his tension seemed to subside. "You don't need a permit to live, either," he added. "It's not so terrible for me—I'm old. But these young ones . . . ." His voice trailed off.

"Why were you selected for deportation?" Joseph asked. "Was it random?"

"I was a medical doctor until they took away my license. Then I supported myself by treating patients in my home. The *mischlings* especially needed my help. Being only half-Jews, they are rejected by the Jewish hospital because they're not Jews, and by the municipal hospitals because they *are.* Somehow the Nazi authorities found out what I was doing, and now here I am, standing here in this train station with my little suitcase—all that they would let me bring."

Joseph glanced back at the office to see if Uncle Oskar had emerged. He had not, so he spoke again to the old man. "I have a Jewish friend who is about your age. I'm trying to persuade him to emigrate to America, but he refuses to go. He says that Vienna is his home, and he will stay here, no matter what. What should I tell him?"

The man turned to face Joseph squarely, his eyes intensely penetrating into Joseph's. "Tell your friend that Vienna doesn't exist anymore!" His voice hoarse and trembling, he added, "*Austria* doesn't exist anymore, and if he doesn't get out immediately, *he* won't exist anymore, either. If he won't do it for himself, then do it for his family —for his loved ones, if there is *anyone* who cares about him. *Get out!*" Shaking with emotion and wiping a tear from his sunken, wrinkled cheek, he picked up the small suitcase and hurried away, disappearing into the milling crowd. Joseph, pale-faced, stood watching him until he was lost to view, and then he slowly returned to where Stephan was standing by the office door.

"Make a new friend?" Stephan asked cheerily. Joseph only sighed, frowned, and shook his head. He had no words. Stephan shrugged, and they waited in silence until Oskar finally came out to join them.

"There's no ladder," he announced, "but I have the key to the utility room. Let's go check the fuse box." The utility room was located beneath the clock, behind metal double-doors. The fuses were all in good working order, but they spied a ladder fixed to the wall, leading up to a hatch panel in the ceiling. Climbing up through the hatch, Joseph saw another ladder which went up to the clock motor bolted to the wall. Taking a flashlight, he went up and inspected the motor.

"There's a lot of corrosion on the power terminal," he called down. "We need to clean it off." They turned off the breaker fuse to the clock, detached the electrical cable, and cleaned the corrosion from the post and clamp. When they reattached the cable and flipped the breaker back to the 'On' position, the clock began whirring quietly and a little wheel began spinning. Joseph didn't know what the wheel was for, but it was clear that the clock was running. With an adjustable wrench he began to turn a crank that rotated the clock hands. Oskar stood in the passenger hall with his pocket watch in hand and signaled to Stephan when the hands were at the correct time. Stephan then yelled up to Joseph to stop turning the crank, and the job was finished. Oskar returned to the office to get a signature confirming that the clock was now working, and then they headed for home.

"How much do you think we should charge the SS for fixing the clock?" asked Stephan. "Fifty marks?"

"At least two hundred marks," said Joseph.

"Two hundred marks!" exclaimed Oskar in disbelief. "Just for cleaning a terminal and resetting the hands?"

"Two hundred marks for knowing the terminal needed cleaning and for knowing how to reset the hands," replied Joseph firmly. "If they could have fixed it themselves they wouldn't have needed us, and besides that, we fixed it the same day they hired us. We're worth every pfennig, if not more."

"I like the way you think, Joseph!" grinned Oskar. "Two hundred marks it is!"

"Yes!" Stephan hooted, pumping his fist in the air. "Wiener schnitzel tonight!"

"You know," Joseph continued reflectively, "the Nazis seem to be very interested in clocks and knowing the time. They're like a machine—like robots—not like real humans."

"Maybe Eichmann should have a clock on his hatband instead of a skull," suggested Stephan and they all laughed, but then Joseph frowned.

"Maybe he should have both," he said quietly. "I think time may be running out for the Jews."

"You know what they say," Oskar said, giving Joseph a direct look. "*Tempus fugit*! You need to get your friends out of Austria—out of Germany—as soon as possible."

"True!" Joseph agreed somberly. "Austria doesn't exist anymore. Time flies for all of us."

17

SUDETENLAND

It was the last day of September and the weather had begun to cool down from the summer heat. Joseph's enjoyment of the pleasant temperatures was moderated by his realization that he now had only a little more than a month before he would leave Vienna and return home. He had come to regard this as his new home and was loath to go back to the noisy and crowded streets of New York. Every day that passed brought him closer to the inevitable separation, and try as he might, he couldn't shake the feeling of dread that increasingly overshadowed his mind. Only when he was in the workshop could he focus on other things and be free.

Miriam still had not received her immigration visa to allow her entry to the United States, and this was another source of worry and concern for Joseph. Her telephone calls to the consulate always met with the same response: "Nothing yet." She was getting discouraged and this weighed on Joseph, who tried to be positive and optimistic even though he was equally frustrated. At least she and Herr Engelmann had not been abused by the Nazis like many other Vienna Jews, but they feared that this would not last long.

On a more positive note, Miriam was enjoying attending services at Christ Church and never missed a Sunday. In fact, just the preceding week she had invited Joseph to go with her and he had cheerfully accepted. He still found the severe lack of ornamentation in the Anglican sanctuary to be stark and almost grim, but he admitted that it seemed to help him listen to the words of the sermon since there was nothing else to compete for his attention.

"How did you like it?" she had asked as they left the building. "Don't you think it's better when you can understand everything that's being said?"

"Yes, I guess so," he replied hesitantly. "It's different though, and I'm not used to hearing English in church. I'd have to get used to it."

"Of course, it's not just the *language*," she continued. "It's what they're *saying* too. I don't know much about Catholicism, but the Anglicans seem more practical and relevant to me. I wish they would all just come together and be *Christians* instead of having so many divisions. Other religions don't have such fragmentation—so many different churches! Why is Christianity like that?"

"I don't know. I guess they just disagree on doctrines and such."

"But don't they all believe that Jesus is the Son of God—the Messiah—and believe the Bible is God's Word? Isn't that what really counts? Why divide over little things?"

"I don't know that either. I've never really thought about it before."

Miriam stopped on the sidewalk and fixed her direct gaze on Joseph. "I think I could really become a Christian, but this is a problem for me, Joseph. If Christians can't get along better than that, why should I join any of their churches? I've been reading about Jesus in the gospels, and I like him—I like him a lot!—but I'm not so sure about these churches."

"I wish I could explain all that," Joseph shrugged, "but I can't. You're asking some deep questions. I agree with you that being a Christian is more than just being a Catholic or Anglican, or something else, but I'm not sure you can really be a Christian without being part of *some* church. Maybe you should ask your priest."

"Maybe I will," she had replied thoughtfully. "I think I will."

As the week progressed the news was full of reports of a political conference to be held on Friday in Munich. Hitler and Mussolini would both be there along with the British and French leaders, Chamberlain and Daladier. The purpose of the meeting was to resolve tensions over the Sudetenland of Czechoslovakia, an area populated with ethnic Germans which Hitler was demanding to be handed over to Germany.

"This is just like what happened with Austria last March," fumed Uncle Oskar as he read the newspaper Thursday evening. "Hitler is threatening to invade and seize the territory if they don't give it to him. Only the British and French can save Czechoslovakia!"

"Do you think they will do it, Papa?" asked Anna Marie.

"They haven't said 'no' to him yet," scowled Oskar. "Why should they start now?"

"Herr Engelmann says that when Hitler gets the Sudetenland, he'll take the rest of Czechoslovakia next," said Joseph. "And after that, Poland."

"Why would he want those countries?" objected Mama Gruber. "They aren't even German! He says he only wants to bring all Germans together into one country. How would taking Czechs, Slovaks, and Poles accomplish anything?"

"I still think his target is Russia," Joseph frowned. "Hitler has always said that he wants to conquer Russia and reclaim the land that Germany took in the Great War but then lost in the Treaty of Versailles. I think he's moving east so that he can eventually attack Russia."

"No, no, no!" Oskar waved his hand dismissively. "It would be insane to invade Russia! Even Schicklgruber isn't that crazy!" He laughed harshly. "No, I think Mama Gruber is right. He only wants *real* Germans—not Slavs. The Sudetenland will be his final acquisition, and then we'll have peace."

"I hope you're right," Joseph said doubtfully. "I really do!"

On Saturday morning the news on the radio was that the Sudetenland now belonged to Germany. Hitler had assured the British and French that this was his last territorial demand and they had believed him. Over the protests of the Czechoslovakian government,

German troops crossed the border and occupied that portion of the country. The evening newspapers featured a photograph of Prime Minister Neville Chamberlain holding up a piece of paper upon his return to Britain, proclaiming that peace had been secured. The fear of an impending war had become intense in the days leading up to the conference and the announcement brought a sense of relief to everyone—except for the Czechoslovakians, of course, but no one cared about that.

The next day Joseph went to the Anglican church service with Miriam again, not so much for the religious experience as to see what the Englishman would say about the outcome of the Munich conference. Hugh Grimes, the clergyman who had baptized Miriam, had recently returned to England, but his replacement, Reverend Fred Collard, was continuing with the baptisms of Jews. Collard delivered the sermon in the service, and to Joseph's disappointment studiously avoided any mention of political developments until his final comments. The focus of the sermon had been on Jesus' miracle of calming the storm at sea, and in his conclusion Collard made an application of the story.

"The storm was so fierce that the disciples feared for their lives. They had no hope, but in desperation they turned to Jesus. With just a word he stilled the waves, calmed the wind, and brought peace! We today are also often afraid, with no hope. However, if we turn to Jesus, he can still calm the storms in our lives. He can bring peace, just as Prime Minister Chamberlain brought peace two days ago, preventing a war that seemed about to erupt. Let us never give up hope, but always trust in the Lord to answer our prayers!"

Another song was sung, followed by a prayer, and the service ended. Miriam grabbed Joseph's hand and pulled him after her, not toward the exit, but toward the front of the church. She made a beeline for Reverend Collard, who was holding the hand of an elderly English woman in both of his and nodding as she talked. They waited for a long minute until the reverend was free, and Miriam stepped forward.

"Hello Reverend! My name is Miriam and this is my friend, Joseph. I'd like to ask you a question, if you don't mind."

"Certainly, Miriam! How may I help you?"

"Why are there so many churches in Christianity? And how can I know which one to join?"

Collard blinked in surprise, and it seemed to Joseph that his smile stiffened a bit. "Well, my dear!" he said, putting his hand on her shoulder. "That is a very good question! The short answer is that there are so many churches because of disagreements about what we are supposed to believe. As for which church you should join, I must confess to being a bit biased!" He laughed while Miriam nodded agreement. "If you want a more thorough answer, I suggest that we get together sometime this week and talk about it. Let me give you a telephone number to call to make an appointment. Would you like that?" Miriam nodded again, and he quickly jotted down a number on a slip of paper in the pulpit. "Just call that number and we'll set up a time to meet." They shook hands, and Miriam stepped aside to let another person speak to the reverend.

Back on the sidewalk Miriam asked Joseph, "What did you think of the sermon?"

"It was interesting. Like I said before, I'm used to hearing church things in Latin, so this was really different. I admit that I do like being able to understand it." Joseph hesitated, and then added, "However, I don't think he should have compared Neville Chamberlain at Munich to Jesus calming the storm. That's taking it too far, in my opinion. After all, there were three other people there, you know, and whether they kept peace and prevented a war remains to be seen. We can only hope that they did."

"You're being too critical. He didn't mean that Chamberlain worked a miracle, and it looked like there would have been an invasion of Czechoslovakia if they hadn't made an agreement, so I think they *did* keep the peace."

"Yes—by giving away important parts of Czechoslovakia! That's like saving someone's life by cutting off their leg. It may have been necessary, but it's not something to be happy about."

"Better to be alive with one leg, than dead with two," argued Miriam with a glare.

Joseph laughed and raised his hands. "I surrender!" he cried. "If the patient survives, then the operation will have been a success. But —" he frowned, "that's a very big 'if.'" They walked a few more steps and he added, "By the time we know how it turns out, I hope you and your Opa will be on the other side of the ocean."

"So do I," she agreed.

"Maybe it's time to pay Roger Thomas another visit?"

"Maybe. But Opa and I must go stand in line to have our passports stamped with a red 'J' by Wednesday, so it will have to be after that."

Surprised, Joseph looked quickly at her. Her face was impassive but her anxiety was not entirely concealed. "Jews are no longer considered citizens of the Reich," she continued quietly. "Our passports will not be valid at all in a few months—by early next year, they have said. Until then we must have the 'J' to keep our Austrian passports."

"We definitely need to talk to Thomas, then," Joseph muttered. "The sooner, the better."

The next Wednesday morning, the Uhrmacher-Gruber workshop was a busy place as they put the finishing touches on several clocks. Unexpectedly, from the front room Uncle Oskar called for Joseph and Stephan to come out and join him. Herr Schneider, mallet and chisel in hand, also came to the doorway to see what was going on. There were three Nazi officers dressed in black SS uniforms with swastika armbands standing in the display room, looking curiously at the beautiful clocks on tables, shelves, and walls. To his surprise, Joseph recognized one of them.

"Herr Hart—I mean, Herr Oberführer—Oberbann—I mean—"

"It's Obersturmführer!" corrected Hartstein, with visible irritation. "Heil Hitler!" He clicked his heels and threw his arm out in a stiff salute, and the other two Nazis followed suit.

"Sorry—Heil Hitler—I can't seem to remember the new German army ranks."

"The SS is *not* part of the army!" Hartstein snapped indignantly. He was really irritated, now. "We are entirely *separate* from the army, and we answer only to the Führer himself!"

"I apologize," said Joseph quickly. "I meant no disrespect."

Still frowning, Hartstein turned to Oskar. "Obersturmbannführer Eichmann sends his compliments for fixing the Aspangbahnhof clock so quickly." He whipped out an envelope from his coat's inside pocket and extended it. "Your fee!"

"Thank you," said Oskar. "It was Joseph who did most of the work. He's a very skilled worker." He accepted the envelope, glanced at its contents, and gave a quick, confirming nod to Joseph. Two hundred marks were all there.

Hartstein gave Joseph a quick, sharp glance and then focused on Oskar again. "The main reason I'm here is to ask about the bookstore on Mariahilferstrasse. There seems to be some confusion as to who actually owns it."

"Are you talking about the Buchhandlung-Gruber, at the corner of Mariahilferstrasse and Amerlingstrasse?"

"That's the one. According to our records, it is supposed to be Buchhandlung-Engelmann."

"It used to be," nodded Oskar, "but I bought it from Engelmann a few months ago—last April, I believe. It belongs to me now. The sale was recorded properly—what's the problem?"

"Do you still sell books there? I was just there and it's locked and the lights are off." Hartstein was perplexed, frowning as he studied a piece of paper in his hand.

"It's still open for business," Oskar replied, becoming a bit uneasy. "I gave the manager the day off to take care of some personal business. It should be open again by tomorrow. If you're looking for a good book to read, we've got—"

"I'm not shopping for books, Herr Gruber," interrupted Hartstein. "As I'm sure you know," he said acidly, "Jews are not allowed to own or operate businesses in the Reich, and we want to know if you are employing Engelmann to manage your bookstore."

"Absolutely not!" laughed Oskar, relieved. "I'm not employing Engelmann or any other Jews, for that matter."

"Well then," persisted Hartstein, "who is it that runs the store? Who have you given the day off?"

"I thought you wanted to know who *owns* the bookstore," Oskar asked, surprised. "Why are you asking about who *sells* the books?"

"Because you can't employ *Jews*, that's why!" Hartstein barked, beginning to get angry. "Do you have something to *hide*? Don't think you can get away with ignoring the law!"

"Did you come here to threaten me?" demanded Oskar, his chin jutting out combatively. "I'll have you know that I fought in the war and was wounded three times! I killed a dozen men, and I still have shrapnel in my leg from Russian artillery! Don't come in here and tell me who can sell books for me!" His voice rose steadily louder until at the end he was red in the face and shouting, jabbing his finger at Hartstein.

Hartstein's face went blank and he took a step back. "Herr Gruber," he said in a more moderate tone of voice, "I'm not here to threaten you. I'm just trying to make sure that Jews are not taking jobs away from good Aryan Germans. I'm sure you wouldn't want that either—true?"

"Hmph!" snorted Oskar. "If you know any good, Aryan Germans who want a piddling, part-time job selling books in a little bookstore, send them to me. Or better yet, sign them up for the SS. If this is all you people have to do, then any broom-pusher can handle it."

Joseph and Stephan exchanged alarmed looks. *Oskar's temper is getting the better of him,* Joseph thought, *and this could be dangerous.* Hartstein looked like he was about to explode at Oskar's insult, when a voice rang out from the workshop doorway. Everyone's head turned to see Herr Schneider in his lederhosen and thick knee socks, with flowing white hair and beard.

"I have a question for *you*, Herr SS man," Schneider said with an edge to his voice. He walked into the showroom, gesturing toward Hartstein with his mallet. "Why did Herr Hitler go to the brink of war to bring Sudeten Germans into the Reich but gave away the Germans in the South Tyrol to Italy?" Schneider's voice trembled with anger and he kept shaking the mallet at Hartstein as he spoke. "Don't we Tyroleans matter to Hitler? Are we not important to the Reich too?"

"Who are *you*, old man?" Hartstein blustered indignantly. "The Führer doesn't answer to you, or to anyone in Tyrol!"

Schneider slammed the mallet down on one of the tables with a deafening crash. Hartstein and everyone else in the room jerked involuntarily. "That's the problem!" Schneider shouted furiously. "The Führer doesn't answer to *anybody*! Do the German people have no rights? Do we not have the right to *be Germans*, and to live in our own German country? What right does he have to hand us off to *Italy*? Mussolini doesn't care about us! We want to belong to the *Fatherland!*" Raising his mallet high overhead like Thor's hammer, and with fire in his eyes he roared, "Tyrol is worth ten of Czechoslovakia! We are true Germans!"

The three SS officers gave each other nervous looks. In a group they backed slowly toward the door as one of them replied to Schneider in a placating tone of voice. "We understand your concern, Herr—ah, we will be sure to pass along your—ah, concern—your love of the Fatherland—we will, ah—" They reached the door to the street and all three, as if on cue, clicked their heels, saluted, and cried "Heil Hitler!" and hurriedly exited the shop.

"Bah!" spat Schneider, smacking the table loudly with the mallet again. "Bastards!" he growled, and stomped back into the workshop. The three Grubers looked at each other in stunned silence, struggling to grasp what had just transpired.

"*Mein Gott*," breathed Oskar in awed tones. "If Oberbahnhofwienerschnitzelführer ever comes back, I want Herr Schneider out here with me!"

Stephan snorted as he failed to stifle a laugh. With an impish look at his father, he grinned. "Sign up any old broom-pusher for the SS? *Really*?" His shoulders shook with silent laughter.

Oskar reddened and then began to smile, and then to grin. "It might raise their standards!" he chuckled.

"Well," Joseph added wryly, "at least you didn't say 'Schicklgruber.'" All three burst out laughing at that. Joseph then added, "Somebody needs to tell Herr Engelmann he's not employed to run the bookstore. Wouldn't want him to have the wrong idea."

"Yes," Oskar agreed a bit sheepishly. "I'll have to talk with him about that. We'll work something out." Exhaling loudly through pursed lips, he waved them toward the workshop doorway. "Let's get back to work. We've got clocks to sell!"

18

THUNDERBOLT OUT OF THE BLUE

"Opa! Roger Thomas says that my application for a visa to the United States has been approved! I should be able to leave by the end of the month!" Miriam practically vibrated with excitement as she hung up the telephone in the bookstore storeroom.

"At last! We've waited so long—that's wonderful, my dear!" Herr Engelmann was beaming with delight and his voice quavered with emotion. "I am so happy for you!" He rose from his chair and gave her a lingering embrace, patting her back. "This is an answer to prayer!" he exclaimed.

"And now *you* must apply for a visa, also!" Miriam's face took on a stern look and she wagged her finger at her grandfather. "You've sold the bookstore, mother is gone, and when I am gone there will be nothing for you here. You can't stay here by yourself! Please say you'll come with me!"

"Ah, Miriam! Wien is my home! I cannot—"

"Vienna doesn't exist anymore!" Joseph inserted. "*Austria* doesn't exist anymore, either. Remember what the man at the Aspang station said! Get out while you still can! It is only going to get worse."

"Opa—you know he's right," Miriam insisted. "How many Jews have disappeared without a trace already? How many have been deported by the train loads? How many have committed suicide? A black cloud is hanging over the Jewish people. The sun doesn't shine anymore for us."

"But Miriam, I just—"

"Herr Engelmann!" Joseph argued. "I'm no expert, but it seems to me that in the Bible, whenever the Jewish people were in a fix, God always made a way out for them. Like when they were slaves in Egypt and he sent Moses to lead them through the Red Sea. He didn't just leave them there to suffer. Maybe the Atlantic Ocean is your Red Sea, and God is giving you a chance to get out while you still can!"

"Yes, God does make a way out for his people," agreed Engelmann, "but it's not for us to say what that escape route might be. Sometimes we just have to wait for God to do it his way."

"But what if the Israelites had not followed Moses?" Joseph persisted. "What if they had said 'This isn't God's way—we'll just wait a while?' They would have continued to be slaves. When God opens a door, we have to go through it! Maybe America is your Promised Land—don't let it slip away from you."

"You make a good argument, Joseph," he conceded with a sad smile, "but my heart tells me to stay here. America is a wonderful place, but it is no Promised Land. My ancestors have lived here for generations, and I will be laid to rest with them here."

"You wouldn't say that if you had been at the Aspangbahnhof and seen the hundreds of Jews with their suitcases being herded onto the trains. I don't know what will happen to them, but I doubt that they will be laid to rest here with their ancestors. I don't think they're ever coming back. You can't take the chance that you'll be the next to go."

Engelmann sighed heavily, and tears filled his eyes. The room was quiet as he took a white handkerchief from his pocket and blew his nose gently. He sighed again and wiped his glasses with a silk cloth. A moment passed in silence, and finally Miriam spoke with quiet resolution.

"Opa, if you won't come with me, then I refuse to go. I won't leave you here alone."

"No, Miriam! I won't let you stay! You must go, and as soon as possible!"

"Not without you, Opa. I mean it."

Joseph rubbed his temples in consternation. "I think she really does mean it, Herr Engelmann. You might as well give in."

Herr Engelmann sighed deeply again, with a troubled expression on his face. He looked sadly across the chess board at Joseph and reached out to take Miriam's hand as she sat at the side. "It breaks my heart," he said slowly, with a crack in his voice, "but I know you are right. To stay here without you would be unbearable. I will call Thomas tomorrow and start the process—but it will take a long time and you must go on ahead. Don't wait for me!"

Miriam threw her arms around his neck, upsetting the pieces on the board. "Oh, thank you, Opa!" She kissed his cheek, wetting it with her tears. "You've made the right decision! We'll be together in America by New Year's; I just know it!"

"It's like you've always told me," Joseph smiled, relieved. "You have to know when to advance your pawns!"

"You're a quick learner, Joseph!" Engelmann smiled. And this time it was not a sad smile.

"That is absolutely the gaudiest clock I've ever seen." Herr Schneider squinted at Joseph's Art Deco masterpiece, running smoothly and quietly as it hung on the wall in the workshop. His voice sounded disapproving, but he patted Joseph on the shoulder and added, "It's not my style, of course, but the workmanship is flawless. I congratulate you on an outstanding job, Joseph!" They clasped hands firmly and Joseph's heart swelled with pride. He had wanted Schneider's approbation more than anything.

"Same for me!" boomed Uncle Oskar, clapping Joseph on the back. "The right customer would pay hundreds of marks for a clock like that! It's one of a kind!" Stephan added his praise, as did Anna Marie and Mama Gruber. This moment was the culmination of months of careful planning and hard work, and Joseph felt that the completion of this stunning clock justified the year he had spent laboring in the workshop. He hoped his father would be as impressed as Oskar's family were. He stood with a radiant smile on his face, gazing at its rich, vibrant colors and bold lines. *It's perfect!* he thought. *If I live to be a hundred, I'll never make a more beautiful clock than this.*

"Thank you, Uncle Oskar! It's not for sale, though. I'll keep this one for myself!"

His reverie was interrupted by the tinkling of the bell over the door in the display room, followed by a loud, harsh voice calling out his name—"Franz Josef Gruber! Joseph Gruber! Come out here immediately!" The Grubers exchanged surprised looks and the family hurried out into the other room. Obersturmführer Hartstein stood with feet apart and hands on hips, flanked by four soldiers carrying rifles.

"What is the meaning of this?" demanded Oskar indignantly.

"This doesn't concern you, Herr Gruber," snapped Hartstein. He extended a paper toward Joseph. "This is for you." Joseph took the paper and scanned over it.

"Conscription? I don't understand," he mumbled, confused. "This looks like a draft notice, but I'm an American citizen."

"Perhaps so," Hartstein scowled, "but you were born in *Austria*—Ostmark, that is—and you are also now a *German* citizen. As such you are required to serve the Fatherland in the Reichswehr! Heil Hitler!"

"But I'm going back to America in less than a month! I can't—"

"Oh, but you *will*! Unless, of course, you *refuse* to serve the Fatherland," Hartstein fixed his icy stare on Joseph. "If you refuse to be inducted into the army you will be taken directly to the Mauthausen camp, and you won't come out for a long time!"

The Grubers raised a collective cry of protest which Hartstein silenced with an abrupt wave of his hand. At that moment Schneider emerged from the workroom, his eyes spitting fire.

"Watch that one!" Hartstein barked, pointing at the old man. "He's dangerous!" The soldiers chambered rounds in their rifles and turned toward Schneider menacingly. He stopped at the counter, grinding his teeth in anger.

"Come!" Hartstein ordered, beckoning to Joseph. "I don't have time to waste. You can make your decision on the way, but remember what I said—it's the army or Mauthausen." In shock, Joseph walked slowly forward. Hartstein grabbed him roughly by the shoulder and shoved him toward the door. The bell tinkled again as they left.

On the sidewalk Hartstein glared triumphantly at Joseph. "I'll make a good Aryan of you yet, Joseph Gruber!" he gloated, showing too many teeth to give a friendly impression. Joseph was loaded into the back of an army truck with the four soldiers, joining a few other forlorn civilian men. The engine roared and backfired, and a cloud of black smoke belched from the tail pipe. The driver shifted into gear with an awful grinding noise, and finally, with a jerk the truck lurched forward, and then it was gone—and Joseph with it.

Two hours later the truck coughed and shuddered to a stop at the army training camp at Döllersheim in north-central Austria, about halfway between the Danube River and the Czech border. There had been no conversation along the way—it would have been impossible due to the noise even if anyone had wanted to talk—so Joseph spent the time immersed in his own thoughts, which were anything but cheerful. Upon arriving at the camp he was grim, anxious, and almost frantic with worry.

The camp itself was rather bleak. It consisted of two long rows of wooden barracks with an unpaved street between them. A few larger buildings were visible in the distance, which he later learned were the armory, mess hall, and other administrative structures. He and his traveling companions joined a sizeable batch of new recruits, forming ranks as soldiers shouted at them and shoved them into place. A captain stood before them and gave a short speech, basically informing them that they would undergo basic training for sixteen weeks and then be sent to other camps for more specialized training. He warned them that the training regimen would be demanding and would require their best efforts. "Nothing less would be worthy of a soldier in the Reichswehr!" he shouted.

He then ordered the men to raise their right arms in the Nazi salute and repeat an oath of loyalty to Hitler: "I swear by God this holy oath that I shall render unconditional obedience to the Leader of the German Reich and people, Adolf Hitler, supreme commander of the armed forces, and that as a brave soldier I shall at all times be prepared to give my life for this oath." Joseph mumbled the words convincingly enough to avoid attracting the attention of the soldiers, meanwhile thinking to himself, *"But God, I don't mean it!"*

The recruits lined up to receive outfits of gray-green fatigues and boots, and then their hair was cut—trimmed short on the sides. They were assigned to barracks in groups of eight, each under the command of a corporal. By early afternoon Joseph was sitting on a stiff, squeaky cot covered with a scratchy wool blanket, and he critically surveyed the other recruits in his group. They did not appear to be in particularly good physical condition, he thought. A couple looked like they might have been football players—*soccer*, he reminded himself—but the rest looked soft. He wondered when their training would begin. He got his answer immediately.

"On your feet!" shrieked a soldier as he stepped through the doorway. Startled, everyone in the room jumped to his feet. This was their barracks corporal. "Outside! *Now!*" he screamed again. Joseph wondered if he would scream everything, and if so, how long his vocal chords would stand the strain. "I am Corporal Schwarz," he bellowed, pacing back and forth in front of them and slapping his high-topped boot with a baton, "and I am your commander for the next four months. You will do everything that I tell you to do without hesitation or I will beat you without mercy!" Joseph believed that he would enjoy it, too—the man was lean and wolfish-looking and gave the impression of being permanently furious. "It is four hours until you will be fed your supper, and by then you will be too exhausted to eat it! Now—follow me!"

For the next four hours the recruits marched, ran, did calisthenics, push-ups, and sit-ups, and carried buckets of bricks until they were dripping sweat and leaning on their knees gasping for breath. They were finally allowed to return to their barracks to shower in ice cold water before marching to the mess hall for supper. The sun was already setting below the distant tree line, and the sky was more black than blue.

Joseph was surprised and dismayed at the sparse fare they were served. *I hope the other meals are bigger than this*, he thought, *or we're not going to be able to survive this punishment.* It took only a few minutes for the men to clean their plates and they looked about with questioning eyes, as if wondering if there was no more to eat. With hardly a minute to spare Corporal Schwarz began shouting at them to line up. The last recruit to join the line was given a sharp whack across the shoulders with the baton. "Don't be the last to line up!" brayed Schwarz. "Always be the first!"

It was dark when they stumbled back into the barracks. The room was filled with exhausted groans and the squeaking of cot springs as the men collapsed onto their beds. After a few muffled moans of "Mein Gott!" and such, all was quiet, except for light snoring.

Lying in the pitch darkness, Joseph struggled to come to terms with his situation. *Surely this can't really be happening,* he told himself. *The Grubers will contact the American consulate, and John Wiley or Roger Thomas will get me released. They can't kidnap an American citizen and force him into the German army, can they? One way or another, I have to be on that ship to New York in less than a month. I need help!* Instinctively he made the sign of the cross over his chest and began to pray. After only a few words, he drifted off to sleep.

19

ROLLER COASTER!

The recruits were subjected to rigorous physical training for the next two weeks. Daily, from before sunrise to after sunset, they were driven to the point of collapse by the screaming Corporal Schwarz and his ever-threatening baton. Fortunately, the October weather was temperate enough that they didn't suffer from extreme heat or cold, but the long days were still more than some could take. At night they fell into bed without even bothering to shower. The small portions of food they were provided contributed to their misery, and all of them lost weight. The obstacle course was the most challenging activity, but due to his strength and athleticism, Joseph actually enjoyed it. He frequently found himself silently thanking Charles Atlas and his muscle-building course for preparing him to weather these trials. He was determined not to let Corporal Schwarz make him vomit like the others.

One of the recruits especially attracted Schwarz's ire—a slightly chubby, pale young man named Engelbert. Unfortunately, when Schwarz had roared at him and demanded his name, he had responded with "Berti," which led to Schwarz ridiculing him for having a child's name. From that time onward the corporal constantly harassed him, contemptuously shouting "Berti! You lump!" whenever he faltered, though he called all of the others by their last names. Berti received more jabs and blows from the baton than any other recruit.

Joseph felt sympathy for Berti, watching him struggle to do the calisthenics, running, and load-carrying. He offered words of encouragement when he could, and he could tell that Berti was nearing his breaking point. At night he was sure that he heard him crying softly in his bed. Observing how Schwarz delighted in demeaning and humiliating Berti made Joseph loathe the man even more, and he soon came to intensely despise him.

After two weeks of hell, a new training regimen was added to the daily program. The recruits began to be trained in hand-to-hand combat techniques. From the beginning Schwarz selected Berti for his demonstrations, repeated throwing him to the ground, pinning him with a knee or elbow, and twisting Berti into painful positions until he cried out. By the end of that week Joseph had had enough of it. He wasn't sure what he could do about it, but he knew Berti couldn't take much more.

One afternoon when it was time for the hand-to-hand lesson, Schwarz ordered them to take their customary positions in a circle around him for a new demonstration. "Berti!" he snarled. "Come here, you lump!" Joseph, standing next to Berti, heard him audibly groan. "Berti!" repeated the corporal. "Get out here! You coward!" Reluctantly, Berti moved slowly to the center of the circle to face Schwarz. "Watch carefully how I deflect his attack and gain control," Schwarz said, and directed Berti to lunge for him. Berti did not move. Schwarz ordered him again, and still Berti did not move. Schwarz stepped forward and slapped him across the face, cursing and belittling him. He continued to slap and abuse him until finally Berti snapped. He lunged forward with a half-strangled cry, reaching for Schwarz's neck. Schwarz grabbed Berti's right arm, twisted it and leveraged him over his hip, throwing him heavily to the ground. Descending upon the prone Berti, he pressed the edge of his hand into Berti's throat cutting off his air. Berti choked and struggled to breathe until he almost passed out before Schwarz finally stood up, flushed in the face, upper lip curled in a snarl. "Get up, little Berti!" he rasped hoarsely. "We will repeat it until you learn what to do—or until you are dead!"

Without thinking, Joseph raised his hand and spoke. "Jawohl, Herr Corporal Schwarz—I think I see how it is done. I would like to practice it with you, mein Herr."

Schwarz was clearly angered by this as he had intended to abuse Berti further, but he could hardly decline the offer. Berti staggered back to the circle and Joseph took his place in the center. "So, Gruber," Schwarz sneered. "You think you can do better than little Berti? Go ahead—lunge at me! Lunge at me! *Do it now!*" His voice rose to a high pitch as he tried to goad Joseph into a sudden move. Joseph suddenly extended his arm and cried, "Heil Hitler!" Taken by surprise, Schwarz hesitated and then responded with a stiff arm and barked, "Heil—"

Joseph quickly grabbed the corporal's arm with both hands, twisted it and threw the corporal over his hip, sprawling to the ground. Instantly he dove onto him and drove the edge of his hand into Schwarz's throat, cutting off his air as he had done to Berti. Schwarz struggled, kicked, and clawed to no avail, and finally Joseph released him and stood up.

Schwarz, red in the face, holding his hand to his neck and coughing violently, rose to his knees. When he regained his voice he pointed at Joseph and hissed, "You will pay for this, Gruber! I'll see you in the brig!"

"What seems to be the problem, corporal?" No one had noticed the long, black Mercedes stopping on the nearby unpaved roadway. The camp commander, Major Grünfeld, had dropped by to observe the training session and was a few yards away, hands clasped behind his back. "How is the training coming along?"

"Herr Major Grünfeld!" Schwarz leaped to his feet. "Heil Hitler!"

"Heil Hitler!" responded Grünfeld with a half-hearted wave. "Is everything alright, Corporal Schwarz?"

"Jawohl, Herr Major Grünfeld! Everything is in order. I was just instructing these men in tactics for hand-to-hand fighting, mein Herr!"

"You appear to be doing an excellent job of it, corporal—especially with this one. He seems to have mastered the technique very well! My compliments!"

"Jawohl, Herr Major!" At a loss for what else to say, he continued with another "Heil Hitler!" and a stiff-armed salute.

"Carry on," replied the major with a nod, and turned to leave.

"Herr Major Grünfeld!" said Joseph impulsively. The major turned back and gave him a frown. Soldiers—especially mere recruits —did not address officers without permission. Joseph realized that he was clearly out of line, but it was too late now. "I apologize for speaking, Herr Major, but—" he hesitated.

"Yes, soldier?"

Joseph cleared his throat. "Is that a Mercedes-Benz Nürburg? I've never seen one in person before."

The major blinked, and then grinned like a boy with a new puppy. "It is indeed! Would you like a closer look? Come on over here!"

Joseph eagerly followed him to the automobile and the other recruits followed behind him. Schwarz was clenching his fists and literally spitting in fury, but did not dare to object in the major's presence. He trailed the group, gritting his teeth.

"This is the Nürburg 500K," said the major proudly, wiping a spot from the hood with a handkerchief. "It has an eight-cylinder, three-hundred cubic inch engine, and produces a hundred horsepower! With the supercharger engaged it makes a hundred-sixty horsepower! It has the five-speed transmission with overdrive and a top speed of a hundred-seventy kilometers per hour."

"I would love to drive a machine like this!" Joseph said admiringly. "It's beautiful!"

"Does one so young have experience driving?"

"Jawohl, Herr Major! I am an American citizen, and have driven in New York City, as well as here in Aust—I mean, in *Ostmark*."

"An American! How is it that you are enlisted in the Reichswehr?"

"I was born in Vienna, Herr Major, so I am also an Austrian citizen—now a German citizen. My family emigrated to America when I was four, and I came back here a year ago to visit my uncle and his family. I was conscripted three weeks ago."

"I see," the major murmured, stroking his chin. "Very interesting. What is your name, soldier?"

"Joseph Gruber, mein Herr."

"When were you planning to return to America?"

Joseph cleared his throat nervously again. "I was to return home in a few days, Herr Major—about a week from now."

"Very interesting," he repeated slowly, as if his mind was elsewhere. He studied Joseph closely for a few seconds and then abruptly saluted with a "Heil Hitler!" and got into the rear seat of the vehicle and was driven away in a cloud of dust.

For the remainder of the training session Schwarz was particularly loud and demanding, but he did not physically engage with any of the recruits. His verbal abuse was more savage than usual, especially when directed at Berti. He threatened with the baton more than once, causing Berti to flinch, but for some reason did not strike. He ignored Joseph completely.

As he lay in bed that night Joseph could not stop thinking about his encounter with the major. Would he find himself in trouble? Would it lead to something good? Would it have no effect at all? He had had no communication with Uncle Oskar's family or with Herr Engelmann or Miriam for three weeks now. They must be worried about him—were they able to do anything to help him? Was the American consulate working on his behalf? Did his parents know of his plight? He wondered if it would be possible to escape and make his way to a seaport without being arrested and sent to the Mauthausen concentration camp. His head was spinning with all these questions, and he felt so sick with anxiety that for a moment he thought he would throw up. He managed to calm his nerves enough that he eventually dropped into a restless sleep, but awakened before the morning wake-up call.

Lying in the dark quiet of the bunk room, he glanced toward

Berti's cot. His eyes adjusted to the faint light enough that he could see the cot was empty. *Berti? Where are you?* Joseph sat up and put his feet on the cold floor. He thought Berti might have gone to the latrine, but he heard nothing. Concerned, he tiptoed to the latrine and found it empty. He walked through to the shower room and turned on the light. Berti's body hung lifeless from one of the shower heads with a belt around his neck, his face hideously discolored, eyes staring, protruding. Stunned, Joseph staggered backward and then approached and touched the body. It was cold. Berti had been dead for at least a couple of hours, he guessed. He started to lower Berti's body to the floor, but then thought, *No, I want Schwarz to see this. This is his fault.* He turned off the light and returned to the bunk room.

Just then the wake-up siren sounded over the camp loudspeakers and the men immediately piled out of their cots, groaning, and quickly dressed. They could already hear Corporal Schwarz outside shouting for them to line up. Everyone visited the latrine, but no one entered the shower room. The seven recruits lined up in the chill of the pre-dawn darkness. Noting that there were only seven of them, Schwarz quickly identified the missing recruit.

"Where is Berti?" he shouted, whacking his boot with the baton. "Berti! Get out here now, you lump!" Joseph stood silently with the others. Schwarz stormed furiously past them into the barracks. They could hear him bellowing, "Berti! You can't hide! Get out here!" It was apparent from the echoing of his voice that he was back in the latrine. Suddenly all was quiet. Joseph tried to imagine what must be happening in the shower room. Grimly, he waited for Schwarz to reappear. *I hope he's satisfied,* he thought. A long minute passed.

Finally, the corporal emerged, walking slowly around to stand in front of the men. Even in the semi-darkness Joseph could tell that he was pale and shaken. When Schwarz spoke it was, for the first time, in a low, controlled voice. "Go to the shower room and get Berti's body. Wrap it in his blanket, and lay it on his cot." Uncomprehending, the men did not move. "Do it!" Schwarz croaked, pointing to the door with his baton. Then, quickly returning to his normal state, he screamed this time—"Go get him! Now!"

The seven men hurried to the shower room and all but Joseph gasped in shock. Two retreated to the latrine and vomited into a toilet. They wrapped Berti in his blanket and laid him on the cot, and then reassembled outside. Somber and repressed, they looked at Schwarz with cold, accusing eyes. He marched them down the camp's main street, which was busy with the stirring of other groups of recruits beginning their morning regimens. He halted the line in front of the main office building and stood on the first step to the entrance.

"Gruber! Take the men to the forest trail for a hike. Do the long route and then go to breakfast." Without another word he turned and disappeared into the building.

"Let's go, men!" Joseph said, and set off at a leisurely pace. For the first time he actually enjoyed the forest trail. There were still some autumn colors to be seen, and birds could be heard singing and foraging for their breakfast. The rosy glow of the rising sun colored the sky, which began to take on a blue tint, with puffy white clouds floating motionlessly. They stopped on a promontory to admire the view and the men began to remark how pretty it was. The conversation turned to the morning's incident.

"Too bad Berti can't be here to enjoy this," one said.

"Berti wasn't cut out for the army life," observed another. "He just couldn't take it."

"Schwarz killed him, just as sure as if he'd strung him up himself."

"I wonder if Schwarz will face discipline for this."

"He'll probably get a medal."

"The best thing that has happened since we got here was when you put Schwarz on the ground and choked him!" exclaimed one, looking at Joseph. The others enthusiastically agreed, laughing uproariously.

"I wish you'd finished him off!"

"Hey, Gruber—what's this about you being an American and supposed to go home? Is that really true?"

"Yes. I'm supposed to be on a boat to New York on the twelfth of

November. That's only a few days away, and it doesn't look like I'm going to make it."

"They oughta let you leave! You shouldn't have to be in the army for some other country!"

"Thanks! Be sure and tell that to Major Grünfeld!" They all laughed at that, and resumed the hike in better spirits.

Later, as they were leaving the mess hall after breakfast, Major Grünfeld stood outside the door along with Corporal Schwarz. "Gruber! Over here!" snapped Schwarz, but without his usual venom.

"Heil Hitler!" Joseph gave the expected salutation.

"My driver is in the infirmary today," said Grünfeld. "I need someone to drive me to an important meeting. Do you think you can do that, Gruber?"

"Jawohl, Herr Major!" Joseph exclaimed enthusiastically. "I can definitely do that!"

"Good! Corporal Schwarz has agreed to release you for the day. Come to my office and get the keys. We'll leave in half an hour."

It turned out to be an entire hour before they left, but Joseph needed all of that time to prepare. He ran to the barracks, washed quickly at a sink, and changed into a clean shirt. He considered using the shower, but the memory of Berti hanging from the shower head was enough to make him reject that thought. When he reached the main building, the major was in his office with the door closed. His secretary handed him a black leather military jacket and hat, leather driving gloves, and a folded road map. Opening the map, he studied it until he found Döllersheim.

"Where is the major's meeting?"

"In Dürnstein. It's a small village on the Danube, near Krems."

"I see it. That looks like about fifty kilometers. Should take us about an hour. How long will the meeting last?"

The secretary glared. "It will take as long as Herr Major wants it to take!" He tossed a small ring of two keys onto the desk. "Go get the car and bring it around to the front. Check the oil, water, and tires. He won't want to be kept waiting."

Joseph was thrilled to be able to open the engine compartment and inspect the powerful motor. Eight inline cylinders! With twin carburetors! He checked all of the fluid levels, belts, and hoses, and wiped some smudges off the valve cover. A shiver ran up Joseph's spine—driving an automobile like this was a dream come true! He pulled the stiff driver's hat down securely on his head, put on the gloves, took a deep breath, and eased into the driver's seat. When he turned the ignition key the engine sprang to life with a deep, throaty rumble. Carefully checking all of the gauges to make sure the oil pressure and engine temperature were where they should be, he adjusted the choke setting, slipped the transmission smoothly into gear, and gently let out the clutch pedal. The Nürburg promptly shuddered and died.

Almost in a panic Joseph looked frantically for the cause and discovered that the hand brake was set, even though the parking pad was perfectly level. With an exasperated shake of his head, he released the brake, restarted the engine, and slowly drove around the building to the front. He let the engine idle, warming up for the coming drive. He used the time to memorize the roads and turns along the route to Dürnstein.

He guessed that this was a meeting of high-ranking German army officers. *What important decisions will they be making today,* he wondered. *Maybe they'll be talking about invading Czechoslovakia, or maybe Poland.* He also wondered if he should ask the major about Berti's death. *Does he even know? Would he care?* He decided to keep his questions to himself.

The major came out carrying a leather briefcase and sat in the back of the car. "Stop in Ottenstein and fill up the fuel tank," he ordered.

"Jawohl, Herr Major," responded Joseph. He did not show his surprise, but he wondered why the major wanted to do that since the meeting was only about fifty kilometers away and the fuel tank was already half full. *This car could go to Vienna and back on a half-tank,* he estimated. *I guess he just likes keeping a full tank.*

Ottenstein was a small town about five kilometers from the camp. There were a few old houses and stores, a small church, and one garage with a fuel pump. Joseph eased the car to a stop in front of the pump and rolled down the window. The station attendant approached, wiping his hands on a rag, but Grünfeld spoke up quickly. "I don't want him to touch this car! *You* fill the tank, Gruber!"

Joseph walked to the rear of the car looking for the cap to the fuel tank, and found it tucked inside the chrome rear bumper, beneath the luggage rack. With its slender chrome neck and cap, it could have easily been mistaken for part of the bumper. Major Grünfeld exited the car and paid the attendant himself, and then to Joseph's astonishment he climbed into the front passenger seat beside Joseph.

"Well done, Gruber! You're the first driver I've had who found the fuel tank cap by himself! I've had to show them all where it is."

"Thank you, Herr Major." Joseph decided that the fuel stop was actually a test to see if he was competent. He carefully navigated the car back onto the road, dodging a bicyclist and a horse-drawn hay wagon. When they had left the town behind and were on the open road, the major rolled down his window and rested his elbow on the window frame, crossed his legs and half-turned toward Joseph.

"So, Gruber," he began in a conversational tone. "Tell me about America! What is it like there? What is New York like?" Joseph's surprise was so obvious that the major laughed. Shrugging, he added, "I'll never get to go there, so I might as well hear about it from you!"

Joseph nodded. "Your driver isn't really in the infirmary is he, Herr Major?"

Grünfeld laughed again. "You're a bright fellow, Gruber! I like you! Now, tell me about America!" They talked for the entire hour's drive, with the major asking dozens of questions, and Joseph talking about the skyscrapers, the traffic, the crowds of internationally diverse people, the ball games, the harbor, the Statue of Liberty, Ellis Island—everything he could think of. Reaching the Danube River at the town of Krems, he turned west and in ten kilometers they were in Dürnstein, a picturesque village on the banks of the great river, overlooked by the ruins of a medieval castle perched hundreds of meters above on a rocky crag.

"Turn left here," directed the major as they entered the town. "I'm going to the Hotel Richard Löwenherz. You can park in the court-yard." The luxurious hotel had a splendid view of the Danube. Encompassed by the walls of a medieval monastery dating to the fourteenth-century, it was a mere stone's throw from the beautiful blue-and-white abbey church's towering spire.

Joseph shut off the engine. "Herr Major, do you want me to stay with the car?"

"Not necessary, but be back here by one o'clock. You'll want to eat somewhere." He handed Joseph three marks. "That should cover your lunch anywhere but here. Make it do."

"Thank you, Herr Major." *Three hours,* he thought. *I'm going to have a decent meal for the first time in a month!* With eager anticipation he headed for the main street to find an inexpensive restaurant. He strolled about the village, enjoying views of the Danube, the narrow, cobblestone alleys, and the castle ruins, and finally picked a quaint-looking place to eat. He chose a small table near the warm tile oven and read the menu. His mouth began to water and his stomach to growl, and he suddenly realized how ravenously hungry he was.

He ordered liver dumpling soup, a slab of roast pork with sauerkraut and a semmel knödel, and a piece of apple strudel for dessert, with a cup of coffee. Finally, when he had cleaned his plate, Joseph leaned back with a groan, feeling as if his stomach would burst. With more than an hour to spare, he stayed at the table for a while, enjoying the warmth of the oven. The three marks covered the bill with thirty pfennigs to spare.

As he was leaving the restaurant, he noticed a telephone booth in the corner. The thought suddenly flashed through his mind that he should call Vienna. He entered the booth and closed the curtain, lifted the receiver, and with a quickening pulse inserted his coins into the slot. They rattled down into the coin return. He put the coins into the slot again, and they fell into the return again. Anxiously he looked for a reason why the telephone was not accepting the coins and saw a handwritten note taped to the wall: "This telephone only accepts groschen." Evidently the telephone had not been updated since the Anschluss and the subsequent replacement of the Austrian currency with Reich currency.

He stepped out of the booth and saw the waiter watching him, his arms folded across his chest. *He knew this would happen,* he thought. "Mein Herr," he said apologetically, "I have only pfennigs. Do you know where I can find some groschen for the telephone?"

"Certainly," the waiter responded impassively. "How much do you need?"

"It says on the telephone that it takes fifty groschen to make a call."

"Of course. I can sell you fifty groschen for one Reichsmark."

"One Reichsmark!" Joseph exclaimed. "That's worth a hundred and fifty groschen!"

"That is my price. If you can find a better price somewhere else, then you should go there."

"But I have only thirty pfennigs! And you can't spend the groschen, anyway! Give me fifty groschen for my thirty pfennigs! *Please!* This is important!"

The waiter eyed him contemptuously. "Follow me," he sneered, and walked through a swinging door into the kitchen. "This floor needs sweeping and mopping," he said, handing Joseph a broom. "Then, wash these dirty dishes. When you finish all that we'll see about your groschen."

It was all Joseph could do to restrain himself from punching the man in the nose. He grabbed the broom and began sweeping madly. He swept the pile of trash into a dust pan and emptied it into the bin, and then did the mopping. The water in the sink was steaming hot, but he rolled up his sleeves, grabbed a sponge, and scrubbed the dishes until they were spotless. Forty-five minutes had passed and he was finished with the tasks. He hurried back into the dining room and stood behind the waiter while he took the food order of a guest.

The waiter was obviously ignoring Joseph, chatting casually about the weather. Glancing at the clock on the wall, Joseph tapped him on the shoulder. "Mein Herr, I don't have time to waste."

The waiter spun about furiously. "How dare you interrupt me while I am taking an order!"

"I am in a hurry and you know it! Pay me what you owe me!"

"I owe you nothing! Get out of here, before I call the police!"

"Fifty groschen! You owe me—"

"I owe you nothing! Get out! Now!"

Joseph turned and stalked angrily back through the kitchen door. He stood scowling, hands on hips, and the cook gave him a nervous glance. Through an open door he noticed a small office in the back. He pushed the door fully open and looked in—sure enough, there was a telephone on the desk. He closed the door, sat in the chair, lifted the receiver and spun the dial to the zero. In seconds a female operator answered with "How may I help you today?"

"I need to reach a number in Vienna, please." He gave her the number of the Uhrmacher-Gruber shop, and in seconds he could hear the ringing tone.

"Uhrmacher-Gruber, Stephan here. How may I help you?"

"Stephan! It's me—Joseph! I need your help!" The brief conversation that followed was excited and emotional, but he made sure Stephan knew that he was in the training camp at Döllersheim, and that he should contact the U.S. consulate for help. "Talk to John Wiley or Roger Thomas! They've got to get me out of here! And please let Miriam and Herr Engelmann know what has happened!" Stephan promised to do as asked, and then Joseph had to go. "Tell Uncle Oskar, Mama Gruber, and Anna Marie that I love them and hope to see them soon! Goodbye!" He shakily put the receiver back on the cradle and stifled a sob, face in his hands. Getting control of his emotions, he opened the door just as the waiter was reaching for the handle. The man's eyes widened in surprise.

"What are you doing in the office? You can't be in here!"

"Keep your damn groschen!" Joseph snapped and shouldered roughly past him.

Realizing that Joseph had been using the telephone, the waiter cried "Stop!" and grabbed his arm, but Joseph jerked free and ran through the dining room into the street. "You owe for that telephone call!" shouted the waiter. "Pay me what you owe!" Joseph never looked back, but ran all the way to the hotel, arriving one minute before one o'clock and climbed into the car, panting for breath.

At one o'clock sharp the major walked out of the hotel, his trench coat flapping in the chilling wind. Halfway to the car he stopped and turned around, and waved to someone in a window on the third floor. Joseph's jaw dropped as he saw a naked woman waving from the window before pulling the curtain closed. *Good Lord! So that was his important meeting? Well,* he thought, *at least there isn't going to be an invasion of Czechoslovakia anytime soon.*

The major got into the front seat again and Joseph turned the key, bringing the powerful engine to life. "How was the meeting, Herr Major?"

"Excellent!" said Grünfeld, and chuckled. "It was an *excellent* meeting!" He glanced over at Joseph, and apparently realized that Joseph must have seen the goodbye wave. He slapped Joseph's shoulder with a boisterous laugh, and then threw back his head and laughed some more. "Yes indeed—it was a *very* excellent meeting!" He was still laughing as they drove out of Dürnstein.

20

BROKEN GLASS

The camp captain investigated Berti's death, interrogating each of the remaining seven recruits. Apparently they all told the same story because Schwarz was promptly reassigned to a regular army unit, and the seven remaining recruits were distributed to other barracks in the camp, filling gaps left by those who had been discharged for various reasons. This meant that Joseph and the others found themselves in new groups with other recruits and drill corporals they did not know. They were glad to be rid of Schwarz, but disgruntled that their squad had been broken up.

Joseph's new group began training with firearms that week. They were issued Mauser bolt-action carbines and spent the first two days learning to disassemble, clean, and reassemble their weapons, along with instructions on safety and proper shooting form. By midweek they were on the shooting range firing at targets a hundred meters away.

Before lunch on Wednesday they were made to run the obstacle course again, but this time with an additional challenge—firing five rounds at a target at the conclusion of the course, when they would be winded and spent. The course had eight lanes so that the entire squad could run simultaneously, which made it obvious who finished first and who was last. The recruits did not know that they were being timed with a stopwatch. Joseph reached the end of the course well ahead of the others. He picked up the rifle and dropped to one knee, resting his left elbow on his knee to steady his aim. He jerked the bolt back and shoved it forward, locking it into place. Exhaling slowly, he tightened his finger on the trigger and squeezed off the first shot. The rifle kicked back hard against his shoulder, and he quickly chambered another round. He had made all five of his shots before the next recruit even began to shoot.

When everyone had completed the course, the corporal ordered them to follow him. They walked to the targets and inspected them. Some of the recruits had hit their target with only a couple of shots, not even within the large target circle. Only Joseph and one other had five holes in their targets. Joseph's had one in the bullseye and the other four were scattered somewhere inside the circles, giving him the best marksmanship score of the group.

"Well done, Gruber!" the corporal nodded. "You need more practice with the rifle, but at least you're hitting the target." Pointing to the group with his baton, he continued, "For the rest of you, this was a poor start! We are going to work on this for the rest of the week! We'll be back out here after lunch!"

After lunch, however, things were different. There was a sizeable crowd of recruits at the starting point for the obstacle course, and a lieutenant with a megaphone gave instructions. There was to be a competition, he announced, and the eight fastest recruits had been selected to represent their squads. Riflery was included in the competition, and seconds would be added or subtracted from their course time for each shot that missed or hit the target at the end of the race. As an incentive, a special meal would be served at supper to the squad whose representative won the race. The recruits cheered enthusiastically at that, and each group began to prep its candidate. Joseph found his shoulders and arms being massaged as his new mates loudly exhorted him to win the race. The atmosphere was like that at a football game. *All we're lacking is a marching band and cheerleaders*, he thought.

He removed his shirt and handed it to one of his group. The chill in the air was invigorating, and he swung his arms back and forth, did a couple of knee bends, and ran in place a few steps to warm up. Each squad was assigned a lane, and Joseph took his place near the middle, bouncing on his toes and taking deep breaths. The lieutenant produced a pistol, counted down from three, and fired into the air. The eight racers dashed forward and their comrades filled the air with shouts and whoops, running alongside the course and cheering all the way.

Following a short sprint from the starting line, Joseph jumped up onto the balance beam without breaking stride and ran smoothly along it. The competitor to his right fell off the rail and had to climb back up. Reaching the end of the rail, Joseph made a prodigious leap to the overhead ladder and swung rapidly, his hands a blur as he surged ahead of the pack. After ten chin-ups and fifty push-ups, he scaled a four-meter-high wall with a climbing rope and crawled through a ten-meter-long pipe. He crossed a water-filled ditch on a log, carried a hundred-pound cement weight twenty meters, and then sprinted fifty meters to the finish line, where the marksmanship test awaited.

He inserted the five-round clip and worked the bolt, chambering a round, and then paused to take a couple of deep breaths before shouldering the rifle. Kneeling as before and bracing his left elbow on his knee, he exhaled slowly and squeezed the trigger. He remembered that most of his earlier shots had tended toward the left of the bullseye, so he carefully aimed slightly to the right. He could hear shots being fired by the others as he worked the bolt and fired his second and third rounds. The noise of their shooting made him hurry his fourth shot, but he forced himself to take more time for the final one. Only after he laid the rifle aside did he begin to shake, his hands trembling from the extreme exertion. His heart was pounding and he rested on his knees, waiting for the others to finish shooting. For the first time he became aware of the hysterical shouting and cheering of the crowd of recruits, rooting for their own champions. *I hope I didn't let my team down,* he grimaced. *They'd never forgive me for losing them their special meal!*

When all of the shooting was finally complete, the captain and the eight corporals collectively inspected the targets and tabulated the results. They spent several minutes working out the final scores, and then had the men gather around for the announcement of the winner. Major Grünfeld stood to one side, observing. The captain took his stance in front of the crowd and began with the obligatory salute and "Heil Hitler!" to which all of the men responded the same.

"We are pleased that Herr Major Grünfeld could be with us this afternoon," he said with a nod toward the major, who nodded in reply. "It is especially fitting that the major is here, because we not only have a clear winner in today's camp's obstacle course and riflery competition, but we have a new course record!" A murmur ran through the assembled recruits, and one of Joseph's team slapped him on the back. "Our new camp champion is—" he paused for a couple of seconds—"is Soldat Joseph Gruber, of Barracks Ten!" The recruits cheered and applauded, and Barracks Ten the loudest of all. Joseph raised his arms triumphantly, and his mates hoisted him to their shoulders in celebration.

As the squads headed in different directions for their afternoon drills, the captain called Joseph's name. Buttoning his shirt, he trotted over. "A fine job, Gruber! Well done! Herr Major Grünfeld wishes to speak to you."

The major smiled with a twinkle in his eyes. "Congratulations, Gruber! That was quite impressive!"

"Thank you, mein Herr!"

"I hate to take you away from your training again, but I need a driver."

"Another important meeting, Herr Major?"

Grünfeld laughed and lowered his voice. "Yes, it actually is! We are going to Wiener Neustadt, to the Theresian Military Academy, for a very important meeting tomorrow. We will return on Friday. Go get cleaned up and meet me at my office in an hour."

The highest temperature that day was less than ten degrees, so

Joseph was glad for the leather driver's jacket, hat, and driving gloves. He studied the road map and determined that Wiener Neustadt was almost two hundred kilometers away, roughly fifty kilometers south of Vienna. *Looks like a three-hour trip,* he calculated. *Good thing it's dry today, though cloudy. Should be a nice day for a drive.*

Once again Grünfeld had Joseph fill the gas tank in Ottenstein, and again he moved to the front seat before they resumed the journey. The major asked more questions about America, this time probing Joseph's personal and family history. He wanted to know about his parents, his siblings, sports activities, school, what kind of work he did, and many other things. Joseph described his wood carvings, the clock shop, his love of Art Deco and jazz music. The major seemed to want to know everything. He talked about President Roosevelt and his New Deal, and asked what Joseph thought about all that. He even brought up the Great War and the Treaty of Versailles, and was surprised at how much Joseph knew about those topics.

"Do you believe that Germany caused the war?" he asked pointedly. "That's what the Big Four said at Versailles, you know. That's why they punished Germany so severely—they wanted to cripple us! But it backfired on them, and now we are stronger than ever!"

"I'm not a historian," Joseph replied carefully, "but it seems to me that there is enough responsibility to go around for several countries. Archduke Ferdinand was assassinated in Sarajevo, and Austria had to punish the Serbs for that. Russia backed the Serbs against Austria, and so Germany backed Austria against Russia, and then France backed Russia against Germany. It was like a row of dominoes falling down—one thing led to another."

"Exactly!" exclaimed Grünfeld. "If Russia had just stayed out of it, then the war would not have spread all over Europe. And if the British had not blockaded our ports and starved our women and children, we would not have had to use submarines against them, and the Americans would not have entered the war!" He threw up his hands in frustration. "Germany was a victim, not an aggressor!"

"Jawohl, mein Herr," Joseph concurred, though he wasn't sure he completely agreed with the major's vindication of Germany's role. "But had none of that happened, do you think that Hitler and the National Socialists would have taken power in Germany?"

"No!" Grünfeld instantly replied with a laugh, slapping his knee. "We would still have our Kaiser, and the Austrians would still have their Habsburgs! And Russia might still have their Romanovs instead of the Bolsheviks! The whole world would be different—and perhaps a better place too!" Then, realizing what he had just said, he quickly added, "But don't tell anyone I said that! Because all those things *did* happen, we have our Führer and Germany will make them pay for what they did to us!" Just then a horse-drawn wagon blocked their lane, and Joseph had to brake sharply and wait for a chance to pass it. He was grateful for the distraction so that he did not have to respond to the major's bold assertion.

Before long the twin towers of Wiener Neustadt's thirteenth-century Romanesque church came into view in the distance. The major directed Joseph over a long bridge spanning more than a dozen tracks at the main train station, past the Stadtpark and the city's picturesque water tower, to the fortress-like Military Academy. By then it was almost six o'clock and getting darker by the minute. He parked the car behind the Academy, and from the parking lot Grünfeld pointed out the adjacent barracks where Joseph would sleep for the next two nights and where he would find his supper with the other rank and file soldiers. "By the way, Gruber," he said, as if suddenly remembering something, "here are your wages for your first month in the Reichswehr—" and handed him an envelope containing thirty-five Reichmarks.

"I didn't know I got paid *anything*," said Joseph, surprised.

Grünfeld burst out laughing. "Seriously, Gruber? You thought you were a *slave*? And I thought you Americans were smart!" He laughed again, and slapped Joseph good-naturedly on the shoulder. "And I almost forgot—you also get expense money while on driving duty, so here are a few more to go with that. Don't spend it all on wine, women, and gambling!" Chuckling at his own humor, the major headed into the inner courtyard and called back over his shoulder, "See you Friday morning at nine!"

Well, what do you know about that! Joseph mused. *The three marks he gave me in Dürnstein were my expense money for driving. And I thought he was just being generous.* He put the money in his pocket and headed for the soldiers' mess hall. Unlike the fare at the training camp the meal was quite decent, with meat and potatoes, bread, and green beans. Afterward he decided to take a walk and see the town. The main square was only a few minutes away, and turning up his jacket collar against the chill, he began walking, hands in pockets.

He had not walked very far when he noticed something strange—the sidewalk was littered with shards of broken glass. The plate glass window of a clothing store had been shattered, and inside he could see that the merchandise was in total disarray. *What happened here?* he wondered. He passed two more shops which had been ransacked, and the broken glass covered the sidewalk and part of the street. In the glow of the street lamps the pieces of glass glistened and shown like crystals, or maybe diamonds, he thought. Perplexed, he made his way into the main square, bordered with a medieval arcade and featuring an ornate fountain in the center.

It would have been a pretty scene except for the mob of men furiously wrecking two more storefronts. A large crowd of people stood and watched, and there were several policemen who stood passively by. The constant shouting and smashing of glass created a harsh din of noise. Joseph turned to a man standing at the periphery of the crowd and asked, "What's going on here? Why is no one doing anything to stop this?"

The man merely shrugged. "Jews," he said, as if that was all the explanation that was necessary. Pointing to the shops, he added, "Getting rid of them."

Joseph stared, disbelieving. Mobs destroying businesses just because the owners were Jewish? He saw a man standing to the side of the destroyed shop, with blood running down his face—apparently the shop owner. *This is going too far*, Joseph thought. Then he saw a plume of black smoke rising into the sky a short distance to the north of the plaza. Concerned, he trotted quickly in that direction. Along the way he passed three more shattered businesses, with broken glass crunching underfoot as he hurried past.

The smoke was rising from the Jewish synagogue. Flames flickered and leaped from its windows, and the roof appeared about to collapse. A fire brigade was on hand, but its water hoses were directed at the adjacent buildings, making sure the fire did not spread to Aryan-owned businesses. Once again there was a crowd of spectators, some of whom cheered as the vandals threw rocks through the windows. Joseph watched as the police arrested the rabbi and took him away in a van.

In a panic, Joseph ran back to the Hauptplatz where he had noticed a telephone booth. This time he had the correct coins, and gave the operator Uncle Oskar's phone number for a collect call. After several rings Mama Gruber answered, and hearing that it was Joseph calling, accepted the charges.

"Joseph! Where are you? Are you alright?"

"Yes, Mama Gruber, I'm alright. I'm in Wiener Neustadt, and something terrible is happening here. Mobs are attacking Jewish homes and businesses, beating them up and arresting them. It's a massacre! I'm afraid for Herr Engelmann and Miriam—are they alright?"

"Oh, Joseph!" her voice was wracked with emotion. "It is the same here! A mob attacked the bookstore and smashed it to bits. Papa Gruber brought Miriam here for safety, but Herr Engelmann wouldn't—"

"Joseph!" It was Miriam's voice, and she was hysterical. "Opa is in danger! He wouldn't leave the bookstore, and those awful Stormtroopers are destroying everything! You must come! Joseph, we need you! Please get here before it's too late!"

"I'm coming, Miriam. I'll be there in an hour. I'll go to the bookstore and help your Opa. I won't let them hurt him!"

"Hurry, Joseph!" she sobbed. "Please hurry!"

"I'm on my way," he replied grimly. "Just sit tight!" He hung up the phone and violently jerked the booth door open, startling a couple passing by. Glancing up at the clock on the face of the city hall, he saw that it was almost eight o'clock. *There won't be much traffic at this hour,* he calculated. Joseph ran all the way to the Military Academy, went around to the back parking lot and climbed into the driver's seat. He turned the ignition key and the Mercedes Nürburg 500 rumbled to life. *Sorry about this, Herr Major Grünfeld,* he grimaced, *but I have no choice. It's time to advance my pawns.* Joseph waited until he was driving away on the main street before switching on the powerful head lamps. Reaching the highway he turned north, passing the sign that read: "Wien 43 km." Shifting gears, he pressed hard on the gas pedal and the Mercedes surged forward like a rocket. "I'm coming, Miriam," he said aloud through clenched teeth. "I'm coming!"

21

A PIECE OF PAPER

As he drove through the dark streets of Vienna, Joseph saw signs of the night's violence everywhere, with shards of broken glass, furniture, clothes, and miscellaneous belongings on the sidewalks and streets. He felt as if he were traveling through a war zone. It was after nine o'clock when he stopped the car in front of Buchhandlung-Gruber. The store was dark, and the sidewalk and street were covered with the glistening fragments of the plate glass window.

He stepped through the window frame into the dark interior. The floor was littered with books, many of them ripped and torn, with loose pages lying about. He turned on the light in the store room. Bookshelves were overturned, the chess board broken and the pieces scattered, but Herr Engelmann was not there. The silence was oppressive. He ascended the stairs to the apartment above and went from room to room, floor to floor. The raiders had been very thorough; little was left undisturbed.

On the third floor he found what was evidently Herr Engelmann's bedroom. The door was ajar. Clothes and books were strewn about, and picture frames hung at angles on the wall, with broken glass. The bed was disheveled. Joseph walked slowly across the room, feeling that he was violating a sanctuary by being there. "Herr Engelmann?" he called softly. "It's Joseph!" Silent as the tomb.

He stopped suddenly, frozen. A dark shape lay motionless on the floor on the far side of the bed, partially illuminated by light from the window. He fell to his knees. "Herr Engelmann!" He shook him by the shoulder and touched the cold face, streaked with blood. "*No!*" he wailed in agony. He clutched his old friend's body to his chest and held him tightly for a long moment, rocking back and forth, tears pouring from his eyes as he shook with sobs. Releasing the body, he gazed in stunned anguish at the peaceful, lined face, and gently closed the sightless eyes. For several minutes he sat holding the arm and patting the hand, groaning as if in physical pain.

Finally, he stood, fingertips to his temples, unable to think. Stumbling to the doorway and leaning against the frame to steady himself, he shakily descended back to the ground floor. He picked up a pawn in the storeroom and put it into his pocket. Reaching the street, he turned and looked one last time at the store—Buchhandlung-Gruber. *Selling the store and changing the name didn't save him, after all*, he thought sadly. Then it dawned on him—*This is Hartstein's doing! He is responsible for this! That devil's spawn! If I could just get my hands on him, I would*—Joseph clenched his fists in rage. He felt himself fully capable of murder at that moment, but he knew that his first priority had to be getting Miriam out of there and safely away to America. He knew he had to focus his mind on that.

He parked the car on a side street and rang the bell at Uhrmacher-Gruber. Uncle Oskar came down and opened the door. It was an emotional reunion with the family, but the news of Herr Engelmann' death was traumatic for everyone. Miriam fainted and had to be laid on the sofa, where she moaned and wept unconsolably. Anna Marie sat beside her and stroked her hair, heartbroken at her friend's tragedy.

To make matters even worse, Oskar informed Joseph that Roger Thomas had called that day from the consulate to say that they would be unable to issue Miriam's immigration visa after all. It was something about closing the Vienna ministry and transferring operations to the U.S. embassy in Berlin. Joseph slumped in his chair, head in hands. After a long moment, he finally spoke. "It's too late tonight to do anything. Tomorrow I will go to the consulate and talk to them. Maybe something can be done. Let's all just go to bed and try to get some sleep." Everyone agreed that this was a good idea, and headed upstairs.

Joseph took Miriam's hand and said, "Come with me for just a few minutes." He led her to the roof, and put his leather jacket around her shoulders, ignoring the cold. "Take a few deep breaths and try to clear your head," he suggested.

Shivering, she moaned, "What is going to happen, Joseph? Mother is gone. Opa is gone. You are leaving. I have nowhere to go. All is lost!"

"Not yet!" Joseph disagreed. "I'm not going to promise anything, but tomorrow we will go to the consulate and see what we can do. I am not going to leave you. We will think of something. Tonight, we must pray like never before! Only God can make a path through this. Don't give up!"

She stared dully into the distance, her shallow breath fogging in the air. Alarmed, Joseph took her by the shoulders and gave her a gentle shake. "Miriam! Don't lose touch! I need you to be focused. Do you remember what you said when Reverend Grimes baptized you?"

"'With God's help, I will,'" she murmured softly.

"Keep thinking like that," he urged. "With God's help, we *will* get through this." She nodded silently. Joseph kissed her forehead and gave her a quick hug. "Let's get back inside."

The next morning at breakfast the atmosphere was quiet. No one had slept well, especially Miriam, who looked haggard and red-eyed. Oskar and Stephan had already been to the bookstore and seen to the removal of Herr Engelmann's body to a morgue. The only sounds were those of eating utensils against dishes and coffee cups on saucers. Finally, Joseph commented with forced cheerfulness, "This is the best breakfast I've had in a month!" This initiated a conversation about what his experience had been like in the army training camp. He described the daily routine, but did not mention Berti or Corporal

Schwarz. He dug out of his pocket a small tin medal, received for winning the camp obstacle course and riflery competition. The family seemed grateful to have something to talk about other than the events of the night before. Miriam, however, was detached and silent.

At seven-thirty Joseph made a telephone call to the consulate and was surprised to get an answer so early. He asked to speak with Thomas, and within seconds the assistant consul's voice came through the receiver. "Roger Thomas, assistant Chargé speaking."

"Good morning, Mr. Thomas," he said, making an effort to sound pleasant. "This is Joseph Gruber—"

"Joseph!" he interrupted. "The last I heard, you had been forced into the Reichswehr! Where are you?"

"I'm still in the army, but I'm visiting at my uncle's place here in Vienna. I want to talk to you about Miriam's visa, if you have a few minutes."

"Ah, yes! That is indeed an unfortunate situation. We were just informed a few days ago that all embassy functions are being reassigned to Berlin. We've been instructed to freeze all immigration visas until further notice. I'm so sorry—we were so close to having that completed, too!"

"Isn't there something you can do?"

"I don't see that there is anything. I have my orders, and well, you understand...." His voice trailed off.

"But Mr. Thomas, you know what happened last night all across Germany and Austria, don't you? I saw it myself in Wiener Neustadt and here in Vienna. Jews are not safe here. Miriam's grandfather was killed last night! Surely you can bend a rule a bit and help her get to safety!"

"I'm so sorry, Mr. Gruber. I really am. And it's terrible about her grandfather! I wish that I could do something, but—"

"Mr. Thomas, I do understand that you have orders to follow. I'm not trying to be difficult, but will you be in your office all morning? I'd like to come see you. I have a suggestion that may make a difference. Please just give me a few minutes of your time. Can you do that for us, sir?"

"Honestly, Mr. Gruber, I don't see—"

"It will take only a few minutes! This is too important to not try every possibility! If you still say 'no,' then I won't bother you anymore. I can be there within the hour."

Thomas sighed and hesitated for two or three seconds. "Very well, Joseph. I'll give you a few minutes—but I mean it when I say there's really nothing I can do!"

"Thank you! Thank you, Mr. Thomas! I'll be there as soon as possible! Thank you!" Joseph hung up the phone, and turned to find the entire family and Miriam staring at him expectantly. "He's agreed to meet with me this morning," he announced. "I have a plan, and I need your help, Stephan!" Turning to Miriam, he said, "Go wash your face and brush your hair—you're coming with us. Put on something nice." She blinked, hesitated, and then hurried upstairs. Joseph gave Stephan instructions on what he wanted him to do and then also went upstairs, returning a few minutes later with his suitcase. Joseph fetched the Mercedes, and when Miriam came down wearing a red dirndl with white blouse and apron and blue wool jacket, they were ready to go.

Miriam sat in the front seat beside Joseph and Stephan sat in the back, holding a heavy-looking cardboard box. "What's in the box?" she asked.

"Joseph's plan," Stephan replied, tight-lipped. She furrowed her brow and gave them both a questioning look, but did not ask again. "Joseph, where did you get such a car as this?" asked Stephan.

"I borrowed it," was all Joseph offered. He cranked the engine and Stephan hooted in delight at the powerful rumble. Joseph steered expertly through the Vienna morning traffic and soon had them at the U.S. consulate. He found a parking space and the three hurried inside, with Joseph carrying the large box and Stephan a second, smaller box. They went directly to Roger Thomas' office on the second floor and knocked on the door.

"Enter!" came a voice, and Miriam opened the door for them.

"Well, you did get here within the hour!" commented Thomas. "What's in the boxes?"

Joseph looked quickly around the room and pointed to the wall opposite Thomas' desk. "We'll put it there," he stated. Taking a pencil, he made a mark on the wall. "Right there." Stephan opened his box and took out a hammer, a nail, a screwdriver, and a large screw. He drove the nail into the plaster-covered wall, and then pulled it back out with a small cloud of plaster dust, and a few small flakes rained down onto the floor.

"What are you doing?" Thomas cried in alarm. "You can't just start knocking holes in my wall!"

"It will only take a minute—you'll see!" said Joseph. Stephan twisted the screw through an angled brace and screwed it into the hole made by the nail. When it was secure, they opened the larger box and Joseph carefully lifted out a gleaming, colorful clock cabinet. He hung it on the screw and then added the crown piece. When the pendulum and the weights were attached, they started the clock and began the process of adjusting its hang so that it ran smoothly. Then, Joseph stepped back and gestured to the clock. "What do you think?"

"What—what—that's—I never—" Thomas was at a total loss for words. He slowly approached with wide eyes and open mouth.

"It's an Art Deco Vienna Regulator," Joseph said softly, his eyes caressing its every line. "It's one of a kind—the only one like it in the world. What do you think of it?"

"It's—it's—it's the most beautiful thing I've ever *seen!*" Thomas finally exclaimed. "It's *gorgeous!* Where did you find something like this?"

"I made it myself. I designed it, carved it, assembled it, and painted it. It's my masterpiece—and it's yours, Mr. Thomas."

"I don't understand. Why would you give this to *me*? It must have taken you *months* to make this!"

"It's been my dream for *years*. I'll never make another like it. It's part of my heart and soul. I would never sell it for any price. It's yours —but not for free."

"I don't understand—if you wouldn't sell it, how can you offer it to me, but not for free?"

"You have something I want more than this clock, Mr. Thomas. A piece of paper. Do you know what I am talking about?"

Thomas blinked and his face went blank, and then a sudden flash of understanding illuminated his eyes. "Oh!" he exclaimed. "Oh!" He walked back to his desk and sat down, shaking his head. "But I don't have that piece of paper! I told you there's nothing—"

"Do you have any of the visa forms that you used to issue?"

"Well, yes, of course I have the *forms*, but—"

"And do you have a typewriter?" Joseph looked meaningfully at the typewriter on a side table.

"Well, of course I have a typewriter, but—"

"Just put one of those forms in the typewriter and fill in the spaces, sign it, and you'll own a one-of-a-kind Art Deco Vienna Regulator."

"But I told you—we have orders to not issue any more visas!"

"When did you receive that order?"

"About a week ago—it was November third."

"Then just type 'November first' on the form and we'll be fine, right?"

"What? I can't just—just—I can't just type—just change the date —why that would—"

"Who would ever know?" Joseph asked, shrugging. "And remember that Miriam's Opa was killed by Nazis last night. She has no one left here. She needs this visa now. Look at her—wearing red, white, and blue! She needs to go to America!"

"I know—it's terrible, but—"

"Mr. Thomas," interrupted Joseph firmly, "look on your wall there." He pointed to the framed print of Klimt's *The Woman in Gold*. "You look at that a lot, don't you?"

"Well, yes, I do. It's beautiful."

"You remember that she's Miriam's aunt, right?"

"Yes—yes, I do."

"Do you want to have to look into those eyes after you've denied her niece a visa because you didn't want to type a different number in a space on a form? After you kept her niece from escaping to America where she'll be safe, and be with the rest of the family? Aren't you going to feel guilty? Will you want to even look at that face anymore? Will it haunt you and make you feel miserable?"

"My God, stop it!" cried Thomas, burying his face in his hands. "All right! I'll change the date on the visa! But don't you dare ever tell anyone—"

"Never!" chorused all three. "We'll never say a word to anyone!"

"It will be our secret forever," Joseph assured him. "Thank you, Mr. Thomas! Can you do the form right now? We are in a bit of a hurry."

Thomas opened a drawer and produced a folder. "This is your folder, Miss Bauer. And this is the main form you will need at Ellis Island." With trembling fingers he inserted the form into the typewriter, cranked it down several lines, and moved the cylinder across the page, all the while shaking his head and mumbling to himself. "Can't believe... I'm doing this... Can't tell... nobody...." A few sharp taps of the keys and he pulled the form out and laid it on his desk, took a pen and signed it. "Now, Miss Bauer, if you'll sign right there —" In seconds the form was back in the folder and Thomas handed it to her. "Go in peace, Miss Bauer, and may God bless you with a safe trip to America." Miriam hugged him and wiped a tear from her eye, unable to speak.

"You have my undying gratitude, Mr. Thomas," said Joseph. "I hope you enjoy your clock."

"Are you sure you want to give me that clock?" asked Thomas. "I don't feel like I've earned it."

"That piece of paper is more valuable to me than any clock could ever be," Joseph replied earnestly. "It's a fair trade." He paused at the door. "A good man once told me that sometimes you have to make a sacrifice to win the game! He was right."

Miriam cried quietly in the car all the way back to the clock shop. Joseph stopped at the curb in front of the store. "Run up and get your things," he told her. "I'll get my suitcase, and we'll be ready to go." In minutes Joseph descended back down the stairs to the workshop carrying his suitcase and set it on the floor, waiting for Miriam. The whole family, plus Herr Schneider, were gathered there. "I guess this is goodbye," he said awkwardly. Suddenly he felt like he was going to be ill. *Could the year really have passed so quickly, and could this really be the final farewell?* His heart rose into his throat and speech was suddenly impossible. He was afraid he was going to cry. The tinkling of the front door bell created a welcome distraction.

"I'll see about that," Oskar said, and darted into the other room. However, he came backing into the workshop immediately, his face pale. A man in a black uniform stepped through the curtain after him, lightly slapping his leather gloves in his hand, followed by a soldier carrying a rifle.

"Hartstein!" blurted Joseph, in shock.

"Soldat Gruber!" barked the SS officer. "Heil Hitler!"

22

LIFE AND DEATH

"What is the meaning of this?" demanded Oskar, regaining his composure. "You can't just—"

"Why aren't you with your unit in the training camp, Gruber?" interrupted Hartstein, ignoring Oskar. "Why are you *here*? And who is driving that Nürburg parked out on the street?" He stepped closer to Joseph, glaring into his eyes. "Answer my questions, *boy*!"

"I drive for the Döllersheim camp commandant. He is in Wiener Neustadt for an important meeting and he allowed me to come visit my family. That's all, Herr Obersturmführer Hartstein."

"Really? Then why do you have a suitcase? Are you taking a trip, *Joseph*?" He stepped closer again, his eyes blazing. Joseph did not answer.

Just then Miriam came clattering down the stairs with her small suitcase. "I'm ready to go, Joseph! Will we be taking the train?" When she saw the two Nazis, she dropped her suitcase and an involuntary cry escaped her lips before she could clap her hand over her mouth. She froze on the bottom step, eyes wide and face white as a sheet.

"So, you *are* going on a trip!" Hartstein smiled coldly. "To *America*, perhaps?" Again, Joseph did not answer. His fingers toyed with the small, wooden pawn in his pocket, and in his mind he recalled the sight of the bloody, dead body lying on the bedroom floor in the moonlight. *I am looking at Herr Engelmann's murderer,* he thought, and his blood began to rise.

"Soldat Gruber, are you aware that the penalty for desertion is a firing squad?"

Joseph's eyes narrowed and he found his voice. "Yes, Herr Obersturmführer Hartstein, I am aware of that. But I will never face a firing squad!"

"Don't be so sure about that!" Hartstein snarled. To the soldier, he commanded, "Take him to the car and secure his hands! We'll take him straight to a cell in the Reichswehr brig."

Before the soldier could take a step, there was a sharp, cracking sound and he pitched forward to lie on his face in a rapidly widening pool of blood. Herr Schneider stood over him, hammer dripping red. Hartstein reached for the pistol in the holster on his hip, and Joseph reacted instantly. Grabbing him by the arm, he leveraged Hartstein over his hip and threw him violently to the concrete floor and fell upon him, driving the edge of his hand into the man's throat and putting all of his weight behind it. Hartstein struggled, but within seconds went limp. Joseph did not relent, but pushed even harder until he heard a snapping sound. Hartstein's body jerked, and then was still.

Miriam sat down hard on the step, hands over her face, peering through her fingers. There was a stunned silence in the room, and then Uncle Oskar said, "Good job, both of you! Now, we need to get rid of these bodies."

"There's a very big river not far away," pointed out Herr Schneider, "and it will be dark in a few hours."

Oskar nodded, taking command. Motioning to Stephan, he said, "Wrap them in those blankets and help Schneider put them in the van. Then let's get this blood cleaned up!" Stephan moved quickly. Getting the keys from the soldier's pocket, Oskar added, "I'll take their car and leave it somewhere far away from here." Mama Gruber and Anna Marie began filling a mop bucket with water and soap and brought out a box of rags for cleaning. Everyone was in motion with a job to do.

Joseph took the pistol from Hartstein's holster. "I might need this," he said, shoving it into the waistband of his pants.

"And this," added Schneider, handing him the rifle. When Joseph hesitated, he insisted. "Better to have it and not need it than to need it and not have it." Reluctantly, Joseph took the rifle. He wrapped it in a blanket and laid it on the back seat of the Mercedes, putting the two suitcases on top of it.

The urgency of the situation made a lingering farewell impossible —there was no time for tears. After quick handshakes and hugs, Joseph and Miriam waved goodbye as the car pulled away from the curb and mingled with the midday traffic. In what seemed to Joseph like forever, but was actually no more than twenty minutes, they found their way to the highway heading south to Wiener Neustadt. Glancing in the rearview mirror, Joseph murmured, "Goodbye, Vienna!"

"Goodbye, Vienna," echoed Miriam. "Goodbye, Opa!" She dabbed her eyes and nose with a handkerchief for several minutes before settling back in the seat with a tired sigh and closed her eyes. She did not open them until they entered Wiener Neustadt, slowing for the local traffic.

"Where are we going?" she asked, rubbing her eyes.

"I'm returning the car—I don't want to steal it. Then we'll go to the train station and buy tickets to Hamburg."

"Do you think it's safe to go into Germany?"

"If we go quickly, I think we can make it." He glanced over at her. She didn't appear to like the idea of traveling through Germany but she said nothing, twisting her fingers together nervously as she looked out her window.

Joseph steered the Mercedes to the parking lot behind the Military Academy and pulled into a parking space beside an army truck. They got out of the car, suitcases in hand, and started to walk away when a voice spoke from behind them. "Gruber? What are you doing?"

Joseph froze. He turned slowly to face Herr Major Grünfeld, who was leaning against the front of the truck. "I came out to the car, but it wasn't here. Where have you been?"

Joseph swallowed hard, licked his dry lips, and searched for the words to explain. Miriam stepped forward and said simply, "I am Joseph's friend. I'm Jewish, and he is helping me get to America, where my relatives are. They killed my Opa last night. Please don't stop us—I beg you!" Joseph couldn't believe her boldness, and gave her an alarmed look. *She's ruining our chances,* he thought.

Grünfeld grunted in surprise. "I see." He studied them for several seconds before speaking again. "I see," he said again, softly, nodding. "And how do you plan to get to a seaport?"

Joseph cleared his throat. "We're going on the train. I left the keys in the car."

"I see," he said once more, cracking his knuckles. "I will have to report you missing in the morning, you know. They will be looking for you. The train is no good. You won't make it."

"Then what should we do?" Miriam asked. "Help us!"

"Take the car," Grünfeld shrugged. "Take the car and go south— to Trieste. North into Germany is twice as far and much too danger- ous. If you go quickly, you can get across the border before it closes." Grünfeld pulled his trench coat open, revealing a pistol in a holster on his right hip. His hand moved toward it, and Joseph felt a stab of fear, but the hand reached further and pulled a wallet from his back pocket. He opened it and took out several bills and extended them to Joseph. "You'll need every pfennig you can get."

Joseph stared. "I don't understand, Herr Major. Why are you doing this?"

Grünfeld's eyes seemed to look past Joseph and Miriam into the distance. "My wife was Jewish," he almost whispered. "My beautiful, sweet Angelica! After the Nuremberg Race Laws were announced in '35, I was passed over for a promotion. I assured her that it had nothing to do with her, but she knew better. She became depressed, and then—" he closed his eyes and sighed deeply—"and then she took her own life! In the note she left, she said she didn't want to hinder my career." He threw back his head, and an agonized cry burst from his lips. "*Mein Gott!*" he shouted. "My career! So, thank you Angelica, yes, I've been promoted now! And I don't give a damn!" He gave his head a violent shake and then focused on Joseph again.

"So, Joseph!" he smiled with genuine warmth. "Take the money. Take the car. And don't look back. They'll give me another one—the Führer owes me that much! And don't stop until you get where you're going!" Looking sympathetically at Miriam, he added, "I'm sorry about your Opa. Forgive us if you can." Without another word he turned and walked back toward the Academy. They watched him in stunned silence.

"Hurry, Joseph!" Miriam said, jolting back to life. "Do what he said! Let's get to the border!"

The Mercedes seemed to understand the urgency of the situation. It instantly roared to life and rolled briskly out of the parking lot, almost without Joseph's direction. In minutes they were speeding down the highway southward. He reached over and took her hand. "Pray, Miriam! Pray hard!"

"I *am* praying, Joseph! It will be alright. I feel it." She returned the squeeze and smiled bravely. He nodded, and gripping the wheel with both hands, focused on the road ahead.

No sooner had they left Wiener Neustadt behind than the road began to climb, gradually at first, but then steeply, with repeated switchbacks as they approached the Semmering mountain pass. The pass cut through the Raxalps at an elevation of almost a thousand meters above sea level, and normally Joseph would have been enthralled at the spectacular mountain scenery, but now he fretted at the slow pace he was forced to make. Finally cresting the summit, the descent began, but constant sharp turns kept his foot on the brake most of the way down. After more than three hours, much of it white-knuckle driving over the mountains, they reached Graz in mid-afternoon and stopped to refuel and eat lunch.

They ate quickly at a würstelstand, and Joseph filled the nearly-empty gas tank while Miriam studied the road map. "We're making good time," she said. "It looks like we are only about fifty kilometers from the border. We should be there in another hour."

"That would put us there just before five o'clock," Joseph calculated. "When does the border close for the night?"

"I don't know, but some of Opa's friends said the border with Hungary closed at seven, so I think we should assume it's the same."

"Let's get going. I don't want to cut it too closely. Have your papers ready to show the guard."

As they were getting back into the Mercedes Joseph noticed a military patrol car slowing down as it passed by, going in the opposite direction. Its canvas top was folded back, and the two soldiers inside stared intently as they went by. Joseph saw one of them say something to the other, and the car began to turn around. Uneasy, Joseph pulled into traffic and kept an eye on his rearview mirror.

"Is something wrong?" asked Miriam, noticing his nervousness.

"Probably not," he muttered. "Two soldiers in a patrol car are following us, but it probably doesn't mean anything." She nodded and proceeded to busy herself with rummaging through her small purse. All the way across Graz, the patrol car played tag with the Mercedes, repeatedly creeping up close behind, but then falling back as Joseph accelerated, taking advantage of relatively open stretches of road. Eventually, just before they could leave the city behind, Joseph found himself hemmed in by slower vehicles and the patrol car pulled up alongside.

"Pull over!" shouted one of the soldiers, motioning with his hand. "Pull over now!" When Joseph did not immediately comply, the command was repeated twice more, emphatically. He frowned and made a gesture of frustration, but slowed and then pulled to the curb, his stomach churning. The patrol car pulled over in front of the Mercedes and the two soldiers were stalking back toward them, elbows angled outward in an aggressive posture.

"Let me handle this," he said tensely. "Just stay in the car."

"No," Miriam replied. "You need my help." He turned to her, about to insist that she stay put, but his jaw dropped in amazement. She had applied red lipstick and unbuttoned her blouse down to the top of the dirndl, revealing soft, white flesh. Her long, dark hair now hung down over her shoulders. She cupped her hands under her breasts and boosted them into a more prominent position. "Leave this to me," she said, and opened her door.

"Miriam!" Joseph gasped, and grabbed for her arm, but she was already out of the car. He felt his heart racing as he exited the car and walked slowly forward, putting on his driving hat to give himself a more official appearance.

"What's the problem, officers?" Joseph asked, trying to sound innocent.

"What are you doing, driving that car?" demanded the one that had been sitting in the passenger seat, apparently the higher ranking of the two. "That kind of car is only provided to high-ranking officers, and you are no officer!"

"He drives for the major," interjected Miriam. "And the major is waiting for me. You don't want to make me late, do you?" She rested one foot provocatively on the front bumper of the Mercedes, tossed her head, and with a hand, flipped her long hair back over a shoulder. "He won't like that!"

The two soldiers looked at each other, unsure how to proceed. "Which major are you talking about?"

"Do you really have to ask?" she laughed. "Don't be silly!"

The driver turned to his sergeant and exclaimed, "I *knew* it! He leaves early every Thursday about this time. Last week I saw lipstick on his—"

"You missed the turn to the camp three kilometers back," interrupted the sergeant. "Where are you going?"

"You didn't think he would have me come to the *camp*, did you?" Miriam scoffed, tossing her hair back over the other shoulder. "This has to be kept *quiet*, you know!"

"So where *are* you going?" he repeated.

"I'm not at liberty to say," she pursed her lips in a pout and tugged at her skirt. "But please give me your names so I can tell him who has delayed my arrival!"

Still unconvinced, the sergeant turned to Joseph. "Why haven't I seen you before? Who are you?"

"I'm not stationed in Graz, so you wouldn't know me."

"Where are you stationed? Who is your commanding officer?"

"He brought me here from Vienna," snapped Miriam, with irritation. "The major likes Viennese women." She stood contrapposto, hand on hip. "Are you going to keep us here all day, asking your useless questions? Give me your names, or let us be on our way!"

The two stepped back and conferred briefly in whispers, glancing sideways at the two of them. After a moment the sergeant took a step forward, and with a quick, stiff bow, said, "Very well, Fräulein! Keep your appointment, and give our regards to the major!" He touched the brim of his hat and they retreated to the patrol car. Joseph and Miriam quickly slid back into the Mercedes, and they were soon motoring out of the city, southbound, feeling greatly relieved.

She buttoned up her blouse. "Well, that was embarrassing!"

"But very effective!" countered Joseph, grinning. "Miriam, you amaze me!"

"Try to forget that happened," she advised sternly. Producing a small cloth, she began wiping lipstick from her mouth. "It would help to have a mirror and a light."

A couple of minutes later, Joseph's eyes widened as he studied the rearview mirror. "Uh-oh!" he frowned. "Those two soldiers are still following us—and they're gaining on us." He pressed harder on the gas pedal. The twists and turns of the road and the frequent villages and small towns limited his speed, and the patrol car continued to creep up close behind, its headlights glaring into the Mercedes.

Miriam turned and looked back, with concern on her face. "Why are they following us?" she said anxiously. "I thought they believed us." Then she added, "Oh!" as if suddenly remembering something.

Joseph gave her a questioning look. "What?"

"When we drove past them as we left, one of them looked into the car. He must have seen the suitcases—and your pistol is on the car seat. Do you think that's why they are following us?"

"I don't know, but they aren't going to catch us," Joseph replied grimly. "If this road will just straighten out a bit, I'll leave them in the dust."

"Even if you can get away from them, will we get through the border before they catch up?" Miriam worried. Joseph hadn't thought of that. Even if he outran them to the border crossing, they would almost certainly arrive before the border guards cleared them to pass. He began to formulate a plan—all he needed was a few kilometers of reasonably straight road. Finally, he got his wish.

The last town before the border was Leibnitz, and after that were several kilometers of fields and farms with gently rolling hills and no sharp curves. The pursuing patrol car was so close that he could hear its horn honking. The sergeant's arm waved out his window, and he appeared to have a pistol in his hand. "Here we go!" Joseph muttered, and pressed down hard on the gas pedal, activating the supercharger. The Mercedes disdainfully spat a small puff of dark smoke out its tailpipe and with a roar took off like an charging bull. The acceleration pressed them back into their seats and the patrol car rapidly receded into the distance.

As they crested a low hill, Joseph said, "Hold on!" and slammed on the brakes on the downside of the hill, stopping in the road with smoking tires some two hundred meters from the summit. He turned off his headlights, and jumping from the car, he jerked the back door open and snatched the rifle off the seat, throwing the blanket aside. He ran to the rear of the car, working the bolt action to chamber a round in the 8mm Mauser. He knelt and rested his elbow on his knee to steady his aim, and waited.

When the patrol car came over the hilltop he aimed at its front left tire and squeezed the trigger, worked the bolt, and fired again. Black smoke erupted from underneath the car, the tire disintegrated into shreds, and the car veered hard to the left. As it ran off the edge of the pavement and its rear end began to slide into a drainage ditch, the driver jerked the steering wheel back to his right, causing the open-top car to overturn and slide to a grinding halt in a cloud of dust and smoke. Joseph aimed at the exposed fuel tank and fired once more, producing a loud explosion and a flaming pyre, which sent a plume of black smoke skyward. *Too bad about those two,* he thought. *They should have left well enough alone.* He flung the rifle into the underbrush and ran back to the Mercedes.

Miriam stared at him with wide eyes, speechless. He said nothing, but turned his headlights back on, shifted into gear, and drove away at a more leisurely pace. Neither said a word until suddenly Miriam gasped and grabbed Joseph's arm. "Joseph! Did you see that road sign?" He hadn't noticed. "It said the border is ten kilometers away, and it closes at six o'clock!"

"At six o'clock!" he almost shouted. "No!" He pressed the gas pedal harder and raced like a mad man, tires squalling through the curves, shifting gears up and down. When the border crossing came into view, his heart sank as he saw that there were three cars ahead of them at the gate.

There were two guards inspecting passports and asking questions at the car windows. The first car was passed through the gate almost as soon as they arrived, and the second car followed shortly after. The younger of the two guards strolled back to the Mercedes while his partner dealt with the car in front.

"Nice car!" he commented with an approving nod. "Is it yours?"

"No, I drive for a major. He has sent me on an important errand, and it is vital that I get through tonight. We have our papers in order. Can we show them to you?"

"Unfortunately, it is just now six o'clock and the border must close until tomorrow morning at six. I'm afraid—"

The guard's Vienna accent was unmistakable, and Miriam leaned over toward the driver's window. "Mir san oba a Wiener!!" she beamed in her warmest Wienerisch. *We are also from Vienna!* She continued in the dialect: "Don't you miss our beautiful city? Wien, the City of Dreams!"

The guard leaned down to peer into the car and smiled broadly, putting his hands on the window frame. "So! Two Viennese travelers! You are far from home!"

"Yes, unfortunately true! I am so sorry for you that you must stand out here in this remote place on a cold, dark night! But could you not find it in your heart to let us pass through? We would be so grateful!" She smiled and held up her Austrian passport.

The car ahead of them drove through the gate, leaving them the only car remaining. The youthful soldier looked at his older colleague and made a questioning gesture. The older shrugged and walked back into the guard booth and turned off the light inside. The younger stood up straight and briskly waved them ahead. "Go through!" he ordered. "Have a good trip!"

The gate bar came down behind them, and the border was closed for the night. The Yugoslav border guards were also ready to quit for the day and did not even ask to see their passports, but casually waved them through.

"Thank God," Joseph breathed.

"I hope I never see another Nazi for as long as I live," Miriam added. "I'm exhausted."

"We're only halfway to Trieste," cautioned Joseph. "But it's the easy half still ahead." *Or at least I hope so,* he thought.

23

BY THE SKIN OF THE TEETH

About twenty kilometers south of the border they crested the summit of some high hills and saw below them the lights of Maribor. It was a lovely sight with the Drava River winding its way through the small city, spanned by several bridges. Church spires rose above the rooftops, and low mountains could be seen in the distance to the west and north. It was a peaceful scene, but as much as they would have liked to rest and eat a good meal, they decided not to stop but to drive on to Ljubljana, about three hours further. After the frightening encounter with the German soldiers, they wanted to put as much distance as possible between themselves and the border.

One advantage to driving into the night was that there was less traffic on the road. Joseph kept the speed down to avoid attracting attention from police, and the Mercedes purred smoothly and easily. It was quite chilly, and Miriam reached into the back seat for the blanket that had covered the rifle and draped it over her shoulders and knees.

"May I ask you something?" she said.

"Sure. What's on your mind?"

"Earlier today, at the clock shop, two SS men were killed. Herr

Schneider killed one of them with his hammer, and you killed the other with your bare hands—what was his name? Steinhart?"

"Hartstein. Does it bother you?"

"I just don't understand why that was necessary. Couldn't we have gotten away without killing them?"

"Maybe, but if we had just knocked them out, they would have put out the alarm when they came to, and the German army would have been looking for us, especially at the border crossings. A few telephone calls and we would have been caught, most likely.

"And whether we managed to get away or not," he continued, "Uncle Oskar's family would have been arrested, and they would have all gone to jail. Hopefully no one will see them dump the bodies in the Danube, and if Uncle Oskar leaves the car somewhere far away, there won't be any connection to them."

"I suppose so," she said hesitantly. "It still seems like it should have been possible—"

"Furthermore," he interrupted, "Hartstein was responsible for me being drafted into the German army. He was trying to make a Nazi of me. And there's one more thing you should know."

"What's that?"

"Hartstein came to the clock shop a few weeks earlier, asking about your Opa and the book store. He didn't seem to believe that it really wasn't Jewish-owned. I am sure he sent the brutes that destroyed the store last night and killed your Opa—he may even have been there with them." Miriam was silent as she absorbed this.

"When I killed him," Joseph added quietly, "I believed I was avenging Herr Engelmann's death, and I did it the way they taught us in the army training camp. If not for him, I wouldn't have known how to do it."

Miriam took a deep breath and exhaled. She reached over and squeezed Joseph's arm. "Thank you for explaining that. I understand now, and I'm glad you did it. He deserved it."

Joseph felt relief that she approved. "As for the other two soldiers, I do regret that," he admitted, "but I did what I felt I had to do. They had no business chasing us, and we could not afford to be arrested. I never expected to ever kill anyone, and today I've killed three men. It's not a pleasant feeling."

She squeezed his arm again. "You are a good man, Joseph Gruber," she assured him. "And they were not. It was their fault that you were in that situation, so don't feel guilty. I am thankful that you have been able to get us this far. I know that God is helping you. We are going to make it!"

In the car's dark interior, he could barely see her face, but he gave her a curious glance. "A few months ago, you said you didn't believe in anything. What changed?"

"I don't know, really," she said slowly. "I've been going to the church services, listening to the songs, prayers, and Bible readings and sermons. I've read the prayer book, and I've read the gospels. All of that matters, but honestly, I think I just *needed* to believe in something. There has been so much to worry about, so much to fear! When you were taken away to the army, I was devastated and horrified. I prayed for you constantly. Without something to believe in, I just couldn't face life each day. I don't know if God really knows who I am or if he cares about me, but I have to believe that he does. I just *need* to believe. Does that make sense?"

"Yes, actually, that makes a lot of sense. I don't think I've ever heard anyone put it quite that way, but it makes perfect sense to me. I need to believe, too. I can't imagine not believing, and I'm glad you're a believer now." He paused for a few seconds and then added, "Thank you for praying for me. Your prayers were answered!"

"I have another question—where are we going to sleep tonight?"

Joseph burst out laughing at the sudden change of subject. "Right here in this car, I guess," he grinned ruefully. "We don't really have a choice."

"True. I just wanted to know."

They filled the time with conversation, taking turns describing books they had read or movies watched, favorite artworks, and anything else they could think of. The drive took longer than expected, and it was almost ten o'clock when they reached the outskirts of Ljubljana. The medieval castle dominating the skyline high over the city was an impressive sight as they approached, reminding both of them of Salzburg's fortress. The city was mostly dark and quiet at this hour, with almost no traffic on the streets.

Joseph drove slowly along a long, tree-lined avenue, looking for an out-of-the-way place to park. Eventually, near the center of the city they came to a small river, and he followed its winding path westward, more because it looked pretty than for anything else. When he came to a bridge adorned with two fearsome, green dragon statues, he impulsively crossed the river on the bridge and drove a couple of blocks along the opposite bank. The street abruptly opened up into a broad space, lined with booths, tables, and awnings.

"It's a market!" Miriam exclaimed. "No one will be here until morning. Let's stop here for the night."

"Sounds good to me," he replied, and eased the Mercedes into a particularly dark place under some trees. When he shut off the engine, the silence was eerie after hearing its rumble all day. Miriam shifted to find a more comfortable position, and the soft squeaking of the leather seat seemed to penetrate his skull. Even the sound of his own breathing was distracting.

"Something wrong?" she whispered.

"Too quiet," he said in a much too loud voice. He grunted in surprise, and then repeated in a soft whisper, "Too quiet!" Miriam giggled. "I think I'll get out and walk around for a few minutes," he said. "I'm still wound too tight."

The cold air helped clear his head, and he could feel it penetrating his sinuses, his brain, and coursing down into his chest. He walked around the market lot, swung his arms energetically, and pretended to be a boxer, bouncing on his toes and punching the air. Reinvigorated, he was ready to go back to the car.

As he approached, however, he saw a movement in the dark shadows. Quickening his stride, he strained his eyes to see. As he drew closer, he could make out the figure of a man, hunched over, creeping slowly and silently at the rear of the car, starting to move up along the passenger side. Joseph's upper lip curled in a snarl as he sprang forward. Hearing a sound behind him, the man whirled about and slashed at Joseph with a knife, the dim light flashing off the blade just enough that Joseph saw it and recoiled just in time. He felt at his belt, and realized in dismay that the Luger was still on the car seat.

The man advanced, holding the knife in his right hand, waving it slowly back and forth. Joseph retreated step by step, drawing the man out of the darkest shadows in order to see him better. He was short and stocky with a thick, drooping mustache, wearing workman's coveralls and heavy boots. Joseph smelled alcohol and knew the man was drunk. With a toothy grin, the man rubbed together the fingers of his free hand. "Denar!" he rasped, and gestured that Joseph should give him money.

"No denar!" replied Joseph, shaking his head and circling around to get between the man and the car.

"Denar!" he insisted, becoming angry. Joseph remained silent, poised in a crouch, waiting for the man to attack. *Make him make the first move,* he thought. The would-be-robber edged closer, muttering as he threatened with the knife. Just then, a car crossed the Dragon Bridge and turned down the street. The approaching car was behind Joseph and its headlights illuminated the face of the assailant, who, blinded by the light, ducked his head and turned away. Joseph seized the opportunity to turn and run to the Mercedes, fishing the key from his pocket on the way. He unlocked the driver's door, and glancing up saw that the man, emboldened now that the car had passed, was chasing after him.

Joseph reached into the car and grabbed the pistol from the seat. As the man rounded the rear of the car knife in hand, Joseph racked the slide, chambering a round, and pointed the gun, scarcely an arm's length from the man's chest. The man scrambled to reverse course so frantically that he sat down, then crawled on his hands and knees grunting like a pig, until he could get his feet back under him. With a panic-stricken look over his shoulder he ran unsteadily across the market square, falling down twice more before disappearing into the shadows.

That was too close, he grimaced. *Glad I didn't have to pull the trigger. Four in one day would be four too many.*

He heard Miriam's sleepy voice from inside the car. "Joseph! Close the door! It's cold!"

"Sorry about that," he apologized as he climbed in and locked the door, holding the pistol down between his knees so she wouldn't see it. "Go back to sleep. Tomorrow will be a big day." She snuggled under the blanket and leaned against her door, and was soon asleep. Joseph slept very little, however. After several watchful hours he dozed off, only to be awakened shortly by the vendors arriving to set up for the market day.

He cranked the Mercedes and gave Miriam a gentle shake. "Time to go!" he said, trying to sound cheerful. She stretched and yawned.

"It's freezing!" she exclaimed. "How did you sleep without a blanket?"

"I'm fine," he lied. "Let's find the road to Trieste, and get moving."

Their roadmap did not include Trieste, but it did show enough of Slovenia that, with the road signs to guide them, they were able to trace a route from one town to the next, following the main road westward, and they were relieved to finally recognize the name of Trieste, Italy on a sign. It took almost two hours to reach the border crossing, thanks to the usual impediments along the way.

The day was chilly, overcast and windy, lightly misting. The Yugoslav border guards, wearing raincoats, showed little interest in their identification papers, probably because they were exiting the country, and waved them through after a casual glance at their passports.

The Italian guards were a different story altogether. They were suspicious of two young people traveling in an expensive automobile, and demanded to see the ownership documents. Joseph produced the packet from the glove box and handed it over. They saw that the car was the property of the German army, and that Joseph was wearing a military uniform and driving outfit. It took several minutes of fractured English interrogation to satisfy their doubts. He managed to convince them that he was the driver for Major Grünfeld, and was delivering a woman to the port on Grünfeld's orders, professing ignorance of the major's reasons. The Italians raised their eyebrows and gave each other knowing looks. Joseph glanced over at Miriam to see if she was cooperating with the ruse, and saw that she had again applied lipstick and opened the neck of her blouse. The Italian guards nodded and grinned, and waved them through the gate.

"You're getting pretty good at that," he said approvingly as he steered back onto the roadway.

"I'm getting pretty *tired* of that," she frowned. "But it's good that men are so stupid."

Joseph snorted, and then laughed. "That's true," he grinned. "We *are* stupid—but we get things done in spite of it."

"I think maybe I should keep the lipstick until we actually get on a ship," she mused. "You never know when it will come in handy."

"First of all, we have to find a ship that's going to America and buy tickets," rejoined Joseph. "I have no idea where to go from here, but I know the port has to be ahead of us, so we should be able to find it." Then a thought occurred to him and he added, "I just hope we have enough money to buy the tickets!"

Miriam began unbuttoning the bodice of her dirndl. Seeing this, Joseph exclaimed in shock, "*Miriam*! I don't think you have to go *that* far!"

She glared at him. "Don't be ridiculous, Joseph! I'm not undressing!" She pulled out a handful of Reichmarks. "This should help. Mama Gruber gave me part of this, and the rest came from the pockets of the two Nazis that were—" she hesitated—" that didn't need it anymore." She thumbed through the bills. "Looks like a couple hundred."

"There were about six hundred in your Opa's box, and Major Grünfeld gave us a hundred, so hopefully that will be enough."

It took almost an hour to find the Italia Line cruise ship office. When Joseph parked the Mercedes in an out of the way car lot, the needle on the fuel gauge was touching the Empty mark. *Running on fumes*, he said to himself. They walked into the office carrying their suitcases and stood in line with others at the ticket counter. The clock on the wall said ten o'clock.

There was only one clerk working at the counter, and he did not seem to be in a hurry. Joseph heard the sound of writing, of papers being stamped, drawers being opened and closed. The conversation was in Italian, and with one traveler, in the language of Slovenia. Finally, the elderly couple in front of them reached the counter, sliding two small suitcases along with them. They addressed the clerk in German, with distinct Austrian accents. He frowned and held up his palm to stop, and beckoned a young secretary from an inside office to join him. She translated their German into Italian.

As Joseph and Miriam listened, they heard the couple request third-class accommodations. Even before the secretary translated the clerk's reply, it was obvious that the answer was not good. "Third-class is full," she said. "Everyone wants third-class these days. There is no more third-class."

"Then we would like second-class, please," the old man replied with a shrug.

"Two-berth cabin, four-berth cabin, or six-berth cabin?" she translated.

"Two-berth, please."

"No more two-berth cabins," she translated. "All two-berth cabins are taken. Only four-berth cabins are left."

"Then we will take a four-berth cabin, please."

She translated this for the clerk, and he again began to shake his head. "Two people cannot have a four-berth cabin," she explained. "You must have four people to get a four-berth cabin."

"But we are just the two of us," protested the man. "We must go to America! Can't you please find room for us on the ship?"

"No four-berth cabin for only two people," she said firmly. "Next!"

"We will share a four-berth cabin with you," offered Miriam, gesturing to Joseph and herself. "We also need to travel to America. This will be better for all of us!"

The couple turned, looking surprised and pleased—until they saw Joseph in his army uniform. Their smiles froze and their expressions were horrified. Quickly Miriam explained, "He is not a Nazi—he is an American! He is going home to his family. Don't be afraid!"

Joseph held up his United States passport and tried to smile. They hesitated and looked at each other uneasily. Lowering her voice, Miriam said, "Ham ata yahodi?" *Are you Jewish?*

They blinked and then their eyes widened. "Ken, anachanu!" *Yes, we are.*

After a brief, whispered conversation in Hebrew, they agreed to the arrangement and turned back to the clerk. "We are four together, and we would like a four-berth, second-class cabin! Please!"

After the translation, the clerk nodded and wrote on a scrap of paper, handing it to the elderly man. "This is the price of the cabin," the secretary explained. "You must pay in full, in Italian lire."

"In lire?" said Joseph, wiping sweaty hands on his pants. "We only have Reichsmarks. Will you accept Reichsmarks?"

"No. Only lire. No Reichsmarks."

Joseph gave the wall clock a worried look—it was almost eleven o'clock. Banks would be closing for lunch soon, and would not reopen until later in the afternoon. "Where is the closest place to exchange Reichsmarks into lire?" he asked anxiously.

Translation again. The clerk shrugged, turned, and walked to the next window at the counter. He opened the speaking port in the glass, sat down on a stool, and put up a sign that said, "Cambio valuta." *Currency exchange.* The four travelers looked at each other in astonishment and quickly moved to the next window.

"How many lire do we need for our half of the room?" asked Joseph. The Jewish man showed him the paper—twelve thousand lire was the total. Joseph pursed his lips in thought and muttered. "We need six thousand lire? That sounds like a lot. How many Reichsmarks is that?"

The secretary translated his question, and the clerk was scribbling some calculations on a note pad before she finished. He tore it off the pad and pushed it through the slot into the paper tray. "Eight hundred fifty Reichsmarks," Joseph said, a bit taken aback. He and Miriam quickly counted their money, and with a sigh of relief tendered the bills through the paper tray. They had fifty to spare.

After the currency exchanges were done, they all returned to the other window and the tickets were issued. The foursome exited the office together feeling greatly relieved. "'*SS Vulcania*,'" said the Jewish man, reading his ticket. "Where might that be?"

"Where is Pier Seven?" Miriam wondered, also reading from her ticket.

"'Leaving at twelve noon,'" Joseph read, and then looked up. "*Twelve noon*! It's almost eleven-thirty now! We better find our ship and get on board! Hurry!"

It was a half-mile to Pier Seven. The wind was picking up, and the mist turned into drizzle. Joseph ran ahead and made sure the gangway was not closed before the others could get there. They almost didn't make it, but huffing and puffing and looking quite bedraggled, they reached the pier where the *Vulcania* was docked just in time. They were the last passengers to board. A steward pointed them to their cabin, which was furnished with two sets of bunk beds, two sinks, and a toilet, but no window or bath.

"You two can take the bottom bunks, if you like, and we will take the top," suggested Miriam. "By the way," she added, "I am Miriam and this is Joseph. What are your names?"

"We are Sarah and Jacob Goldberg, from Vienna."

"Vienna! Well!" smiled Miriam, "We have so much to talk about!"

In response, the Jewish couple smiled for the first time that day.

24

"BUON VIAGGIO!"

"I'm glad to see you out of that Nazi uniform," Miriam said. "That was bothering me quite a lot."

"It's a relief to me too," Joseph agreed as they sat alone at a table in the second-class dining room. "I feel normal now. I'll keep the leather jacket, hat, and gloves, but the rest I'll toss in the trash as soon as I can."

"What did you do with the pistol?"

"It's in my suitcase. I'll get rid of it, too. Probably will throw it overboard."

"Major Grünfeld said he would have to report you missing this morning. Won't they be looking for you? And what about the SS men and the two army soldiers who died? Will they suspect you were involved in that? And what about the car? We just left it parked in Trieste. Will—"

"Miriam!" Joseph protested, holding up both hands. "Don't be so anxious! We can't control any of that, so let's just hope for the best."

"But what is going to happen? I'm worried, and I can't help it."

"I was supposed to meet Major Grünfeld this morning at nine to drive him back to camp, so he would have probably waited a little while before reporting it. By noon, they would probably have checked my home address and would have looked for me there. I'm sure that confused them, because I put the address of the SS headquarters at the old Rothschild mansion as my home address on the induction form. Only Hartstein knew I was at Uncle Oskar's place, so they'll have a hard time connecting me to the family. There are a lot of Grubers in Austria, so that's no help."

"What about the SS men who died?"

"It should be a few days before Hartstein's body washes ashore in the Danube. If Schneider weighted the bodies, they'll stay under for a long time. I'm sure Uncle Oskar left their car somewhere a long way off, so I don't think they will make a connection to me or the family.

"The two army soldiers in Graz had their car's top down, and when the car flipped and the gas tank exploded, their bodies would have been cremated. I don't think there will be a connection to me for that, either."

"But what about our car? Can't they identify it by the license plates?"

"Yes, but it is parked away from a busy street, and it should take a day or two before anyone notices that it hasn't been moved. Then the police will notice that it has German military license plates and will make telephone calls to see why it is there. Before long they will find out that it is the car assigned to Major Grünfeld, and then things will begin to get interesting. They will probably assume that I drove to Trieste to board a ship, and will start checking passenger lists. With any luck, the *Vulcania* will be far away before they figure out that I'm on board. Surely they wouldn't turn a ship around and bring it back to port just to catch a deserter from another country's military."

"That makes me feel better, but won't they be waiting for you in New York?"

"I'd like to see the Germans arrest an American citizen on American soil for deserting the Germany army!" Joseph smiled confidently. "No, I'll take my chances there, gladly."

"Alright," she said, still looking uncertain. "But I hate having to wait eleven days to find out if you are going to be in trouble. I'll be worried all the way across the ocean."

At that point, Sarah and Jacob joined them at the table and they enjoyed a hearty dinner and good conversation. Joseph decided he liked them. They were quiet, mild people, and Jacob reminded him of Herr Engelmann. He was pleased to learn that Jacob liked to play chess, and they planned to have a game later.

That evening, back in their cabin, Sarah emerged from the small toilet having changed into her nightgown. "You know," she said with a slight frown, "I would have expected second-class cabins to be a little more spacious than this. I saw a brochure in the ticket office with pictures of the first-class cabins, and they were like luxury hotel rooms. They even have balconies!"

"You should see the third-class berths," smiled Joseph. "Last November, Miriam's Opa and I came over in third-class. There's no sink and no toilet—just a bed. The plumbing is all down the corridor in the washroom!"

"Oh, horrors!" Sarah exclaimed. "I guess I won't complain, then! I'm just thankful that the two of you were there so we could get this cabin. What a blessing!"

Everyone said 'good-night,' and went to bed. Lying in their top bunks, Miriam and Joseph were almost close enough to reach out and touch hands. She smiled at him and silently mouthed the words 'Sweet dreams!' He studied her face as she rested peacefully, eyes closed. After a few minutes, the Goldbergs turned off their reading lights and the room was completely dark. Joseph suddenly was overcome with an overwhelming sense of fatigue. He had hardly slept for two nerve-wracking days, and he was more exhausted than he had ever been. He sank quickly into the darkness and knew nothing until morning.

The *Vulcania* stopped for only an hour at Patras, Greece in the afternoon. Joseph watched a number of passengers board the ship, headed for third-class, and then the ship was underway again. They arrived at Naples, Italy around noon the next day for a two-hour stop, picking up more passengers, most of whom also headed for third-class. The scenery that was visible from the ship was not all that interesting in either place—low mountains in the distance, crowded cities packed along the coast, with occasional church spires rising above the rooftops.

Joseph found it impossible to be in a good mood—it seemed that a dark cloud was on his horizon, and he fought a sense of dread. He paced the deck impatiently, anxious to be on the ocean and out of reach of the German Reich. He longed to see the skyline of New York again, with its skyscrapers looming behind the Statue of Liberty. *I can't get home soon enough,* he fretted. Miriam's anxiety had eaten its way into his mind, and he could not find peace.

Naples receded into the distance, shrouded by a misty rain and overcast skies. Forced indoors, Joseph and Jacob found a chess set in the reading room and proceeded to play a game. Jacob, playing the white pieces, opened the game with a sequence of moves that Joseph had not seen before. "That's different!" he commented. "I don't think I've ever seen anyone begin like that."

"It's an opening called 'the Vienna Game,'" nodded Jacob, with a wry smile. "It's an aggressive opening that can be very effective if one's opponent is not familiar with it."

"Very interesting!" replied Joseph. "I'll have to learn it." At the moment, however, he found himself at a disadvantage, struggling to avoid disaster. Despite his effort to focus on the game, his mind still wandered, and a few minutes later Jacob tapped the board lightly with a pawn to get his attention.

"Is something bothering you, Joseph?" he inquired politely.

"I'm sorry!" Joseph apologized, turning red. "No, everything is fine. Is it my move?"

Jacob looked at him intently. "Everything is not fine, is it? I don't mean to pry, but it's clear that you and Miriam are dealing with a situation that is distressing both of you. Do you want to talk about it?"

Joseph rubbed his forehead and gestured helplessly. "I don't really know what to say, Jacob. It's—it's—it's just a big mess, that's all. I'm sure it will all work out alright."

"Are you?" Jacob furrowed his brow with concern. "You arrive in Trieste driving a German army car and wearing a German army uniform, traveling with a Jewish girl who is not your wife, and board a ship for America. Obviously, there is something going on that puts you both in danger, yes?"

"You are very perceptive!" Joseph grimaced. "I can't tell you everything, but as you can probably guess, I have deserted from the Reichswehr. I should never have been in it to start with, since I am an American citizen, but if they catch me, I'll face a firing squad. I won't be able to relax until we're in the Atlantic Ocean, out of reach."

Jacob contemplated him in silence for several long seconds. "Well, that *is* a big mess," he said finally. "Do you think the Germans will figure out that you're on this ship?"

"Yes, I'm sure they will, but it should take them a few days. At least we've left Naples now, and the next stop is New York, so I think my chances are good."

"Yes," Jacob nodded thoughtfully, "so far, so good. Italy is Germany's ally, but they won't turn the ship around just for you. If they can overtake the ship, they might board it, though. I'd be concerned about Spain, too. The Germans and Italians are helping the fascists in the civil war there, and might be able to get some help from them as we pass through the Straits. Hopefully, Franco will be too busy with his own problems to bother with catching a German deserter."

"Overtake the ship?" Joseph's eyes widened. "Do you think they could—that they *would* do that?"

Jacob shrugged. "No offense, Joseph, but I just can't believe you are that important. Unless there's more to it than you have told me, I doubt that they would go to that much trouble. Desertion is not that uncommon, and it seems to me they would just let it go, especially since you are an American."

"I hope you're right," Joseph mused. *But there is a lot more to it than you know. I just hope it's more than the Germans know, too.*

For two days the *Vulcania*'s diesel engines drove her through the Mediterranean toward Gibraltar and the open ocean. When she was only a couple of hours from the Straits, the ship's engines suddenly were cut to idle and she rapidly slowed, coasting to a near stop. All of the passengers noticed this immediately and began stirring about, venturing out to the decks for a look around and asking the crew for an explanation. The word began to spread rapidly throughout the ship—"We're being boarded by the Italian navy!"

Joseph and Jacob were in the reading room playing a game of chess when another passenger came in with the announcement of the boarding. Joseph's jaw dropped and he froze, with a panic-stricken expression. Jacob reacted quickly. "Joseph, give me your ticket receipt." When Joseph hesitated, confused, Jacob repeated his command and extended his own ticket to Joseph. Still not comprehending Jacob's intent, he exchanged receipts. "You're Jacob. I'm Joseph," explained the older man. "Keep quiet, and let me do the talking."

Twenty minutes later two officers in Italian naval uniforms entered the reading room, accompanied by the ship's captain. They glanced around the room and then walked directly to the table where Joseph and Jacob sat.

"Joseph Gruber?" They spoke in German, their eyes on Joseph.

"Yes?" replied Jacob casually. "What do you want?" Joseph did not look up from the chessboard.

The officers were taken aback, and stared at the old man. "You're not Joseph Gruber!"

"But I *am*!" Jacob objected, without any sign of unease. "What do you want?"

"Show us your ticket receipt," demanded the ship's captain. Jacob reached into his coat pocket and produced it.

"See for yourselves," he frowned. "It says 'Joseph Gruber'—read it right there."

"But you can't be Joseph Gruber," argued the Italian naval officer. "You're too old!"

"Ha!" laughed Jacob derisively. "Gruber is the most common family name in Austria, and Joseph is also a very common name. There must be at least dozens, if not hundreds of Joseph Grubers in Austria! Why am I too old to be a Joseph Gruber? That's ridiculous."

Frustrated, the officer turned to Joseph. "Show me your receipt!"

Joseph looked up for the first time, and with an air of impatience, wordlessly handed over his receipt.

"'Jacob Goldberg,'" read the officer aloud. They handed the receipt from one to another so that they all could see it.

"The Joseph Gruber you are seeking must be on a different ship," suggested Jacob helpfully. "Whoever searched the passenger lists must have stopped looking as soon as they found my name, and assumed that I was the one they wanted. There must be another Joseph Gruber out there somewhere, and he's getting away while you are standing here talking to me."

The ship's captain made one more try. "Show your passport, Jacob Goldberg. The Joseph Gruber we are seeking is an American, and will have an American passport."

"If he is an American," Jacob said incredulously, "then what right do you have to detain him, anyway? This ship is in international waters, and you have no authority here to arrest anyone, especially not an American!"

The three looked very uncomfortable at that, and the officer who did the talking appeared to be getting angry. "Show your passport!" he snapped at Joseph, jabbing his finger at him.

Joseph patted his pockets with a perplexed expression. He looked up apologetically and said in his best Wienerisch, "I schein's ned bei mir z'ham. Des muas in mei Kabinen sein." *I don't seem to have it with me. It must be in my cabin.*

The three stared blankly at him for some seconds. "What did he say?" one asked Jacob.

Jacob smiled indulgently. "He speaks Wienerisch—the dialect of Vienna. Only Vienna natives speak it." They continued staring. "I can translate for you if you like," he added.

The captain and the officers stepped away from the table and carried on an animated conversation in Italian, with a flurry of hand gestures by all three. Finally, the lead officer turned back to them, made a quick, stiff bow, and said curtly, "Buon viaggio!" *Have a good trip!* And the three marched briskly away. Within a few minutes the diesel engines revved up again, and the *Vulcania* resumed its course.

Joseph and Jacob continued to sit quietly at the table and finished their game.

Miriam and Sarah joined them for lunch. The Rock of Gibraltar could be seen through a window as they passed, and Joseph pointed to it. "I thought we would never get to the Straits! Now we will finally be crossing the Atlantic!"

The women had been in the library during the boarding and had not heard anything about it. "Did the ship stop for a little while back there?" Miriam asked. "It felt like we stopped and then started again. Is that normal?"

Joseph and Jacob exchanged a knowing look. "Jacob saved me from being arrested," Joseph said confidentially in a low voice, and quickly described the encounter with the Italian officers. Miriam turned pale, and she grabbed Joseph's arm and held it tightly. "For now, I'm Jacob and he's Joseph, in case anyone asks," he concluded.

"That was brilliant!" beamed Sarah proudly, patting Jacob's arm. Then, stroking his white hair, she added, "I'm so glad they didn't arrest you and take you off to a firing squad."

"So am I!" he chuckled. "It was a close call!"

"Thank you, Jacob—I mean, *Joseph*!" Miriam threw her arms around his neck and gave him a tight hug. "If you hadn't thought so quickly, it would have all been for nothing! You saved us." With a trembling smile she wiped a tear. "God is truly with us!" she whispered.

"I think this calls for some ice cream and chocolate cake for dessert!" exclaimed Joseph.

"And a cup of coffee!" added Jacob. They stayed at the table, talking, laughing, and sharing stories about life in Vienna, until they were the last passengers to leave the dining room.

By evening the *Vulcania* was well beyond Gibraltar, and Europe had disappeared from view in its wake. Feeling safe at last, Joseph and Miriam were more relaxed than they had been for the past week. During the seven-day crossing of the Atlantic, they spent a great deal of time strolling arm in arm, talking, and just sitting quietly. They were virtually inseparable, eating three meals each day together, along with the Goldbergs. Joseph liked to walk with her on the outside deck, despite the blustery cold wind—it gave him an excuse to put his arm around her, which she didn't seem to mind at all. He knew he wanted to be closer, but didn't know how to make it happen. He felt that to pursue her more aggressively would be inappropriate, since he had helped her to get her visa and make her escape. He feared that she would feel obligated to him, and struggled to think of a way to get past that.

On the final day before reaching New York, as they huddled together against a gusty wind on the deck, he impetuously kissed her forehead. Miriam looked up and fixed him with her direct gaze. "Your aim is a little high," she said, with strands of her dark hair blowing across her face. Joseph hesitated only for a second, and then pressed a long kiss on her lips. "I thought you never were going to do that," she murmured, and then shivered. "It's cold." They stood kissing for several minutes before surrendering to the wind and returning indoors.

"I love you," he blurted.

"I know," she smiled demurely. "I've known for a long time. I probably knew before you did." She squeezed his hand. "Now I have to go fill out some immigration papers before we dock. Let's hope that goes smoothly! I'll see you at lunch." She hurried away, leaving Joseph gaping after her.

In fact, things went more smoothly with immigration than they could have imagined. Unbeknownst to them, first and second-class passengers did not have to be processed at Ellis Island, but received only a perfunctory check of their papers on board the ship, and then were allowed to enter directly into the city. Thus, contrary to their fears, Joseph and Miriam were not separated during the landing, but went ashore together.

Joseph had converted their remaining Reichsmarks into dollars on the ship, so they were able to hire a taxi to take them to Joseph's home. Otto was shocked when Joseph walked through the front door of the clock shop, suitcase in hand. Not normally an expressive person, he shouted for joy and dashed from behind the counter to embrace his son, leaving a customer standing there dazed. It was an emotional reunion with his mother and three siblings.

Miriam contacted her relatives by telephone, and they arrived that afternoon in a car to take her home. Both families stared as Joseph and Miriam shared a lengthy kiss while saying good-bye. "I'll call tomorrow," Joseph promised. She blew him a kiss from the car and mouthed the words 'I love you.' He stood waving until the car rounded a corner and was gone. He turned to find his family with mouths agape. "What?" he demanded. "Haven't you ever seen two people in love before?" His siblings roared with laughter and attacked him with hugs again, and his parents joined in.

He wanted to let Uncle Oskar know they had arrived safely, but in a way that would not bring suspicion on him in case the Nazis were monitoring his mail. Otto decided to send him a postcard saying, "Dear Brother, your package has arrived safely. Thank you." Joseph also sent an unsigned postcard to Roger Thomas at the Vienna consulate saying simply, "The Woman in Gold thanks you."

EPILOGUE

Joseph returned to working in his father's clock shop, applying the skills learned in Vienna during the past year. Miriam was also working—one of her uncles employed her as a typist in his office. Joseph spent a great deal of time showing Miriam the city. They visited the Chrysler Building, the Empire State Building, the Statue of Liberty, Central Park, and other famous attractions. She was duly impressed, despite being homesick for Vienna.

In mid-December they attended a memorial service in honor of Herr Engelmann, held at the Temple Emanu-El Synagogue. The synagogue, one of the world's largest, had a seating capacity of twenty-five hundred. Because Herr Engelmann was a victim of what was now being called "Kristallnacht," or the "Night of Broken Glass," the massive synagogue was packed with Jewish mourners paying their respects. It was a moving ceremony, and tears flowed freely from the eyes of both Joseph and Miriam.

A few days after Christmas the Gruber family, along with Miriam, were all gathered in the family apartment eating lunch together. Joseph was quiet and kept reaching into the pocket of his black leather jacket to feel the ring he had purchased a week earlier. Having bought it, now he was anxious, wondering if his timing was right or was he moving too fast? He fidgeted nervously, eating only half of his lunch.

A bell rang, indicating that someone had entered the shop on the floor below. Otto rose from the table to go see. He was gone for several minutes, and returned with a curious expression on his face. "There's a big crate downstairs. It's addressed to you, Joseph."

"To me? I wonder what that could be."

The whole family hurried down to investigate. It was a sturdy wooden box, about two feet wide, one foot deep, and five feet long. It was marked "Fragile" and "Zerbrechlich" on all sides in large letters. Joseph's name and address were written in bold black letters, and in smaller letters was a return address in Vienna. Fetching a crowbar from the workshop, Joseph pried the lid off the box, and found that the contents were thickly wrapped in blankets, with newspapers and padding packed all around. A white envelope lay atop the blanket, also addressed to him. He opened the envelope, took out the hand-written letter, and stood silently reading it for several seconds.

"What does it say?" asked Miriam, touching his arm.

Joseph uttered a strangled cry—an inarticulate outburst of emotion. He abruptly handed the letter to Miriam and frantically began removing the blankets and packing material from the crate. As the object within was exposed to view, the family gasped in amazement and Miriam squealed with delight. The box contained a fantastically beautiful Art Deco Vienna Regulator. Its brilliant colors seemed alive and vibrant, leaping into the air.

"What is this?" Otto asked in awe. "I've never seen anything like this in my life!"

"It's my clock," Joseph breathed. "I made it."

"But—how—why—" the family was stammering, eyes wide and mouths open.

"Read it!" Joseph said to Miriam. "Out loud!"

She held the letter shakily in both hands and in a tremulous voice, began to read:

. . .

Dear Joseph and Miriam,

I am glad that you made it safely to America, and I am glad that I was able to play a small part in that. However, my part was so small that I have felt guilty every time I looked at your beautiful clock on my wall. The Woman in Gold glares down at me with an accusing stare, and I cannot abide her harsh judgment of me. Therefore, I am returning your clock. Thank you for letting me enjoy it for a while. When you left my office that day, you said that piece of paper was more valuable than any clock. Well, the good esteem of The Woman in Gold is worth more to me than the clock. Yes, sometimes you do have to make a sacrifice to win the game.

Auf Wiedersehen,

Roger Thomas

"I don't understand any of that," said Otto, shaking his head. "What is he talking about?"

"I'll explain it all," Joseph replied. "Later." He turned and embraced Miriam, and as they kissed, the letter floated gently to the floor.

HISTORICAL NOTES

1: Planting Seeds

- The SS *Europa* was an ocean liner owned by the North German Lloyd company. Almost a thousand feet in length, it was longer than the RMS *Titanic* by about fifty feet. Third-class was the cheapest fare available, but much more comfortable than the steerage quarters suffered by poor immigrants in earlier years.
- Otto Gruber's cry, "Mir san jetzt Amerikaner!" is not standard German, but is in the Vienna dialect known as Wienerisch (pronounced "*Veenerish*"), commonly dismissed as inferior to High German. When Wienerisch is presented in these pages, the translation comes from the website mr.dialect.com, with input from my wife and sister-in-law, who are natives of Vienna.
- The "Vienna Regulator" was a distinctive style of pendulum wall clock associated with the city for which it was named. The styles evolved over time, but usually involved ornately carved wood cabinets.

- Herr Engelmann quotes from "The New Colossus," by Emma Lazarus, which is inscribed on the pedestal of the Statue of Liberty. His grammar reflects his German-language background, putting the verbs at the end of the sentences. He sometimes uses German words in place of English, such as "Wien" (pronounced "Veen") for Vienna, or "und" for "and." Vienna is sometimes called the "City of Dreams." After this, his grammar is correct because they are speaking in German, though presented in English for the reader.
- The Habsburg emperor, Franz Josef, ruled the Austro-Hungarian Empire from 1848 to his death in 1916. His 68-year reign was the longest of any European monarch.
- Hitler had attempted to overthrow Germany's Weimar Republic government in 1923 in an insurrection beginning in a beer hall in Munich. This resulted in his being sent to prison for a year, along with several of his National Socialist (NSDAP) followers.
- The Madison Square Garden event described here was in 1934. That building was demolished in 1968. "German Day" celebrations had been held on October 6 each year for decades, interrupted only briefly during World War One. Nazi symbols were featured prominently at these gatherings after Hitler came to power in 1933, and German-Americans were divided over how to respond to this.
- A Sam Browne belt is a leather belt with a strap over the right shoulder, typically worn by soldiers and police.
- It probably doesn't need to be explained, but the word "Führer" is German for "leader," and refers to Adolf Hitler. "Sieg Heil" translates as "Hail Victory," and Deutschland Über Alles" as "Germany above everything." *Mein Kampf* can be translated My Fight, My Struggle, My Battle, etc.
- Fraktur script had been voted the official German typeface by the Reichtag in 1911, and remained so until 1941.

𝔉𝔯𝔞𝔨𝔱𝔲𝔯 𝔖𝔠𝔯𝔦𝔭𝔱

- Charles Atlas's body-building course was advertised in comic books and newspapers during this era, with millions of sales internationally. It is still available.
- Eel soup is a Hamburg specialty—a must-eat dish for visitors. A gasthaus is a guest house, or restaurant, pub, etc.
- Names sometimes convey meaning: Hartstein means literally "hard stone," and according to Ancestry.com originally referred to someone who is "mean, harsh, or inflexible." Engelmann transliterates to "angel man." Gruber is the most common surname in Austria.
- The reader should assume that all conversation after this point is in German, though written in English.

2: Settling In

- "Buchhandlung" is German for "bookstore." It was customary for store names to state the business and the owner's name, though the words were not hyphenated. I chose to do it this way for the sake of clarity for English-language readers.
- The "Südbahnhof" (south train station) was completed in 1874, and remained largely unchanged from 1874 to 1945. The description given is accurate. It was torn down in 2010.
- The Apollo Kino Theater still stands. The interior has been dramatically altered since its construction, and it now offers 12 screens with 2160 seats combined. Originally there was just one theater, with 1500 seats. Red is said to be the dominant color, both inside and out, but the exterior looks pink to me. I haven't seen color pictures of the

Apollo from the early days, so my description is influenced by its present appearance.

- "Uhrmacher" is German for "clock maker." Uncle Oskar's surname is Gruber, of course.
- Coffee houses (Kaffeehaus, singular) have been a cultural fixture in Vienna for centuries. Perhaps comparable to English pubs, they are often gathering places for locals, who drink coffee, eat pastries, read newspapers, and talk.
- Stephansdom is the German name for St. Stephen's Cathedral. Built in the 12th century, it is the most famous landmark of Vienna. The mountain barrier north of Vienna consists of a half-dozen summits rising from 1500 to 1800 feet elevation.
- There was certainly antisemitism in the U.S. and in New York at that time. Joseph may not have been aware of the extent, or may have chosen to downplay it.
- Anna Marie is correct about the number of Jews in Vienna. They constituted about ten percent of the population and tended to live in neighborhoods together, though not always by choice.
- Everything said by Oskar and Stephan at the dinner table is historically sound. Hitler had held the rank of corporal during World War One, which was commonly called The Great War until World War Two.

3: "Nothing Lasts Forever"

- Tyrol is the most mountainous region of Austria, sandwiched between Germany to the north and Italy to the south. Its capital city is Innsbruck, which is sometimes called "the capital of the Alps."
- Catholic Mass was always in Latin until the 1960s, when vernacular languages were mandated by the Vatican II council.
- Mariahilfer means "Mary's help." Strasse means "street."

4: Reality

- The description of the process for getting a visa to the U.S. from Austria is taken from the online Holocaust Encyclopedia. Of the 1,413 visas allowed for Austrians by the U.S. quota in 1937, only 409 were actually issued (U.S. Dept of Labor, Immigration, and Naturalization Service, annual report).
- Just FYI, Christmas was on a Saturday in 1937.
- The movie *King Kong* was released in 1933 and was an international success.
- Jewish tradition was to bury the deceased as soon as possible, with no embalming. The "meal of condolence" description is taken from online sources.

5: Portents

- Engelmann's narration of Hitler's actions is historically correct, though the cessation of reparations payments took place in 1932, the year before Hitler came to power, and was due to the effect of the Great Depression.
- Kurt von Schuschnigg was the Austrian chancellor. He met with Hitler at the latter's Berchtesgaden retreat in Bavaria, in February, 1938.
- The comments about the Nuremberg Laws are accurate.
- It is true that Hitler's father was originally named Alois Schicklgruber, and changed his name to Hitler as an adult. Alois was an illegitimate child, and rumors that his biological father was Jewish have persisted to this day, but are not endorsed by historians.
- *Hitler: A Biography* (2 vols., 1936–1937) was the first major biography of Hitler. Written by German journalist Konrad Heiden, in exile in Switzerland, Herr Engelmann could have possessed a copy in his bookstore. An English version appeared as *Der Führer – Hitler's Rise to Power* (1944). The

details Engelmann described about Hitler's background are all found in this book.

6: Anschluss!

- The event of March 1938 in which Austria was unified with Germany is called the "Austrian Anschluss," referring to the annexation, union, merging.
- What might have been revealed by the plebiscite (referendum) is debated by historians. The true feelings of the Austrian people about the annexation will likely never be known with certainty. Schuschnigg predicted that 65% would vote for independence.
- In March 1938, German troops crossed the Austrian border. Hitler followed later in the day, visiting his birthplace at Braunau-an-der-Inn, and then going on to the city of Linz. He arrived in Vienna the next day, March 13. The military columns that advanced into Austria were crippled by mechanical breakdowns and were many hours behind schedule, with most of the tanks eventually arriving in Vienna a couple of days later by train.
- The Anschluss was accompanied by violence against Jews, seizure of Jewish property, and the arrests of opponents of the annexation.
- Nazi banners were ubiquitous during the annexation, but I don't know that one was actually on the Mariahilfekirche. The highest representative of the Roman Catholic Church in Austria, Cardinal Theodor Innitzer, endorsed the Anschluss and urged Austrians to vote for it. However, many Catholics in Austria protested, using the slogan "Our Führer is Christ."
- Hitler did shovel snow at the Hotel Imperial as a poor laborer in pre-World War One Vienna. Where Joseph might have run across that story, I don't know, but Hitler made no secret of his desire to avenge his earlier

humiliation by lodging at the hotel. He stayed in the "royal suite."

7: Desperation

- The Hofburg is the massive Habsburg palace which had long served as the seat of Austrian government. Hitler gave a speech to perhaps a quarter-million Austrians from its balcony on that date. Heldenplatz is literally "heroes place." The quote attributed to Hitler is accurate.
- John Cooper Wiley was officially the "Chargé d'Affaires ad interim" in Vienna for several months in 1938. By all accounts, he was sympathetic to the plight of would-be emigres and treated them fairly. The legation was closed in April, as Austria was incorporated into Germany. Roger Thomas, Wiley's assistant, is fictitious.
- Between March 21 and April 1, approximately 25,000 visa applicants visited the U.S. consulate in Vienna, but only about 800 interviews were given. Wiley hired more staff to handle the work load, and paid them out of his own pocket.
- Klimt's *The Woman in Gold* was privately owned but was well-known, having been publicly exhibited several times. The identity of the model, however, was not generally known.
- The Austrian schilling was replaced by the Deutche Reichmark in 1938 at a ratio of 1.5 schillings per mark. The schilling was resumed in 1945, and then replaced by the Euro dollar in 2002.

8: Closing Jaws

- The annexation plebiscite on Sunday, April 10, 1938, was preceded by intensive propaganda and was not a secret ballot. The German government claimed the final vote tally was 99.7561% in favor. About 70,000 people were arrested and detained between the Anschluss and the plebiscite a month later. Jews were not allowed to vote.

- The Austrian young men would have been familiar with Tarzan. The first Tarzan movie was a 1918 silent film. Johnny Weissmuller's first Tarzan movie was in 1932. These movies were international successes, and by the mid-1960s, Tarzan had become the highest grossing film character of all time.

- As previously explained, according to Germany's 1935 Nuremberg Race Laws, anyone who had 3 or 4 Jewish grandparents was considered fully Jewish.

- Joseph saw a notice taped to the jewelry store window. Adhesive tape was introduced commercially in the 1920s and was widely available in the 1930s. "Aryanization" of Jewish businesses was widespread, leaving their former owners destitute. Jewish employees in other businesses were fired. Jewish teachers and university professors were dismissed. Suicides were frequent.

- Charlie Chaplin's film, *The Great Dictator*, in which he parodied Hitler, was not released until two years later, in 1940, so Joseph's mimicking of Chaplin's walk would not have been inspired by it. The policeman would likely have interpreted it as mockery, especially since Joseph did not return the Nazi salute.

9: Whatever It Takes

- A Pension (pronounced pen-si-ON) is a small, owner-operated boarding house, or guest house, usually more economical than a hotel.

- Austrians mostly drove on the left side of the road until 1938 (It's a little complicated, actually.) After the Anschluss, Hitler ordered all to drive on the right side.

Vienna traffic drove on the left side until September, 1938, for some reason.

- This describes a possible route from Vienna to Salzburg. Since the Autobahn didn't exist in 1938, it's a guess as to which roads they would have used.
- The exchange ratio of German marks to US dollars in 1938 was approximately 2.5:1. The monetary value of the clocks is pure guesswork on my part. I wanted it to sound like a lot of money.
- Hohensalzburg is the largest intact medieval castle in Central Europe. It sits at an elevation of more than 500 meters.
- In German, a "Dom" is a cathedral, not a dome. However, the Salzburger Dom's cupola over the apse was large enough that it is sometimes called a dome.
- The 2-volume biography of Hitler by Konrad Heiden, mentioned above in the notes to chapter 5, asserts that the swastika originated with the Mongols, Finns, and Chinese. Other sources point to India's Hindus and Buddhists. The fascist salute was borrowed from the Italians, who got it from ancient Rome.

10: Storm Clouds

- *The Adventures of Robin Hood* was one of the top movies of 1938.
- The street incident witnessed by Joseph and Miriam is based on the story of Anna Rath, which took place in Nuremberg, Germany, in August 1933, according to three American witnesses, including journalist Quentin Reynolds. The story has been recounted in numerous sources from 1933 to the present, most famously perhaps in Erik Larson's *In The Garden of Beasts*. However, its authenticity has been challenged by a German archivist, Gerhard Jochem, who specializes in German-Jewish

history and is no apologist for the Nazis. See the website rijo-research.de for his arguments.

- Engelmann's comments about author Konrad Heiden are historically accurate.

- "Abentbrot" is a common term for supper in Austria. Apfelstrudel is apple-filled pastry, and topfenstrudel is cream cheese-filled pastry.

- "Nazi" was a contraction of National Socialist German Workers Party, or in German: Nationalsozialistische Deutsche Arbeiterpartei.

- The Sudetenland was a crescent-shaped area on the border between Germany and Czechoslovakia where about 3 million ethnic Germans lived. It was assigned to Czechoslovakia in the aftermath of World War One.

- Joseph's summary of Hitler's declared intentions toward Russia is correct. The German army invaded Russia in the summer of 1941.

11: No Smiles

- Unemployed World War One veterans began selling würstel from buckets on the sidewalks, and the würstelstand became a vital part of Vienna culture. "Würstelstand Leo" still exists, and is famous as the first and oldest würstelstand in Vienna. The fare is basically a hot dog. It is located about a 15-minute walk from the US consulate, which was at Boltzmanngasse 16 in the 1930s.

- Nazi Stormtroopers frequently forced Jews to clean the sidewalks with acid and brushes (or even toothbrushes) in what were called *Reibpartien* ("cleaning squads"). They sometimes urinated on their victims while crowds of spectators watched and jeered. Pants were still buttoned in the 1930s—zippers were not yet widely in use.

- "Schweinfleisch" is literally "pig meat," usually translated pork.

- "Mench" means "man." In this context, it could be translated "fella," or something similarly curt and impersonal. Whether someone who defended a Jew would have been treated so leniently or not is hard to say, but he was certainly in danger of getting a severe beating. Joseph's blond hair and blue eyes probably worked in his favor.
- *Mein Kampf* was written in 1924 while Hitler served a prison sentence for his failed Beer Hall Putsch of 1923. It was first published in 1925.

12: "Im heilgen Land Tirol"

- "Tirol" is the German form of the name, and "Tyrol" is the English version. "Im heil'gen Land Tirol" means "In the sacred land of Tyrol."
- It is true that Tyroleans were generally sympathetic to the Nazis. "The Great War" was World War One. Schneider's descriptions of Tyrolean history and the South Tyrol land dispute are accurate. However, I have committed an anachronism by having him explain the agreement between Hitler and Mussolini to let Italy keep the Südtirol and let the people choose to leave or stay. That agreement was not actually promulgated until the next year, 1939. The Tyroleans had hoped that Hitler's Pan-Germanism would restore the unity of the entire Tyrol. Agitation over the division of Tyrol continued into the 1960s, and occasionally became violent.
- The Alpbach church described here is St. Oswald Parish Church. Interior and exterior pictures can be found online.
- Joseph's journey to Herr Schneider's home in Tyrol is fictionalized, but based on numerous credible sources, both current and historical, and on personal experience. I chose to use the old spelling "Alpbachthal" (Alpbach

Valley) instead of the modern "Alpbachtal" in the interest of reflecting contemporary practice of the time. "Der Opa ist do!" is a rough dialectical equivalent of "Grandpa is here!"

- Tyroler Groestl consists of roasted potatoes, onions, and bacon, cooked and served in a skillet and topped with a fried egg.
- As already noted, "Im heil'gen Land Tirol" means "In the sacred land of Tyrol." This is often seen on traditional houses in Tyrol. It is a repeated line in the provincial anthem commemorating the martyrdom of Tyrolean hero Andreas Hofer by the French in 1809.
- The burning of the fires to celebrate the Sacred Heart of Jesus continues today in Tyrol. In 1938, the church "solemnity" was Sunday, June 5. In 2025 it is Friday, June 27. It is always 19 days after Pentecost Sunday. Pictures are available online.
- I am possibly guilty of another anachronism in describing swastika fires being burned in 1938. This actually occurred mainly in 1933-34 to celebrate Hitler's coming to power in Germany, and was banned by the Tyrolean government, punishable with a year in prison. However, I don't actually know that it did *not* happen in 1938, so it might have been possible. It seems to have been something inspired by the tradition of patriotic mountain fires in the region.
- Adler = eagle.
- The Brenner Pass is on the Austro-Italian border. The blowing up of a power station described by Schneider did happen, but in the early 1960s (it was several power stations, actually). Another anachronism.

13: "I will, with God's help!"

- Schönbrunn Palace had been the summer residence of the

Habsburg royal family, famous for its gardens, walking paths, and world-famous zoo, which was founded in 1752.

- You can find interior and exterior pictures of the Christ Church, Vienna online.
- Vienna's Anglican Christ Church baptized almost two thousand Jews in 1938—229 in one day in July—providing baptismal certificates which were thought to help with Jewish emigration. Reverend Hugh Grimes initiated the practice, and after his recall to England, his replacement, Reverend Fred Collard, continued the rites. The Church later stopped this out of concern that the "conversions" may have been politically motivated (!). Those who went through the process said that they received a few hours of instruction before and a prayer book afterward. The question asked of the baptism candidates by Grimes in my fictionalized account is not based on historical sources, but reflects questions that may be asked in an Anglican baptism.
- Anglican adult baptism may be by immersion or by pouring water over the head.

14: Powder Keg

- The riot at the soccer game happened in Vienna in the fall of 1940, so it's a bit anachronistic to put it here in 1938, but it illustrates the attitude of some Viennese toward the German regime. The Admira and Schalke teams played in the game when the riot occurred.
- "Piefke" was a derogatory term used by Austrians to refer to Germans. It probably referred to Johann Gottfried Piefke, a composer of German military marches whose music was favored by Hitler and used frequently at his public appearances. German military music was often used as a symbol of the alleged rigidity and bluntness of

German behavior, in contrast to the Viennese waltzes, characterized by grace and fluidity of motion.

- The youth rally at Stephansdom described here is based on an actual event involving eight thousand young people in October, 1938, at which Cardinal Innitzer told the crowd that Jesus was the only Führer. There was singing of religious songs, but beyond those details, my description of the event and message is fictional. The next day, Hitler Youth broke into the archbishop's residence nearby and slashed and stabbed a painting of Jesus.

15: The Belly of the Beast

- The palatial residence at the Prinz-Eugen-Strasse address was one of the former homes of the fabulously wealthy Jewish Rothschild family, who fled to England after the Anschluss. The description of the building's exterior is based on photographs and historical sources, as is the description of the entrance hall. The SS appropriated it as their headquarters in Vienna, and Adolf Eichmann set up the Central Agency for Jewish Emigration there in the late summer of 1938. The building was demolished in 1954, and today it is the address of the "Kammer für Arbeiter und Angestellte für Wien" ("Chamber of Workers and Employees for Vienna").
- Obersturmbannführer = lieutenant colonel, a rank held by Eichmann by 1941. My description of him is based on photographs from that time. He probably wouldn't have had a skull emblem on his hat in 1938, since the "Final Solution" mass exterminations had not yet begun at that time. Possibly another anachronism.
- Obersturmführer = first lieutenant.

16: *Tempus Fugit*

- The S.A., or Sturmabteilung, were commonly referred to as the Stormtroopers, or Brownshirts.
- The Aspang Train Station (Aspangbahnhof) in Southeast Vienna was where the transports of Jews from Vienna to the concentration camps departed during World War II. The description of it is based on photographs. It was torn down in the 1970s, and a memorial commemorating the Jewish victims of the deportation now marks the place. The description of the station's clock is imaginary and not based on any historical sources.
- "Grüß Gott" (ß = ss) is literally "Greet God," a common Austrian greeting even today.
- "*Mischling*" means someone who is of mixed ancestry, specifically Jewish. US consul John Wiley, in a 1938 report to the State Department, described the plight of Vienna's *mischlings*, and cited the example of being rejected by hospitals.
- There are 100 pfennigs in a mark. In the late 1930s, one Reichsmark was worth about $2.50 USD.
- The term "robot," meaning a mechanical human, was introduced in 1920 by a Czech playwright. Joseph and the others could have been familiar with it.
- *Tempus fugit* is Latin for "time flies."

17: Sudetenland

- British PM Neville Chamberlain has been mocked ever since for his naïve trust in Hitler's promise to cease his expansionist ways. The Munich Pact—the paper he displayed at the London airport upon his arrival home—is regarded as a prime example of appeasement and failure.
- It is true that Grimes was recalled back to England, and that his replacement, Fred Collard, continued the baptisms of Jews. The comments attributed to Collard are

fictitious, but credible, in my opinion, considering his participation in the baptisms.

- In the Roman Catholic Church, priests usually preached sermons in Latin until the mid-1960s.
- It has been difficult to find detailed information about the status of Austrian passports after the March 1938 Anschluss. Based on my sources, all Austrian nationality status was changed to German Reich status by spring 1939. Jewish passports had to have a red 'J' by October 5, 1938, so I have assumed that the passports would continue to be valid for a while beyond that date.
- The Nazi Schutzstaffel (translated "Protective Echelon," or "Protection Squads"), commonly referred to as the "SS," was not part of the German army, as Hartstein correctly states. The organization was directly loyal to Hitler, and was entrusted with preserving the "racial purity" of the Reich. The SS ran the concentration camp system.
- "Oberbahnhofwienerschnitzelführer" is humor. Oskar is mocking Hartstein and his elaborate title.

18: Thunderbolt Out of the Blue

- After the Anschluss, Austria became officially known as "Ostmark," literally "eastern frontier," a province of Germany, and Austrian citizens became German citizens —except for Jews, Gypsies, and other undesirables.
- Döllersheim was the main training camp for the German army in Austria at that time.
- German recruits typically had been well-prepared for military life by the Hitler Youth organization, but Austrians had not had that kind of training pre-Anschluss. Joseph, you will remember, had been following the Charles Atlas muscle-building program, which served him well now.

- The 8-man barracks groups ruled by a corporal was actual practice. My description of the training regimen is based loosely on online research, and may not accurately represent German military methods of the era. Limiting the quantity of food served to recruits seems to have been intended to toughen them up, along with harsh treatment and brutal workouts.

19: Roller Coaster!

- "Jawohl" (pronounced ya-*vohl*), translated "Yes indeed," is a customary address used by a soldier to his superior. "Mein Herr" derives from the antiquated "my lord," and basically means simply "sir."
- Herr Major Grünfeld, as you will see, is not exactly the stereotypical Nazi officer.
- The description of the Mercedes-Benz Nürburg 500K is accurate, with the technical details converted from metric. It was a high-performance automobile for its time—one of the very few capable of 100 mph—and Nürburgs can be seen in some historical photos of the German army in action, though I can't say whether those had the high-performance options that Grünfeld describes. See www.kfzderwehrmacht.de. To view, select Motor Vehicles, Germany, Daimler-Benz.
- The fuel cap on this model car would not really have been hard to find. Concealing gas caps didn't begin in earnest until the late 1940s, so this is somewhat anachronistic (or maybe the previous drivers were just stupid). The Nürburg 500K had a fuel capacity of 110 liters, equivalent to 29 U.S. gallons. Fuel consumption was about 8-9 mpg with the supercharger engaged. I've been unable to learn its fuel efficiency under normal driving conditions, but I assume that it might have had a maximum range of close to 400 miles (more than 600 km).

- The Hotel Richard Löwenherz is a real 4-star establishment in Dürnstein. Its name refers to England's King Richard the Lionheart, who was imprisoned in the castle above Dürnstein in 1192-3. His subjects paid 35 tons of silver as a ransom for his release.
- Before the Anschluss, the Austrian currency was the schilling, which was worth 100 groschen. After the Anschluss, schillings were exchanged for Reichsmarks at a ratio of 1.5 AS to 1 RM. Telephones of that era were rotary dial, and an operator had to place long distance calls for you.

20: Broken Glass

- "Soldat" means "soldier," and was the term used to refer to the lowest ranking soldiers, equivalent to a private. The obstacle course competition is fictional, and not based on any historical sources.
- The Theresian Military Academy is named for Empress Maria Theresia, who founded it in 1751. It is still today the training facility for Austrian military officers. Wiener Neustadt (pronounced roughly "veener noy-shtaht") is located about 25-30 miles south of Vienna.
- The temperature is given in Celsius degrees. 10 degrees C is equal to 50 F, so the temp that day would have been in the 40s F. The daily temperatures in Vienna are available online as far back as 1855 at www.extremeweatherwatch.com.
- Grünfeld's comments about World War One are basically consistent with the view expressed by Hitler in *Mein Kampf*.
- The fifty-meter-high water tower is a well-known landmark of the city of Wiener Neustadt. The city's rail lines and industrial facilities made it an Allied bombing target in World War Two.

- 35 Reichmarks was the monthly pay for German soldiers at that time. It is equivalent to about $315 in 2025.
- November 9, 1938 was the infamous *Kristallnacht*, or Night of Broken Glass, when thousands of Jewish businesses, homes, and synagogues across Germany and Austria were destroyed.

21: A Piece of Paper

- The Jewish synagogue in Wiener Neustadt was destroyed in the *Kristallnacht* pogrom, along with many Jewish businesses and homes. Many Jewish men were arrested, and some were never seen again. Vienna was also the scene of widespread violence against Jews, and there were fatalities, in addition to many serious injuries. The police and fire brigades monitored the destruction but did not attempt to mitigate it.
- The U.S. State Department did centralize consular functions in Berlin, closing offices in Nazi-controlled areas, but it is not entirely clear to me exactly when that occurred. Emigration from German-controlled areas eventually became impossible. According to The Holocaust Encyclopedia, by September 1938 there was a waiting list in Germany (which included Austria) of 220,000 applicants for an immigration visa to the U.S., and if all available visas were issued, it would have taken 9 years to empty that list—and the list grew longer each year.
- I have undoubtedly oversimplified the process of getting an immigration visa, but elsewhere I have described the tortuous requirements necessary to get to the point of actually obtaining the form, so that will have to do.
- Dirndl is the traditional Austrian dress. Pictures are easily found online.

22: Life and Death

- It is difficult to estimate the amount of time required to drive to destinations in Europe in the 1930s because today's modern expressways did not exist then and Google Maps doesn't help much. I have used my best judgment.
- Border controls are another difficult topic for the 1930s, especially those of the German Reich. The daily closing times have been impossible to discover, and all I've found is that there were significant differences between countries, and that Germany was probably more restrictive than most.
- Yugoslavia was a popular destination for Jews fleeing the Reich because it regarded Jewishness as a matter of religion, not race. The Anglican baptismal certificate could have been helpful for that reason.
- The two German soldiers were in an Einheits-PKW, similar to an American jeep. There were light, medium, and heavy versions. The lightweight version boasted a 4-cylinder, 47 hp engine. It would not have been able to keep up with the Mercedes Nürburg 500K on the open road.
- Joseph's rifle would have been the standard German infantry rifle, the K98k, a 7.92 Mauser, commonly referred to as being 8mm.

23: By the Skin of the Teeth

- As mentioned in the notes to the previous chapter, it is impossible to estimate accurately the time required to travel between points at that time due to slower driving speeds, frequent villages and towns, narrow rural roads, and the problem of animal-drawn conveyances on the right of way. Modern highways were rare, and Slovenia in the 1930s was rather poor and agricultural. Three hours travel from Maribor to Ljubljana (pronounced loo-bi-*ahn*-ah, roughly) seems plausible for that era, though today the trip could be made in half that time or less.

- The river described in Ljubljana is the Ljubljanica River. The Dragon Bridge is a landmark of the city, and an open-air market is nearby, with plenty of trees for shade.
- FYI, on that day, Trieste really was "chilly, overcast and windy, lightly misting." It's amazing what you can find online.
- The Mercedes Nürburg would have had a glove box located in the dashboard in front of the passenger seat for storing maps, owner's manuals, etc.
- The Hebrew dialogue between Miriam and the elderly Jewish couple is courtesy of Google Translate.
- The plural of Italian lira is lire. The exchange rate in 1938 was 7.6 lire per Reichsmark. I estimated the probable cost of the four-berth 2nd class cabin using limited data.
- The SS *Vulcania* was a transatlantic liner of the Italia Line. The four-berth 2nd class cabins had bunk beds and two sinks. Photos available at www.italianliners.com.

24: "Buon viaggio!"

- On a voyage leaving Trieste in July 1938, the SS *Vulcania* stopped in Dubrovnik, Patras, Naples, Palermo, Algiers, Gibraltar, Lisbon, and the Azores enroute to NYC. However, sometimes there were fewer port calls. On the *Vulcania*'s maiden voyage in December 1928, there were port calls only in Patras, Greece and Naples, Italy, which is the itinerary I adopted here. I have found conflicting estimates of how many days the trip would require. The differences may be due to differences in the number of ports of call. Another Italia Line ship, the *Saturnia*, left Trieste on Nov. 2, 1938 and arrived in NYC on the 17th, a 15-

day voyage, but my source did not identify the ports visited along the way. All things considered, eleven days seems to be a safe estimate, with four days in the Med and seven on the Atlantic.

- The descriptions of the different classes of accommodations on the ship are consistent with historical sources.
- Jacob Goldberg makes reference to General Francisco Franco, the fascist who initiated an insurrection against the Spanish government, resulting in a three-year civil war, 1936-39. Hitler and Mussolini provided military support for Franco's eventual victory.
- The SS *Vulcania* had diesel engines that gave her a relatively slow cruising speed of 21 knots. Other liners of her day were much faster, some with speeds approaching 30 knots.
- Passengers were instructed to keep their ticket receipts with them at all times for their identification and to help them locate their rooms if they got lost on the ship. It was probably also to keep third-class passengers from invading the more exclusive areas of the ship.
- "First and second-class passengers arriving in New York Harbor were not required to undergo the inspection process at Ellis Island. Instead, these passengers received a cursory inspection aboard the ship; the theory being that if a person could afford to purchase a first or second-class ticket, they were affluent and less likely to become a public charge in America due to medical or legal reasons." (www.statueofliberty.org)

25: Epilogue

- Miriam could hold a job because legal immigrants could begin work immediately in the pre-war era, though during the Depression jobs were hard to find. The U.S. government did not begin issuing "green cards" until after the war.

- The memorial service at the Emanu-El Synagogue is fictitious, but the synagogue is described accurately.

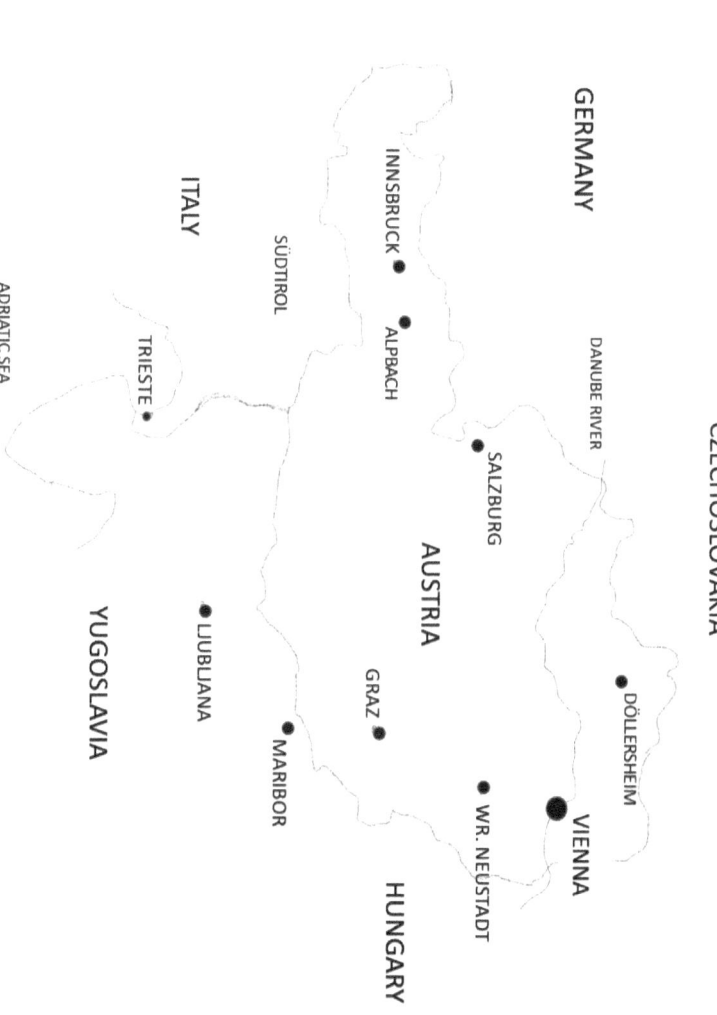

CZECHOSLOVAKIA

GERMANY

ITALY

SÜDTIROL

INNSBRUCK •

ALPBACH •

ADRIATIC SEA

TRIESTE •

DANUBE RIVER

SALZBURG •

AUSTRIA

DÖLLERSHEIM •

VIENNA

WR. NEUSTADT •

GRAZ •

LJUBLJANA •

MARIBOR •

YUGOSLAVIA

HUNGARY

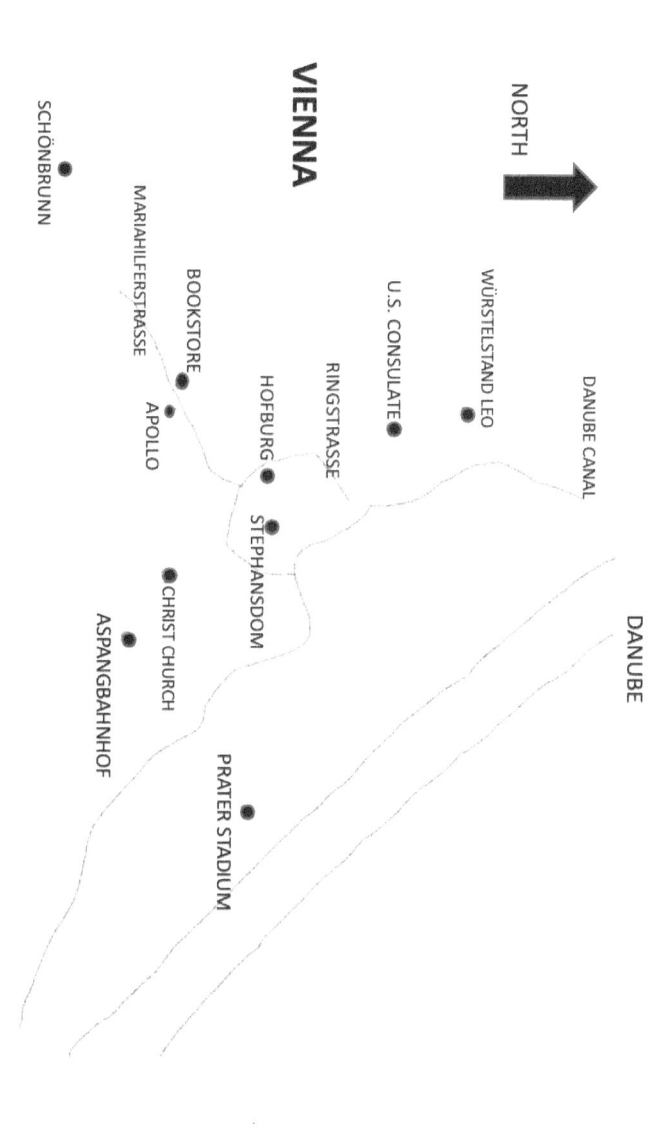

NORTH

VIENNA

DANUBE CANAL

DANUBE

SCHÖNBRUNN

MARIAHILFERSTRASSE

BOOKSTORE

APOLLO

HOFBURG

RINGSTRASSE

U.S. CONSULATE

WÜRSTELSTAND LEO

STEPHANSDOM

AMALIENBAD

CHRIST CHURCH

ASPANGBAHNHOF

PRATER STADIUM

ACKNOWLEDGMENTS

I would like to thank the following for their contributions during the writing of this book. In alphabetical order: David Anguish, Linda Glenn and Reggy Hiller (Wienerisch translation), Wayne Joyner (cover design), Adam Knierim (title), Scott White, and Andy Womack.

ABOUT THE AUTHOR

Michael Glenn earned his master's degree in history at the University of Mississippi and is retired from a career of teaching history. He lives in metro Atlanta with his family and a neurotic Sheltie. This is his fourth book and his third historical fiction novel. Be sure to read *The Odyssey of Walker Garrett* and its sequel, *Walker Garrett, Secret Service*.

www.ingramcontent.com/pod-product-compliance
Lightning Source LLC
Chambersburg PA
CBHW031312170626
46807CB00001B/382